HEATHER BLACKWOOD

A TWICE TOLD TALE

A TIME CORPS NOVEL

CHAPTER 1

NO ONE WANTS TO WITNESS their own conception. This is doubly true if one was conceived in a ritual of fire, blood and death. Neil had no desire to watch what was about to transpire.

"You don't have to do this if you don't want to," whispered Elliot, Neil's partner in the Time Corps. "I can do this alone."

"I'm going," said Neil. He forced himself to pass from the empty hallway into the adjoining high-ceilinged room, a surgical amphitheater that seated about fifty. Neil was acutely aware that he and Elliot might be noticed in such a small group.

Sure, they were seasoned Time Corps agents and their disguises used technology that didn't even exist in this time, 1995. But discovery meant death.

Elliot was in his late twenties, while Neil was in his early forties. They worked together at all ages, but Neil liked their missions best when they were closest in age. They argued more when they were young together, but had more interesting adventures. When they were both older, they slipped into a comfortable camaraderie, using experience and cunning more often than force. When they were far apart in age, they tended to irritate each other. But today, that wasn't the case. Today was too important.

The amphitheater was half-full already, with ordinary-looking people, men and women, even a few children. The chairs were upholstered and soft, the air-conditioning set at a comfortable temperature. It was nearing three o'clock in the morning, but even though the desert air outside was cool, there were no windows here to open, for they were two stories underground. High above them rose a modern house of glass, chrome and wood, isolated on the far edge of Palm Springs.

Neil and Elliot took seats at the topmost row, near the end of the aisle, as far from anyone as they could get without being obvious about it. At the center of the room, two tables waited. One was empty with three large drawers beneath it. The other held a body. A white sheet covered the figure, the feet and nose making peaks in the fabric. Neil knew the exact dimensions of that body, for it was his own.

A thick-bearded man in the bottom row played with a large coin. He moved the thing from finger to finger on one hand, making it do little flips across the backs of his knuckles. Then he palmed it and with a little flourish, pulled it from his pocket. He wasn't doing it to entertain a child, and no one but Neil was watching him. Neil studied the man's hands. He knew them already, each hair and wrinkle, for those hands existed in his own memories. He remembered doing coin tricks with those hands.

Other people filed in and took seats until the amphitheater was three-quarters full.

"You okay?" breathed Elliot, so softly that it was less than a whisper. A normal person would not have heard it, but Elliot knew Neil, with his sharp hearing, would.

Elliot glanced at him, concerned, and then looked away as a second door, a small one at the far end of the room, opened. Mr. March walked in, and a surge of terror ran through Neil. He didn't betray it with any physical movement, but he felt Elliot stiffen slightly. March was the man who had made Neil, the man who had then killed him before Neil's wife, Hazel, had brought him back to life.

March was a slight man, with fair skin and white hair.

2

He wore an expensive gray suit, simple and classic in its cut. This was the first version of March that Neil had known. The man had been killed and had come back with a new body years ago. But tonight, this older version of Mr. March would hopefully give Neil the answers he sought.

March greeted the group and thanked them for coming. Neil vaguely registered his words, but was more interested in the woman behind March. She was young, perhaps twenty-five, buxom and sturdy, but soft and rosy-cheeked in a German milkmaid sort of way. Her blonde hair was tied back in a sensible low ponytail and she wore a cornflower-blue dress that matched her eyes. But there was a cunning and coldness in those eyes that gave Neil pause.

The bearded man with the coin rose from his seat to stand beside her, listening to March as he said that they were accomplishing a great thing today, a fine thing. He used the words "freedom" and "self-determination," "justice" and "truth." Neil had heard all of these words from this man before.

"My brother and sister will be assisting me. May I introduce April and Noel."

Neil heard Elliot draw in a surprised breath at the two names. These were two of March's siblings. He and Elliot had met a few of the Twelve: Julius, September Wilde, Mr. Augustus, June Yee and Red Fawn who used to be May. They varied in ethics and personality as greatly as the humans they resembled. They were also secretive by nature, with only Julius revealing once that they were watchers of some sort.

April and Noel dipped their head at their brother's acknowledgment, but no one in the amphitheater made a sound. Throughout everything, no one had spoken or even coughed. The silence was unnatural.

After a minute, during which March briefly outlined the activities of the evening, two men, both wearing black rubber aprons, pulled a gorilla into the room. Each of the men gripped a long rod with a wire loop on the end that hooked over the animal's head. The gorilla was clearly drugged and shuffled in on all fours, staring at the floor, then gradually up at the people. He touched his lips, and then ran his paw over his face.

"An animal of great strength and intelligence," said Mr. March. "Of sensitivity and cunning."

Neil knew what was coming next and he forced himself to be still. Elliot was having more trouble, but Neil knew he wouldn't interfere. These events had to come to pass. The two of them could not stop them. This was Neil's conception, his birth, and if he ever wanted to understand his origins, he had to face them. Elliot knew this as well as he did.

Mr. March injected the gorilla with another drug, as even a sedated gorilla would fight ferociously for its life. He then slit its throat, sawing at its furry neck until he broke the skin and severed the artery beneath. Noel helped him collect a bowlful of dark, thick blood. The poor animal's heart beat for a while before he bled out and died in silence and without struggle. March then severed its right paw, splattering blood on his expensive suit. He didn't seem to care. The two men dragged the body to one side while March set the bowl of blood and the giant curled black paw on the table beside the sheeted figure.

Neil felt Elliot relax beside him. The worst was over. Now, they would somehow animate the body on the table.

But the two men returned with another animal on a wide, low, rolling cart.

"The Galapagos tortoise," said Mr. March. "For strength, invulnerability and longevity."

They did not drug this animal, which blinked placidly up at March as he approached. The creature was huge and had to be very old already. Its shell was scored in places, but it looked otherwise healthy. March opened a drawer and drew out a long, heavy machete.

April pulled a piece of sliced yam from her apron pocket and offered it to the tortoise, holding it a few inches out of reach. The creature stretched its leathery neck for it, opening its mouth and then taking a ponderous step toward her.

March stepped up, aimed and hacked at its long neck, severing it with one brutal stroke at the base of the skull. The body collapsed on the cart and the head hit the floor with a sickening thud and rolled a few times, stopping with its small black eyes staring at the ceiling. Its mouth was still open, anticipating the piece of yam. March slipped a bowl beneath the neck and caught the blood, and April picked up the head and set it on the table. The two men rolled the cart with the headless body to sit beside the gorilla.

"Three," whispered Elliot, and Neil knew what he meant. These things came in threes. Or sevens. Or twelves. Whether Elliot was predicting three animals or praying that there would only be three, Neil did not know.

The next animal was a dog. She was a pit bull, white with dark patches and a torn left ear. Under her belly, he could see that her teats were swollen. She was still nursing pups.

Neil needed this to stop. These deaths were unbearable. But he was frozen in place. To interrupt this event would halt his own creation. He knew enough about time travel to understand that it would not create a paradox. He would still be born, but it would be in another place or another time. March would simply perform another ritual, costing the lives of other innocent creatures.

On a more practical level, tracking down this date and location had taken almost a year of detective work, and Neil was not willing to do it all over again.

The dog's stump of a tail wagged, though her staggering gait told Neil that she was also drugged. The men held her with the same looped poles they had used on the gorilla.

"A dog, for loyalty, tenacity and a ferocious heart."

Ah, how that had backfired on March, thought Neil, deriving a tiny shred of satisfaction from this evil ordeal. He had indeed inherited those characteristics, along with a fighting spirit. But his loyalty was not to his master, but to something else, something better.

The dog licked March's hand just before he injected her with something, and she dropped her head and staggered sideways. He lifted her chin, slit her throat and gathered the blood. Neil caught Elliot looking away as Mr. March rolled the dog onto her back and put his weight into sawing open her chest. Neil forced himself to watch. If the dog had died to give him life, he owed her this much.

March removed the heart, slicing it free of the tissue that connected it to the body and then cupped it in two hands and set it on the table. A pool of blood collected under the heart, head and hand, dripping from the table onto the floor, but it was nothing compared to the great rivulets of blood that ran from the bodies to the floor grates along the edges of the room.

The unveiling of the body on the table was, surprisingly, less traumatic. Neil already knew what to expect. His wife, Hazel, another member of the Time Corps, had already described his earthen body to him. March tore off the white sheet and tossed it aside. On the table lay a man-shaped piece of stony, crumbling earth.

"I have used earth collected with great effort," said March. "From three great rivers, the sources of life, from the last life blood of a priestess, a prophet and a king. I traveled far, through time and over great distance. The first portions of earth were taken from the Nile, moments after an Egyptian priestess had her throat cut. I gathered more earth from the banks of the Euphrates, where a prophet was murdered. And finally, I collected the blood-darkened earth from a king killed at the edge of the Amazon River."

The two men assisting March returned with a three-legged bronze brazier and lit it. It was then that Mr. March began to speak, this time in another language. Neil had encountered many languages in his years of travel, but never this one. This was an ugly language, full of brutal sounds and low, dark notes, like a piece of music in a minor key, but with long hisses and deep-throated, choked sounds.

Thankfully, the crowd was not asked to participate, as Neil and Elliot would surely have been discovered. Mr. March waved the head, heart and hand through the fire with a few words, and then balanced the head carefully on the earthen man's forehead, set the heart on his chest and placed the gorilla hand so it covered the figure's right hand. He then pulled a small piece of paper from his pocket and slipped it into the man's mouth. Neil knew what letters were on it. The letters would fuse onto the roof of his mouth where they would remain for the rest of his life. They were gone now, but it had taken his own death to remove them.

March mixed the three bowls of blood, then spat into the bowl. April and Noel, likewise, spat into it. They poured this mixture into the stone man's mouth, filling it until it poured down the sides of his face and pooled beneath his head.

Then Mr. March bent down, kissed the bloody mouth and blew into the man's nostrils.

"It has begun," he said and removed the heart, hand and tortoise head. He stood, gazing at the body while the two men cleared away the brazier, bowls and animal parts.

Still, the crowd did not move.

The stone man's finger twitched once, then his hand curled and his leg jerked. Little by little, he came alive, but his skin was still stone and his eyes blind.

"And now, my esteemed friends, I ask you to bestow a boon upon my new son. Each of you has a gift to offer, a memory, a thought that will become his own. You will be creating him, his very self, from your words and memories."

Neil glanced at a teenage girl who rose. He saw her face now in his memory. A friend from high school. An older man beside her was his chemistry teacher. A couple came next, and he recognized his foster parents. His memories had always been spotty and confused, but seeing these people brought them into sharp focus.

Elliot touched his shoulder, reminding him to rise, and they got into line. Each person bent down and whispered something into the earthen man's ear, and the golem lay there, sometimes writhing, sometimes still, sometimes turning toward the sound.

When Neil's turn came, he didn't know what to say, so he whispered softly, "Be better. Find Hazel." He hadn't known what else to say, nor did he know if the being on the table would understand. He certainly had no memory of it himself.

They returned to their seats. The golem had now taken on flesh and the skin of his face and hands was softer now. Within minutes, he was fully human looking, and he opened his eyes, a simple earthen brown color. He sat up and touched his face.

"Have you chosen a name, brother?" April asked March. She and Noel had been the last two to whisper in the golem's ear.

"I have. He will be called Neil. The champion. He will be my champion of the gray shadows."

March took the golem's hand and helped him to rise from the table. The young man was about eighteen or nineteen and no one seemed bothered by his lack of clothing or offered him any covering. Mr. March led him away, and Neil tried to remember this event in his life, but he could not. His earliest memories, hazy as they were, were of school and foster parents. The other people rose and left, as silent as they had been throughout the evening. He and Elliot followed.

Some of the people remained in the house, moving upstairs and helping themselves to refreshments that March had set out. Others got into their cars to leave, and Neil and Elliot followed them. Once they were far from the house, Elliot pulled a tiny electronic storage device from the glove compartment. It was only the size of a child's finger and it received input from a removable implant Elliot wore in his eye. He took a moment to download information from his implant onto the device and handed it to Neil.

"I don't think that was any human language they were speaking," said Neil.

"No one in that room could possibly be human," said Elliot. "No one but me, I guess."

"Why do you say that?"

"Just a feeling. They were all so still and silent."

Neil didn't know if he agreed, but he sometimes did not understand things that his friends intuitively knew.

"I remembered many of those people from my past," said Neil. "I think some of them gave me my memories. Even so, I don't think I'm any closer to understanding things."

"I wouldn't say that. We now know how to make a golem of our very own. We also know that he only made one of you."

"I'm only an amalgamation of their memories and words."

"Not true. You have twenty years of experiences. And when you were only one or two years old, you made your own free choice to leave March and strike out on your own. Either you're stronger than they meant for you to be or they performed the ritual incorrectly."

"It was terrible to witness," said Neil. "So unlike the joy accompanying a human birth."

"I'm not going to deny that. It was all I could do not to jump up myself and lop off March's head. But it's over now. And you're not like them. You're not what they created you to be. Don't forget that. Out of all the one billion people walking this earth, you're unique.

They drove in silence for a while, heading back to the Time Corps safe house in Los Angeles. When they arrived two hours later, Elliot woke up Julius, the owner of the Time Corps safe house, while Neil set up the computer on the kitchen table to play the recording.

Still in his plaid pajamas and robe, Julius came downstairs. He was heavyset with a white beard and hair, the oldest-looking of the Twelve. Julius leaned on the back of a chair as he watched. Again, the animals were killed, the blood was collected, the body parts cut off. When March began to speak in the strange language, Julius stepped back.

"Turn it off," he said.

"Why? What is—"

"Turn it off!"

Elliot stopped the playback, and Julius pulled out a chair, the one farthest from the computer, and sat down with a sigh.

"What is it?" asked Elliott.

"That recording has no place in our world. Destroy it."

"Aren't you going to study it? Don't you want to translate it?" asked Elliot.

It was a good question. Julius loved research and learning and spent most of his waking hours reading. Another thought occurred to Neil.

"Or do you already understand it?" asked Neil. March and Julius were brothers, after all.

"Just destroy it."

"Is it because someone else can use it to make a golem?" asked Neil. "All of the people there heard the words. Could they recreate the ritual?"

"Unlikely. Months of preparation had to go into such a dark nativity. Maybe years. March would never have revealed every part of the preparation he had done to the people witnessing the event. That device needs to be destroyed. The words of that evil tongue will not be spoken under this roof."

Neil took the device from the computer.

"On second thought, give it to me," said Julius. "I'll destroy it."

Neil handed over the recording. He already knew everything he was going to learn. He had been conceived in a bloody, dark ritual, and his early memories were false. There was nothing more.

Julius shuffled out of the room, presumably to spend some time in his study or to destroy the recording.

"I'm tired, but it's too late to go to bed," said Elliot, putting on a pot of coffee. After a minute, he looked up at Neil.

"I'm all right," said Neil, knowing what his partner was thinking. "Aside from the sacrifices, nothing about it was even very troubling. I'd like to know who all those people were, but I'm not willing to find out. They can't be nice."

"As much as I hate to say this, perhaps it's best left alone. You are who you are, regardless of how you came to be. I know you wanted to satisfy your curiosity. I hope it helped."

Elliot poured himself a bowl of cereal, and Neil took a coffee mug from the cupboard.

"Elliot? What did you whisper in my ear back when I was lying on that table?"

Elliot glanced at him sideways as he poured the milk. "I said I wanted you to have a soul."

CHAPTER 2

THE DEAD WOMAN'S SOUL WAS stuck in the drain of the bathtub. Her foot was trapped up to the ankle and the poor geist stood, watching Astrid from under lank, dripping tendrils of her white hair. The shower was still running.

"I always knew this was going to happen," said the spirit. "Even when I was a little girl, I knew I'd go down the drain."

She looked to be about eighty, but Astrid knew that spirits did not always look identical to their mortal body. The woman's corpse lay in the empty tub, presumably dead from a fall and a blow to the head or a broken neck. There was no blood, and Astrid had no inclination to examine the body. She wasn't interested in how the woman had died, only that her spirit was stuck in this world. It was her job to free it.

"I'm going to pull on your foot," said Astrid. "It won't hurt."

As a rule, she hated touching spirits. Under normal circumstances, the spirit would not be trapped, but would simply refuse to go to the afterlife. It was Astrid's job to convince it otherwise. If necessary, she could physically force a geist through the Doorway, but she disliked the practice.

"If you pull my foot free, the rest of me will go down!" cried the woman.

"No. No, you won't. You're dead, and you're going to get

free and then go where the dead souls go." Astrid said it gently, but firmly. She had practiced the tone and delivery for more than four years, all her years as a psychopomp, an escort for the dead.

She climbed into the tub for leverage, careful to stand without touching the corpse. She ignored the warm water that soaked her shirt and jeans and she reached around the woman's ankle, finding it as solid as a living person's.

She counted to three and pulled, then tried again. No luck. She grabbed the bar of soap and showed it to the woman, then rubbed it on the ankle. The soap didn't matter, but the woman's perception of it did. She was only trapped because she thought she was, but often spirits reacted to physical things as if they were still affected by them. Astrid no longer tried to argue with them. She had a job to do, and she wanted it done quickly.

She managed to pull the foot free, then made a Door at the other end of the bathroom and a misty disk appeared, growing larger and opening, an undulating mirrored surface at its center. This was the Doorway to death, what Astrid created and what she was.

She convinced the woman's soul to go through and the Door closed, pulling itself shut and vanishing. Astrid's clothing was creating a dripping mess on the floor and she sighed. None of her kind left any DNA or physical evidence, which was handy when they attended a murder scene, but they could affect the physical world. A pool of water on the floor would cause questions. She left the water running, hating the waste but knowing that disturbing a death scene would look suspicious. No one turned off the water after they died.

She pulled a towel down from the rack, mopped up the water, and shoved it into the hamper, hoping it would dry by the time anyone found it. Then she heard a low moan.

The woman had lived alone. She was sure of it.

Oh, but there was something else. She still felt the

pull of the place, the tugging sensation that each of the psychopomps felt when there was a sticky soul, a geist. The feeling had not gone away when the woman had gone through the Door.

Astrid grabbed her phone from the bathroom counter where she had set it and shoved it into her damp pocket. Then, she let her instincts guide her.

The kitchen. A soul was in the kitchen. The room was bright and cheerful, if about twenty years out of date, with hand-drawn pictures from grandchildren on the refrigerator and a floral painted tea kettle on the burner.

A thin, balding man in the corner glowered at her with a look of pure hatred.

"It's not you!" the man hissed and slid into the dining room. "There's nothing else! It's a balloon, but it was before. Not now. You weren't even there. You can't know!"

This geist was not only troubled, it was insane. The spirit felt stale. Old. Embedded. That was bad. The whole reason for her existence as a psychopomp was to prevent these things from happening. Souls were in pain when they were trapped in the mortal world, and that pain intensified until they went insane. This man was a tragic example.

She tried talking to the man, using all her normal lines and tricks. She tried reaching into his mind to pull on strong threads, hoping to trip a thought that would encourage him to go through the Door she made. Nothing worked. The spirit made a circuit through the dining room, living room and kitchen, always moving, raving and shouting the entire time.

Why had he appeared now instead of when Astrid first arrived? Perhaps he was connected with the dead woman. Was he her husband? And if that was the case, why had they both been trapped here? Few souls remained in the human world after death, and two in the same house was unusual.

She tried talking about the woman, asking him

14

questions, reaching further into his mind to find thoughts, still with no success. She needed a new tactic. If she couldn't get him to go willingly, she'd force him.

As he passed the door to the dining room, she leapt out and grabbed for him, but he slipped sideways out of her grasp. He screamed, shoving his face up into hers until their noses almost touched. She jerked back, banging into the dining room table, knowing consciously that he couldn't hurt her, but afraid all the same. She had been raised as a normal human being for her first eighteen years and still felt like one. True, she wasn't human by birth, but she hadn't known that at the time. Geists could still frighten her. Still, she took her job seriously and she wasn't going to call for backup just yet

She tried a few more times from different positions, but could not catch the wily geist. Her phone dinged with an incoming text from Jeff, the head psychopomp. There were five psychopomps in the world, and Jeff was the de facto leader.

She had an idea. Slipping back against the wall, she waited for the spirit. When it appeared, she made a Door directly in its path. It leapt back, but she expanded the Door and moved it, forcing it over the spirit like a net.

The thing screamed, but she continued pulling the Door tighter until the geist passed through the mirrored surface and into whatever afterlife awaited it.

She waited for a minute, making sure she didn't feel any other sticky souls. Nope. The house was clear. She made a Door to Jeff's bookshop in Nebraska, the place the psychopomps typically met.

"Why are you all wet?" asked Jeff, turning from his bookshelves to look her up and down. He was a middle-aged man of ordinary looks and inquisitive mind. Astrid liked him and found her psychopomp colleagues easier to deal with than most regular people.

"A geist was stuck in a drain and the water was on,"

she said. "But more importantly, I ran into an older geist. It was an elderly man, but I don't know how long he'd been stuck."

"Did he speak in sentences?"

"Yes, but they made no sense."

"But he still had the capacity for basic grammar?"

"Yeah. And he kept making this loop from room to room."

"Always in the same direction?"

"Yes."

"I'd say six months to five years, depending," said Jeff. "At least it could still talk and had human form."

She thought about it, making a mental note to add to her growing list of experiences. One day, she would know as much as Jeff did.

"Your text said you had news for me," she said.

"I do. The Seelie finally called."

A feeling of relief flooded her, followed immediately by dread. She hadn't heard from the Seelie in years. Due to a complicated past in which she had cheated the Seelie out of her cousin Elliot's execution, she was obliged to perform three tasks for them. She had completed two tasks already, but the Seelie were saving the last one. She could be waiting a lifetime for them to give her the last task, and as time went on, she found herself wishing they'd give it to her and be done with it.

"They have a task for me?"

"So they say. Now, you know I'll help you if I can. We all will."

Astrid knew they would. The other psychopomps, Jeff, Gopan, Robin and Graciela, were all decent people. And as the only psychopomps in existence, they were family, in a sense.

"Where do they want to meet me?"

"They said to come through to the Seelie version of Luna Park. They'll call you tomorrow when they're ready."

"I wish they'd just come here. I hate being in the sidhe

worlds. Time passes so strangely there."

"Yeah, but at least after this, it'll all be over."

She hoped he was right. She said good-bye, made a Door to her apartment in New York and changed into dry clothing, then heated leftovers for dinner.

She thought of Sister, her human twin. Astrid was born to the Unseelie, the cousins of the Seelie. But when a human infant had been in danger of dying, Astrid was given the child's appearance and was swapped with her. Astrid was a changeling. That human girl was Sister, who had been raised and tormented by the Unseelie until Astrid had gotten her out of their terrible world and sent her to another. She missed Sister.

The Seelie, though claiming to be opposed to the cruel and lawless ways of the Unseelie, were not so different from them when it came down to it. They had threatened Astrid by threatening Sister, so Astrid and the Time Corps had sent Sister to live in another world with a much older version of Hazel, one of the founding members of the Time Corps. Once her third task for the Seelie was complete, Sister could come home and Astrid could breathe easy, free of her obligation.

It wasn't only the Seelie who were trouble though. She had other ties that she could not break. She had made a deal with a drake and had to have dinner with him fortnightly. But Yelbeghen never threatened her or her loved ones.

After washing her dish, she found her little iron owl bell on a bookshelf. The thing was made of cold iron from a meteor, one of the things that all sidhe, both Seelie and Unseelie, hated. It caused them intense pain. Though Unseelie born, she was immune to this particular piece, and she set it on her nightstand. If the Seelie came early, they'd have a tough time approaching her in her sleep.

It was raining, and she looked down on the wet street below where cars hissed past on the wet pavement and people hurried along, umbrellas up. She wanted to change into her aspect, an owl, and go flying, but she wouldn't. Not in New York City and not tonight. She needed to get a good night's sleep so she'd have her wits about her for dealing with the Seelie.

CHAPTER 3

Professor Seamus Doyle tore a page out of his notebook and pushed it across the table toward Frieda, a striped tabby cat.

"See if you can figure it out," he muttered.

The cat looked it over while Seamus tried the mathematical problem again on a fresh sheet of paper.

"This part is incorrect," said Frieda, setting a paw on the page. "See? Simple error."

Seamus growled a curse, made a note on a clean sheet of paper, crumpled the older paper and threw it toward the trash can where it fell to the floor to lay among its discarded kin. He ran his hands through his hair and heaved a sigh.

"Even without that error, it still won't work. It's impossible."

He shoved himself back from the desk and stood, toppling the chair with a crash. He cursed and picked it back up, only to catch his foot on a coil of spare tubing he had left on the floor. Banging his thigh on the edge of the worktable, he let out a stream of cursing. He regained his balance, disentangled himself, jammed the chair against the desk and turned as the laboratory door opened. Frieda darted through the open door. Like all cats, she hated a commotion.

"You all right, Professor?" asked Hazel. She was in her mid-twenties, but to Seamus, she seemed much younger. He supposed she always would.

"I'm not blowing things up, if that's what you mean."

"I only heard banging and yelling, and—"

"I know what you heard. I'm busy."

"Don't you get cross with me. I was only checking on you."

"You ought not to talk," he said. "You've been prowling around the house all week, looking for trouble."

"Not looking for trouble. Only waiting."

"With you, it's the same thing. You can't keep still to save your life. You and that ship, gallivanting all over the place. And then you marry a golem."

"It's Neil, and you've known him for years. And you gave your blessing."

"Under duress."

But he smiled as he said it, and Hazel tiptoed to kiss his cheek.

"Now, what are you upset about?" she asked.

"The machines," he said, starting to pace between the window at the far end of the room and his worktable. "The vials of blue fluid. I can't figure out a way to make more time machines without more fluid. There's simply no way to use the amount we have and make the numbers work."

They currently had four time machines, but Seamus wanted the security of being able to make more. His wife, Felicia, had come through to his world years ago and still could not return to her home world. Her nephew was suffering from a rare form of cancer and she needed to return home to put his mother in touch with a Brazilian doctor who could save him. No matter how hard he worked or what he tried, he could not find a way to get from this world, the hub world, to Felicia's.

Traveling to the world where he and Hazel had originated was simple, as was traveling to a few other worlds. But Felicia's world eluded him. It was entirely closed off, and yet she had somehow come through.

"We'll just have to be careful with the machines we

have," said Hazel. "And perhaps Felicia will return with useful information."

"Unlikely. Unless she can analyze the blue fluid and duplicate it. So far, all of our efforts have been unsuccessful."

"Professor," said Frieda, poking her striped head through the door. "A package has come for you."

They went downstairs and Seamus found the package on the front step.

"It has no postage or return address," said Seamus. "In this time, people typically don't hand deliver packages."

"I know that, Professor," said Hazel. "They also tend to put addresses on it, and this one just says your name."

"In my own writing."

"Yeah?" Hazel grabbed the package, clearly excited at the prospect. As for Seamus, he was chilled by the notion.

"What would I send myself?"

"Open it up and see!"

"But what if it makes another unstable time loop?"

"Many things we do create time loops," she said.

Hazel was correct. The origin of the time machine had been an unstable time loop. It still was. He tried not to think about it, but the fact hung over him like a specter. All time loops were dangerous. They destabilized the worlds. Sometimes, they tore holes in time. The Time Corps existed to repair these holes, either through technology, or by inserting itself into events to make sure no object, idea or person created a time loop.

In short, unstable time loops were bad. Stable time lines were good.

Each object needed a stable origin, a lifetime and an ending. Under normal circumstances, with time passing in a linear fashion, this took care of itself. Every item, idea or person was created, had its span of existence and then, in the case of physical things, decayed. It was a universal constant. But when time travel was involved, things became complicated.

21

The first time machine, the one he had used years ago, the one he had duplicated for the Time Corps, had come to him from an older version of himself. He had not invented it, not yet, and as the years passed, he found this more and more troubling.

At this point in his personal time line, he could make as many time machines as he liked. He understood the technology fully, except for one aspect. Hazel and Felicia could recreate the machines as well, as he had written the instructions down in the event of his death. But that wasn't the problem.

The problem was the vials of blue fluid. The first machine had come with two inexplicable items. One was a book of coordinates. That was still a problem. True, Seamus had recently created a book and had written in it extensively, but he would never have done so if he hadn't received the same book when he was younger. The second item was the vial of pale blue glowing fluid that was a necessary component in every time machine.

He never knew what the fluid was, nor was he able to make more. Long ago, his former friend, prison cellmate and colleague, Oren McCullen, had received the blue fluid from a man named Mr. March. But March hadn't bothered them in some time, and even when Julius and his siblings had known where their brother was, they did not pursue him. March would never have given up the secret of the liquid.

Seamus found a kitchen knife and slit the tape holding the box closed. He knew already what was in it. How could it be anything else?

CHAPTER 4

"HERE'S EVERYTHING I HAVE," SAID Elliot, pulling the recording device from the time machine and handing it to Seamus. "I hope you can do something with it."

"I'm not sure," said Seamus, inserting the device into the computer in his laboratory. He downloaded the files, and Elliot watched as he scanned through it.

For a man born in the early 1800s, Seamus had adapted well to the technologies of the early twenty-first century. For Elliot, these things were second nature, but some of the older members of the Time Corps had trouble with them. Elliot loved technology, especially the devices of his personal distant future. While others hesitated to embrace their use, he had received removable implantable devices with delight. Why wouldn't a person wish to improve themselves if at all possible?

"Did anyone see you?" asked Seamus.

"Of course people saw me, but you didn't, and neither did Felicia. That's all that matters."

"Are you certain you got close enough to the time rip?"

"I got as close as I could. It did involve an omnibus crash. I couldn't get too close without getting killed."

Seamus grunted and scrolled through the data. Like all people except for Neil, he could not travel to a place and time within ten miles of himself. Since he, Hazel and Felicia had all been in New Orleans when Felicia had accidentally stepped through a time rip in 1857, Elliot had volunteered to go to Seamus's home world and take readings on the rip. It had required him to get very close to an omnibus accident and to avoid detection by a disoriented Felicia and by Seamus, who lived across the street. Neither of them had met him yet, so he was just another face in the crowd.

"The readings are just like my world. My world and Hazel's," said Seamus. "And they're also like your home world. So close to both. Almost as if—sweet Jesus. It's as if her world is between them. But that can't be right. I've tried every setting and combination of coordinates, even the ones listed here."

He continued talking, and Elliot half-listened, knowing the Professor's proclivity for working out problems by talking through them. Eventually, Seamus took to muttering to himself and Elliot turned to leave.

"Wait, I need one more thing," said Seamus. "A few weeks ago, Felicia and I went to San Francisco to try to get readings from their great earthquake in the early twentieth century. It's one of the times when there is a super synchronicity. It touches multiple worlds at one spot. But with this," he motioned to the screen, "I'll need something else. Give me two or three hours and I'll give you specifics. Then you can go."

"Do I need to go right away?"

"Do you mind?" Seamus asked, blinking up at him in surprise.

"Well, no, not precisely." Elliot didn't want to tell him the real reason he was hesitant. It was because of a woman, a woman he had met while trapped in the Library, a woman he wanted to find once again. Every day he spent doing other jobs for the Time Corps was another day apart from her. But how could he deny Neil the right to see how he had been created or do anything other than try to get Felicia home? She had been far from her home world for so many years. He couldn't ask his friends to delay their own trips through time so he could indulge his romantic impulses.

"I can go," Elliot said.

"Void wyrms," said Seamus, licking the tip of his pencil and then writing something down. "From what I gathered on my last trip, there seems to be excessive void wyrm activity in San Francisco around that time."

The void wyrms were the creatures that lived between worlds, in the black, empty place where nothing existed. They were serpentlike things, gigantic and terrifying.

"Did they cause the earthquake? Or are they a symptom?" Elliot asked.

"Hard to say," said Seamus. "Which is why I need more information. But take Neil with you. He's immune to the monsters."

Void wyrms were attracted to the holes between worlds. Any type of hole would do, from the time rips that the time machines created to the randomly occurring natural tears through which people could accidentally step. They even liked the Doors created by people like Elliot's cousin, Astrid. When the void wyrms appeared, they had a way of pulling a person toward them. Neil was the only one of them immune to this effect.

"I exchanged a lot of gold for money when Felicia and I went on our trip. There's still plenty left." He opened a drawer and pulled out a stack of money. Elliot thumbed through it.

"This is a lot, especially in that time."

"I suppose."

"Anything else?"

"Yes," the Professor hesitated with one finger raised, and then turned back to his desk. "No. Never mind."

Elliot knew why he would not speak his thoughts. Occasionally, they had to keep knowledge from each other to keep from creating time loops with information.

"If it's about Yukiko, I already know she'll be there.

When we first met, she recognized me. I know she lived in San Francisco back then."

"There's that, I suppose. Yes."

Elliot waited, knowing that there was more.

"It's just the time loops. You know you'll meet Yukiko because she told you that she'd met you already. All of our friendships, even my marriage, are the results of time loops. We try to restabilize things, but we'll never manage it. It's not a paradox, not precisely, but it is a problem."

"We're not old men yet, Seamus. We'll figure it out and fix it."

"That's just it. I'm not sure we will."

"Time?" asked Elliot.

Neil checked the machine. "Looks like we got it. April 1906. We have until five in the morning on the eighteenth."

"Plenty of time, then?"

"Unknown. Let's find a clock and a newspaper and verify the date."

It was nighttime in San Francisco, and before dawn on April 18, the city would experience an earthquake and resulting fires that would devastate it. But for now, the city was beautiful, the air was cool and moist and without bright electric city lights, the sky was full of stars. Though most of the city was asleep, a few people walked along the streets or rode in carriages, completely unaware that two men from another century moved among them.

"How's the eye implant working?" asked Neil as he closed up the trunk that held the time machine and straightened his hat. They walked down the street, headed east along Pacific Street, Neil pulling the wheeled trunk that contained the time machine.

Elliot tested the ocular camera, taking a few photographs of the buildings nearby. Julius would want them for research. Of course, they would all be digital, in color,

26

and in a resolution so high that no picture could possibly come from a camera of this era. They would have to be for Julius's own archival purposes, not for any general use.

Neil asked the time from a passerby and reset his watch. Elliot did the same with his implant. It was 3:32 a.m. They headed south for a few blocks and found themselves in front of the Hall of Justice at Portsmouth Square.

"We're close," said Neil. "Seamus said to take readings as close to the center of the Barbary Coast as possible."

"Ah, two young men visiting the red light district of San Francisco. A grand adventure."

"I'm not so young," said Neil. "And I'm married."

"And I'm kidding."

It wasn't that Elliot didn't appreciate a fine-looking woman, but he knew better than to think that the ladies of this area were here because they enjoyed the trade. On the whole, he adored his job. The smells, the food, the music, the people and the technology all were a delight to him. But he also knew desperation and suffering when he saw it, however smiling and brightly colored it might be.

"We need to find Yukiko," said Elliot. "She's here somewhere."

"There's not much time. Less than two hours," said Neil.

"I owe Yukiko a favor," said Elliot.

"Because she helped get you out of the Library?"

"She helped me then to return the favor I'm about to do for her tonight."

"And what favor is that?" asked Neil.

"I have no idea. We should find her and ask."

"She won't know who you are."

"Nope. I'd better make a good impression." He pulled his coat straight, knocked a bit of lint off his hat and grinned at Neil. His partner kept walking.

They headed east, toward the bay, past closed fish stalls and cheap clothiers and shuttered bakeries and grocers. Then came the music and low din of talk and music from the concert saloons, dance halls, opium dens and parlor houses. A pair of prostitutes called out to them, and they passed by before Elliot turned back.

"Actually, you might be able to help me," he said to them. "I'm looking for a Japanese woman, a particular one. Her name is Yukiko and she'd be about twenty."

He didn't say that he had no idea how old she actually was. Even now, at over a century old, she looked like she was in her early twenties. As a Kitsune, a Japanese fox spirit, she would not age further.

"Lots of Chinese girls here," the woman said, tipping her head to the brothel behind her.

"She's Japanese. And I'm not looking for an evening with her. She's my friend. Yukiko Sato."

He didn't know if she'd be using that last name in this time, but it was all he had to go on.

Both women said they didn't know her.

"You look sweet, though," said the shorter of the two. "You can always look for her tomorrow, right?" She smiled, but it didn't reach her eyes.

"Is your friend shy?" the other woman said, winking a heavily made-up eye at Neil who shoved his hands into the pockets of his duster.

"You're both very pretty," said Elliot, "and I'm sure if we weren't in a hurry we could stop for a pleasant night. But we are in a terrible rush."

The woman sighed and looked up and down the street, searching for better prospects.

"I'll give you five dollars," said Elliot softly, knowing it was a huge amount of money. "Just tell me a few of the places where Japanese women might go. Not Chinese, though she might be there too." He pulled out a five-dollar bill and the woman unfolded it, examining it.

Then she looked him up and down, as if that might give her a clue to the bill's authenticity.

"I suppose it depends," she said. "If your friend is new

off the boat and doesn't have any money, I'd check the cribs. There's one on Clay Street that's taking new girls."

"What if she spoke perfect English and she was pretty? Good skin, perfect teeth."

"Well, it's possible she'd be in one of the better parlor houses. Can she dance?"

Of course. How had he forgotten? When he first saw her, Yukiko had been dancing at the Luna Park boardwalk for a stage show. She had been able to draw power from the willing audience. Oh my, how willing he had been. She had looked like a vision, a beautiful dream, dancing with the sea wind in her hair.

"Yes, she can dance. Very well, in fact. She might be in a cabaret or dance hall."

"Elliot," said Neil.

Elliot held up a finger to his partner.

"Which ones are around here?" he asked the woman.

She got a thoughtful look and bit her lower lip. She and the other prostitute spoke for a few moments about the various locales where a dancer might work.

"There's a fire," said Neil quietly.

"Where?" Elliot moved up close to Neil, but didn't question his word. "Nothing is supposed to burn until after the earthquake."

"Not sure. The smell of smoke is faint. But there's also yelling. I hear both women and men. It's that way."

"We got three places," said the woman. "The first one—"

"Is it that way?" said Elliot, pointing in the direction of the fire.

"There's one there too."

"We have to go," said Elliot. "Here." He dug another five-dollar bill out to give to the other woman. "Stay outside between five and five thirty in the morning. Don't go inside. Something bad is going to happen, an earthquake. Just try to stay safe."

He could tell by their looks that the women didn't believe

him. He wasn't surprised. He sounded like a lunatic.

"We're scientists," he said. "The machine in that trunk measures tectonic tension and an earthquake is eminent. Just stay outside. It's coming a little after five. Oh, and the whole city is going to burn."

Neil was already partway down the street, dragging the time machine, and Elliot ran to catch up. His partner didn't speak of Elliot's breach of Time Corps rules. Technically, he shouldn't be warning people about disasters or giving them large amounts of money. One of those women might have been destined to die. Anything could happen, and the more interference they engaged in, the more chance they had of creating an unstable time loop.

They could meet and help Yukiko tonight because Elliot knew that he already had done so. Of course, that too was a time loop. He never would have sought her out if she hadn't already recognized him in the future.

The cabaret was called the Pearl of the Pacific, and flames lit the windows from within, giving it an eerie orange glow. Two fire trucks stood outside with men rushing to put out the flames. Yukiko stood across the street in a form-fitting red and gold dance costume. Her face and arms were soot-smudged and her hair was mostly out of its pins. Two policemen were speaking with her. So was another man. Elliot knew him at once. This was Santiago, the Coyote, friend of Julius and a generally tricky bastard. Elliot and Neil approached them.

"You are a filthy, lying mongrel!" Yukiko shouted at Santiago. "You lie to them."

Santiago crossed his arms, his expression full of pity and concern. "I told them what I saw."

"You know I didn't do it. Why would I burn the place down with myself inside?"

"He says you were angry with your employer," said the policeman. "That you had an argument."

Yukiko gave Santiago a look of hatred, but Elliot knew

her well enough to see the hurt beneath it. The young Kitsune had trusted the Coyote and had been betrayed. The police turned to one another, consulting.

"I've been looking for you. I am a friend of Inari," said Elliot to Yukiko.

The name hung in the air between them, the name of the god she served, the one from her home in Japan.

Her face froze and then her eyes widened in happiness. Elliot thought she might hug him or burst into joyful tears. It tore his heart to see her so lonely, so desperate, that any word from home would have this effect on her.

She had never told Elliot the story of her life, but he knew she had come to California unwillingly, as a bride, and that she had suffered being so far from home.

"May I speak with her for a moment?" he asked the policemen.

"Don't go anywhere," said one, who then turned to Santiago.

"You're from back home?" she said, and he could tell she was smelling him. Only someone watching for the long inhalation through her nose would notice. "You're not Kitsune," she said.

"No, I'm not. But I might be able to help you."

"My word won't hold up against his," she said, jerking her head toward Santiago. "I'm just a Chinaman and a whore to them."

"I know Santiago and I know he's often a liar. Now, tell me what happened."

Neil stood near the policemen, listening in unobtrusively, as was his specialty. Yukiko stole at glance at him before turning back to Elliot.

"You know Inari?"

"There's not much time. They look like they believe Santiago."

"I suppose they do. There was a wager. The owner of the cabaret is a foul man, but I needed work. I'm a dancer, not

31

a doxy. Well, he and Santiago made a bargain. If Santiago won, he would take ownership of the cabaret. If he lost, Santiago promised he could bring back the owner's wife, who left him six months ago. Santiago promised that if I helped him and he won, he'd let me be the bookkeeper and administrator for the cabaret. It's better than dancing, and he has no head for honest business. He's no good with numbers and running anything in an orderly fashion. I'd be good at it, and he'd get more customers to patronize the show. Naturally, I wanted him to win."

"What was the wager, exactly?"

"It was a contest for who could get the most money in the door one week versus the next week."

"And you helped Santiago by charming the customers?"

"Yes."

They both knew what he meant. She could create illusions and induce a near-hypnotic state. Men would pay over and over to see her and she would draw energy from them. It wouldn't hurt the men. No, Elliot had experienced it himself, and it was pleasurable. It hurt the heart a little, but in a good way, like a small painful longing that couldn't be fulfilled. But the feeling didn't last, and it did no real damage.

"When Santiago won the wager," said Yukiko, "the owner refused to transfer ownership of the place. He said it wasn't legal, that nothing was in writing, so he wasn't obligated to do a thing. Santiago threatened to burn the place down."

"And then he did?"

"I don't know. I only know it wasn't me. I was in my room and smelled smoke. I helped as many of the girls as I could."

He saw the cuts on her hands, the black on her knees. Young as she was, she upheld the Kitsune code to aid humankind in distress.

"Now Santiago is trying to make it out like I knocked

over a lamp or some such nonsense."

"Why would they believe that? Anyone could have started the fire."

"Because I smelled the smoke first. I screamed for everyone to get out, and it was a minute or two before the humans—the other people—smelled the smoke and started to leave. The ones who didn't dance tonight and who have rooms upstairs were already asleep."

"That doesn't seem like enough evidence for the police to think you were guilty."

"It's not. But the owner survived and talked to the police as well. The three of us are the only ones who know about the wager, and since Santiago won, the owner wouldn't mind getting rid of me. The wager would never hold up among humans, but he knows Santiago is something not human, and he's afraid. He also knows I helped Santiago, but he doesn't know how."

"Do you think Santiago burned it?"

"I do. But I can't prove anything."

"Can you use your magic to get away? Change your appearance?"

"How do you know about me? Did my family send you? Can I go home yet?"

Her face was so hopeful, so sweet, that Elliot wanted to say yes. But he also knew that her hard years in America would make her into the person she would become.

A police officer approached. "We're going to take you to the station," he said to Yukiko.

"I didn't do anything!" cried Yukiko. "Santiago, tell them!"

"There's no proof, officers," said Santiago. "It could have been anyone. I was only speculating."

"Well, the owner did some speculating too," said the officer. "We'll sort it all out at the station."

They put Yukiko in a wagon, and though Elliot saw the tears standing in her eyes, she did not cry or beg. She sat ramrod straight, chin high, like a small queen in her blackened dancer's costume.

"We don't have time for both," said Neil from behind him. Elliot had not heard his partner approach, but he never did.

Elliot checked the clock implant in his eye. "Half an hour," he said.

Neil said, "We can split up. I'll deal with the void wyrms, and you get Yukiko out. If they lock her up when the quake hits, she could be trapped and burned."

"You shouldn't go alone."

"And we can't leave Yukiko," said Neil. "Look, there were never any reports of wyrms or things like them in the witness reports after the quake, even though Seamus detected wyrm activity. That means we dealt with them. And since I don't get pulled toward them the way the rest of you do, I ought to be the one to use the machine to close their rips. I can do it alone."

Elliot couldn't disagree with that logic, and they made a plan to meet up back at Portsmouth Square after the earthquake. By the time Elliot reached the police station, there were only fifteen minutes remaining.

"She's my employee," he explained to the exhausted man on duty. "She dances on the side, but she's my housekeeper. I need to take her home."

"The sergeant will be in at eight in the morning, sir, as will everyone else. You have to wait until then. Also, the woman still needs to be questioned."

He argued with the man, coerced, explained, vaguely threatened and tried to bribe him. He nearly got thrown into a cell himself.

Then the earthquake hit.

Elliot was born and raised in Los Angeles, but this earthquake was beyond anything he had experienced. Luckily, he was prepared for it. The other people were not.

First came the mighty slam as the quake smashed into

the buildings and the floor lurched. Then came the shaking which went on and on. He ran inside, past the panicking policemen, found the man with the keys, grabbed them and then found Yukiko's cell.

By the time he had unlocked it, things had stopped moving. The policemen were shaken, but returned to their posts.

"Use your magic to get us out," he told her.

"I don't have enough."

"I know. Take what you can from me."

He held her hands and faced her, knowing that if she could draw energy from a person by dancing, then perhaps a willing donor could help her.

He looked into her eyes. She was so young now. Though her features were unchanged, she was a different person.

"You love someone," she said.

"I love a few people."

"Think of her."

He did. He thought of Bennu, the desert woman, of the faint markings on her face and collarbones that only appeared in a certain light, of the sounds she made in her sleep. Then, the vision left him, as if a black curtain had been pulled. He felt hollowed out, but as if the act had been done by a gentle hand. He knew it was only temporary.

"Let's go," said Yukiko. "Take my hand."

She led him out of the station, past the officers who turned to look in the opposite direction from them, as if they had heard a voice call their name. Yukiko led Elliot along, her steps sure and light, her gaze straight ahead.

"Did you do this?" she asked.

"The earthquake? Are you serious?"

"I don't know what you are. I cannot tell."

"I'm just a man. A human. I'm no one."

"Why help me? I have offered you nothing."

They reached the street. "You'll see me again. A long time from now. Here." He gave her the rest of his money, and she looked from the stack of bills to his face and back again.

"I am not agreeing to any sort of deal or exchange."

"I know. Just stay alive."

She looked away then, at the destruction and the rising smoke. A horse-drawn fire truck clattered by and a nearby woman yelled something in Cantonese. The men did not stop.

"I should go help them," she said. "But I intend to do as you say. I will stay alive."

He left her there, on the street in her dancing outfit, and headed for Portsmouth Square. Neil was waiting with the time machine and held a large, flat, cloth-wrapped parcel.

"A painting," said Neil before Elliot could ask. "I had to save it from the fire. The house was empty."

Elliot didn't bother to question or protest. If Neil wanted to run into a burning building for a painting, Elliot couldn't stop him. Neil was a mental curator of sorts, always wanting to listen to music and view pieces of art. He was captivated by it all, though he usually only sought to enjoy the art, not to own it.

"Any void wyrms?" he asked.

"Yes. I forced them back and closed the rips. I also got some good readings for Seamus. He'll be pleased."

They walked back to their entry spot into this time, knowing it was a safe location from which to travel. It was only later that Elliot realized he had never given Yukiko his name.

CHAPTER 5

F ELICIA SANCHEZ-DOYLE HAD TWO IMPORTANT things to tell her husband, but first she had to find him. He wasn't working in his upstairs laboratory or reading in the bedroom they shared in the Los Angeles safe house. He wasn't in the backyard, nor had he taken a walk around the block. His mobile phone was sitting on his desk, the battery dead.

In fact, no one at all was home. That in itself was concerning, as the Los Angeles safe house almost always had someone coming or going.

"Nothing worse than having news and no one to tell," she muttered and got herself a glass of water.

A moment later a sleek white cat glided into the kitchen. This was Pangur Ban, mother of the two younger cats, Frieda and Diego.

"Is the news good or bad?" asked the cat. She must have heard Felicia from the next room.

"Good. But where is everyone? I thought Hazel was home for a while."

"She is. Everyone is looking for Julius."

"Where is he?"

"If we knew that, then we wouldn't be looking. But I understand your meaning. We noticed this morning that he was gone. Apparently no one has seen him in days. We all assumed he was in his room reading."

"A fair assumption," said Felicia. "He usually is."

"Indeed."

"Have you called September or Augustus?"

"No one can reach Augustus either. September is back in nineteenth century New Orleans in Seamus and Hazel's world, so no one has gone to visit her yet. The group decided to check on Julius's usual haunts and there are a few private libraries that he had mentioned wanting to visit."

Well, then there was nothing to do but wait. She took a shower and made a sandwich. When Seamus finally returned home, he scooped her into a tight embrace and kissed her. Hazel hung her car keys near the kitchen door and hugged her.

"How long have you been gone?" asked Seamus.

"Three weeks for me."

"Only one week for me."

"Did you find Julius?" Felicia asked.

"No. He's just gone."

"It's not like him to leave. He's always here. That's why it's the safe house."

"Precisely." Seamus looked out the window. It was overcast but warm with a little electric thrill in the air, as if a thunderstorm was coming. "I wish it would rain already. I miss the rain."

"You miss Ireland."

"That I do. So tell me, did you have any luck on the blue material?" asked Seamus.

"Lots of luck," said Felicia. "We couldn't figure it out in this time because we don't have the proper technology yet. But in twenty years, we do. I've spent a good number of hours in a medical lab at UCLA and I can tell you this. The blue stuff is biological material."

"From what?" asked Seamus. "What on God's green earth has fluid that glows pale blue? Is it one of those plants in the Amazon? Or perhaps a creature from under the sea? I've seen programs on the television about the animals down there."

"Not that I know of. I need to go forward farther in time to get more information."

"Then go! I'll go with you."

"It's not so easy. I need to do more studying to learn how to even use the scientific findings developed between now and then. If I go waltzing into a laboratory without knowing what I'm looking for or how to use the lab equipment, I'll get thrown out. It takes time."

She followed him up to his laboratory and told him about her findings while he searched through the mess for one thing or another.

"It's not like any biological material we've encountered before," she said. "It's not plant, that's for certain. It lacks the cell walls and other cellular differentiators. There was never any question on that. But it's not animal precisely either. That's what got me. On the one hand, it has a typical structure to the cells, well, some of them. Most had nuclei, but some didn't. It wasn't until the second day that I knew what I was looking at."

Seamus glanced at her but didn't interrupt.

"The plasma was bizarre. Completely strange. But was, without a doubt, plasma."

"And that means what, exactly?" he asked.

"It's blood."

"Glowing light blue blood?"

"Yes."

"Blood from some strange animal we've never encountered before."

"As far as I know, yes."

"And in order to make more time machines, we need to find this animal and get its blood."

"Correct."

"Can you duplicate it? Don't they clone things in the future? Can you clone the blood?"

"They do know about cloning, but I'm not sure if I can. I'd need to do a lot of research."

"Well, crack your books, because I learned something as well. I haven't figured it all out yet, but I've had Elliot get me some readings from your original time rip in New Orleans as well as the earthquake in San Francisco. I haven't figured it out yet, but I'm close. I think I'm near to being able to get you home."

"But what about you getting back here afterward? Or to your home world? If it's this hard to get to my world, what if you can't get back?"

"I've already left my home world once," he said.

"I meant Hazel. Wherever she is, you'll want to be too. And I'm sure you want to visit your family in Ireland some day."

He got a wistful look and turned to straighten things on his desk. The entire room was a disaster, and she knew that if he was cleaning, he was worried.

"I'll find a way. Or, maybe she can come with us."

"And Neil?"

"The whole gang. The cats too. I don't know yet, but as long as I've breath in my body, I'll not leave you without your family."

"Speaking of which," she said, sidling up to him, leaning back against the desk and watching him from the corner of her eye. She didn't want to miss this moment, and she paused until he looked up at her.

"I'm pregnant."

The change on his face took a few moments, and she watched the words bounce around the pinball machine of his mind. Then he gave a cry and scooped her into his arms, first silently and then with an endless stream of rapid words on boy and girl names based on his countless relatives, preparations and how she ought to be resting. Then he kissed her again and again.

Hazel poked her head in the door. She glanced away, as seeing open displays of affection still bothered her. You could take the girl out of the nineteenth century, Felicia thought, but some things ran too deep to be removed by moving between centuries. Hazel still hated revealing clothing and public kissing.

"Augustus seems to be gone too," Hazel said. "He's not at the boardwalk or his house. And June Yee in San Francisco isn't answering her phone. Neither is Red Fawn."

Pangur Ban slid in behind Hazel and watched them with unblinking eyes.

"They're all gone," said Seamus, glancing at Felicia, then at the others. "The watchers on the ramparts, they've deserted their posts."

"Or maybe they've gone to man them," said Felicia.

"If that's happened, then may God help us all," said Pangur Ban.

CHAPTER 6

ASTRID LET YELBEGHEN PUSH IN her chair after she unfolded her napkin and spread it on her lap. The drake looked like a man, with dark hair, wide-spaced, grayish eyes and a wide, pleasant mouth. And though Astrid had never seen him in his true form, after four years of meals together, she thought she almost understood him.

Because of a deal she had been forced to make on behalf of the Seelie, she was required to dine with him once every two weeks. He was not an unpleasant companion, and she didn't mind visiting him. She usually enjoyed it. He was lonely, which was largely his own fault, and she had told him so a few times. But tonight, something else was on her mind.

"Have you ever known of anything that might cause souls to be more sticky than normal?"

"Why do you ask?"

"I've run into a few lately. More than usual. Jeff isn't worried, but I am."

"You could have called me to take a look."

"I only promised to take you on three jobs with me. I've fulfilled that part of our bargain."

"Yes, but you've taken me on far more than that. You enjoy my company."

"Forget about that," she said, feeling her face grow warm. "I want to know if there were any time periods or events that caused more souls to be stuck here. I'm finding a few that have been stuck for too long and no psychopomp was ever summoned."

"Time periods, no. Events, yes. Well, events coincide with time periods, so in that respect, yes to both."

She could tell that he was in a feisty mood, wanting to banter and flirt, while she wanted information.

"And what events were those?"

"Times of great change, of upheaval or when there were lots of deaths. World Wars, famines, the Black Plague. Events like that."

"What about now? These people didn't die in wars or famines."

One of the servants took their empty salad plates and replaced them with dishes of steaming eggplant parmesan with pasta and grilled zucchini. Astrid, being Unseelie by birth, could eat no meat without becoming ill. The drake always remembered this each time they dined.

"I don't know," said Yelbeghen. "Interesting you should mention it though. There have been other disturbances. I was forced to seal off a Door in Tangier recently. Some of the Seelie were harassing the locals. It became serious. Stealing children, causing people to become lost, that sort of thing. Some people were even being led into Seelie and returning months later."

"You can do that? You can seal off openings to other worlds?" Astrid could open and close her own Doors, but could not seal the Doors of others.

"It's difficult, but yes."

"I can't do that."

"You're barely over two decades old. I have far more experience." He gave a little, self-satisfied smile.

She forgot that sometimes. The drake, for all his years, often seemed unsure of himself, vulnerable even. As much as he ruled over his possessions, he was ruled by them. He was lonely, occasionally cruel, intelligent, eccentric and unusually selfish. He was also completely devoted to her.

43

Yelbeghen collected things, people and animals, but most of the people were there willingly. He had servants, but they were treated kindly. His animals were well cared for and any being who was too freakish and strange to live in the regular world was welcome on his Mediterranean island. The place was beautiful and was part sanctuary and part prison. At times, Astrid wondered which one it was for her. She was obligated to dine with him fortnightly, but she enjoyed the experience for the most part. Also, using her Doors, she came and went as she pleased.

"I saw the movie you recommended," he said. "The one with the aliens."

"Pretty good, didn't you think?"

"It was. But I think the humans who made it let on more than they mean to. I mean, really. Beings from the dark of space, from another world, taking people and returning them later? They're sidhe."

"I only said you should see it so you could participate in the normal world. You're too isolated here. I thought you'd enjoy it."

"I did. But I still think it's telling more than it means to."

"Sometimes a cigar is just a cigar. Aliens are just aliens."

"Well, one type of being I've never met. One I have. Simple."

"Maybe it's not about the sidhe. Maybe it's about all things in the void. Like your kind. Drakes are void creatures."

"As are all Doors."

"So you're saying that humans know about Doors on a subconscious level?"

It was odd for her to categorize people as "humans," but when she was with Yelbeghen, she allowed the distinction. She was human by choice, but could never live honestly among them.

"Yes," he said. "They know something. And I think you knew that when you recommended the movie."

"I didn't."

They debated the points of the movie and then moved on to a discussion of a book they had both read, followed by a brief argument about one of his new sculptures. At the end of the meal, Astrid gave him a gift, an original painting from an artist in San Francisco whose house had burned down during the great quake of 1906. Yelbeghen studied the painting and thanked her.

"I will care for it. Where did you get it?"

"A friend of mine from the Time Corps who loves art saved it before the house burned. He said you'd care for it better than he could."

"Was this your Neil Grey? The golem?"

"That's him. And no, he's not interested in meeting you."

"Pity. And is Captain Hazel Dubois considering retiring from sailing?"

"You won't get her ship either."

"She won't live forever."

From anyone else, it would have sounded ominous. But from the drake, it was a matter-of-fact statement of desire. He wanted Skidbladnir, the living Viking ship, and he wanted to meet a golem. Both were rare, and he loved rare things.

At least he was up front about what he wanted. It was refreshing after dealing with the rest of humanity with all their unconscious manipulations and unspoken desires that they themselves were hardly aware of. They all simply hurt so much, were so hungry inside, and all of them thought they were more hurt and more hungry than the others. So they smiled and made small talk and drank their coffee and drove their cars, and each and every one of them was alien to her.

"Have you made any more art for me?" he asked.

"You've rejected every piece I've shown you."

"I still want to see them. Do you have your sketch book?"

She carried one in her purse at all times, but she didn't

want to show him. She said as much.

"You still owe me an original piece of art."

Their bargain was threefold. First, she had promised to take him on three psychopomp jobs to send souls to death. Though Yelbeghen was a Door, he was not a psychopomp, and he was fascinated with witnessing such a rare occurrence as a soul being escorted to the afterlife. Second, she had to dine with him every two weeks for a ten-year period. And third, she had to make him a piece of art.

"You never gave a time limit for how long I've got to make it," she said.

He smiled and gave a little shrug. "It wasn't my cleverest bargain."

Her phone rang and she excused herself to answer it. It was Gerard, the Seelie who usually served as the spokesmen for his people when dealing with her. He instructed her to come to the Seelie version of Luna Park immediately.

"I'll be there in an hour," she said to him and hung up.

"Only an hour?" said the drake. "I was hoping we could go to the opera. There's one tonight in Vienna, but its starts in three hours."

"Sorry. I have to meet up with the Seelie. My third task."

His face went blank, and she knew he was disappointed. But more than that, he was unhappy. Worried even. If he had been merely disappointed, he would have covered it with a joke or a jab.

"Be careful with them," he said. "You know to call on me if they give you any trouble."

"I'll be fine. They can't imprison me. I can get out of anything they've got."

"They have other ways to hurt you."

Yes. She knew.

An hour later, she made a Door to Luna Park, then another Door from the boardwalk in her world to the one in the Seelie world. She walked to the main office, noting the Seelie with their animal and human parts and their beautiful or strange clothing. A few studied her, but she kept walking. As beautiful as the Seelie world was, with its apricot sky and green sea, and as delicious as the spiced, sugar-sprinkled fruit at the snack stand smelled, she did not want to linger. Like the drake, she was no friend of the Seelie. Their tasks were set as much as a punishment for her as they were selected as a benefit to the Seelie.

She found Gerard, the small, sturdy centaur with a powdered wig and smartly cut coat sitting in the manager's office, chatting with twin girls. They wore matching yellow dresses with ribbons tying their brown hair into sleek ponytails. They looked at each other once and then smiled, exposing triple rows of wickedly pointed teeth.

Once they left, Gerard closed the office door behind them.

"You said you had my final task," said Astrid.

"I do. But first, tell me how your Door-making is going."

Gerard had been her first instructor on the art of making Doors. After years of being a psychopomp, she was as skilled as any of the others at it. Perhaps Yelbeghen was better than she was, but Gerard would already guess that.

She told him that she was doing well and asked after his health. He asked her a few more questions which she deflected with polite but uninformative answers. He got a grim look and finally sighed in exasperation. "I know you don't like me, but I am on your side."

"You're on your own side. Let's not pretend."

"Very well." He fiddled with a button on his jacket. "I want to make it clear to you the magnitude of what we are asking. We do not do it lightly or without great thought and deliberation. It has taken us years to get to this point. There's a person who has caused great harm to the Seelie. He has now committed a deed so grave, that it must be answered."

"What did he do?"

Gerard gave her an assessing look. "He closed one of

the few openings we have to the human world. It's gone now. Completely vanished. The Seelie are more trapped than ever."

Understanding hit her, and her stomach tightened.

"Not only that. We know that a drake will open the void further, to free the void wyrms."

"How do you know that?" she asked, a touch more defensively than she would have liked. She hated her inability to conceal, to trick and manipulate. Gerard's expression changed. He knew that she understood.

"You forget our far-seers. They are, sometimes, correct," he said. "And the drake is a danger."

"He hasn't harmed anyone."

"You are too fond of the monster. But I suppose that's to be expected from someone like you. Even your own mothers, both human and Unseelie, couldn't love you. And you only seem to enjoy the company of the wicked and the strange."

"I won't be baited with this."

"Consider it. The golem assassin? The ship's captain who killed one of the Twelve? The monkey-footed convict professor who destabilizes entire worlds? The Kitsune who lost her tail for bad conduct? The Coyote with the lying silver tongue? You see? The wicked."

"I'm not going to argue good and evil with you. Your words don't make you good any more than your passivity in the face of conflict does. Besides, some of them are innocent. There's Sister and Elliot."

"The tongueless mental patient and the man with his brain unwinding? Those would be the strange."

"What do you care? It's nothing to you whom I associate with. Why not tell me the task and be done with it?"

"Because I want you to understand what's at stake. There are people you care about. If you don't complete your task, the Seelie will find your friends and either kill them or drive them mad or torture them. Maybe all three."

The viciousness of the threat hit her like a blow. Never had Gerard spoken to her like this. Sure, he was not her friend, not really, but he had always been cordial. He had been her teacher, once.

"I've upset you," he said and moved forward to take her hand. She stepped back.

"Don't touch me."

"I may be the only friend you have left after all this is done."

"You're not even my friend now."

"And the drake is your friend?"

"His name is Yelbeghen."

"You still believe that? Years of dining with him, and you don't even know his name. Yelbeghen is the type of drake he is. Not his name."

She hadn't known, and the revelation left her feeling small and alone. He was her friend and she didn't even know his name.

"It hardly matters though," said Gerard. "Your task is not to learn his name. Your task is to kill him."

CHAPTER 7

NEIL GREY STUDIED THE SKY and inhaled. The air was warm and heavy and the scent was off. Not unpleasant exactly, but wrong somehow. Massive dark clouds gathered, altering the quality of the ambient light and changing the color of the streets to darker tones. That itself wasn't unusual. There was something else. It felt as if the hairs on his body were about to stand up and his spine felt electrified.

"I wish it would just go on and rain," said Elliot. "LA needs the water."

Thunder rumbled in the distance and Hazel got a look of delight. She loved thunderstorms. Neil wondered if she missed her home in New Orleans. She never seemed at home in Los Angeles. But she never seemed at home anywhere, really. Only when she was on her ship was she ever really at peace.

"It's just up this street on the right," she said.

There was one last home to check, one last person who might have heard where Julius had gone. The woman who lived in the house kept an extensive collection of old microfiche from back when libraries used them.

"You two go on ahead," said Neil. "I'll buy lunch and we can take it home."

Hazel and Elliot went on without him and he watched the pair of them, Elliot's blond head turning toward Hazel's shorter brown one, her small upturned face and the way she looked into the distance when she spoke. He saw the small bit of discontent in her posture because she was traveling on foot, unable to go fast the way she preferred. Elliot's manner and laugh were so easy, so relaxed, unlike Neil's own emotions which always left him feeling overwhelmed when he could not keep them tightly controlled. Pictures, plants, paintings, voices raised in song, they all were too beautiful for him to bear sometimes, and it seemed to be getting worse the older he got. It was as if he might break open one day, and all the tiny cracks in him would fill until his interior could hold no more and he would split open, spilling everything. He tried to keep himself in check, with silence, with stillness.

He wondered how much of this Elliot and Hazel knew instinctively. Hazel was a more solitary being than Elliot, who got along with almost everyone and loved socializing, even with strangers. In their own unique ways, they both understood human nature in a way he never would.

"To love someone is to have one's heart walking outside one's body," said a man.

He knew the voice, though he had only heard it once before, right before the man had killed him. It was Mr. March. This was not the elderly pale man who had brought him to life, but rather the one who had come after, the same man in a new body. This man was dark-haired, more robust, taller, younger and more muscular.

"I loved you like that, once," said March. "You were my son, in every way that mattered."

"Normal people don't turn their sons into killers. Normal people don't murder their sons when they want to quit killing innocent people."

"And normal people don't have their fathers murdered by their future wives. But you and I aren't normal people. Come, walk with me."

Neil felt none of the old compulsion to obey him. The discovery lit him with a new fire. He had wondered before if March's power over him still applied, but now he knew.

He was free. Truly free.

He didn't move, didn't turn with March. He had no reason to speak with this man.

"Or would you rather we ask your best friend and your wife to join us?" said March. "I can run and fetch them."

Hazel and Elliot had turned the corner and moved out of sight. Every protective instinct in Neil told him to keep March away from them.

"I'll go."

They walked together in the opposite direction from Elliot and Hazel, Neil sizing up the man beside him. They were roughly the same size, and Neil had no idea how strong March was in this body. But March's power over him had never been in physical strength.

"Your Professor Seamus Doyle, is he still alive?" asked March.

"You know he is."

"Well, I wouldn't be surprised if he did something vastly stupid and got himself killed."

"You're the only one who has tried to kill him."

"I was correcting a mistake. I never should have given Oren McCullen the blue fluid. I thought I was being like Prometheus, giving fire to a suffering mankind. The fluid allows the creation of wonderful engines. Did you know that? Before the time machines, McCullen used it to make engines that could produce more power than anything the humans could come up with on their own. I wanted to help humanity to advance. The fluid allows them to make tiny pinprick holes between worlds and McCullen was able to make such brilliant use of them."

"By stealing Seamus's designs."

"He improved upon them. The two of them together could have created such wondrous machines."

"They did. Seamus made the time machines."

"Yes, but there is a problem. When I gave McCullen the fluid, I knew he could use it inside the engines and make those pinprick holes between worlds, like tiny holes in skin. Those holes can heal themselves. Tiny ones usually can. All was well as long as the holes were small. It's the giant rips that Seamus made that became a problem."

"Then why not take it back? You could have confiscated the machines years ago. Instead, you tried to kill Seamus and let McCullen get away with another machine. God only knows where he is now."

"He's safely tucked away in his own home world. The machine did not work again once he used the coordinates I gave him."

"You gave two inventors something without forethought and then punished them for using it."

"I was punished, rather."

"How? By getting killed by Hazel? She was defending the Professor. He's like a father to her. She loves him."

"And she was defending you. Don't forget that she loves you too."

March purchased two cups of coffee and handed one to Neil along with two sugar packets.

"Two sugars, no cream, correct?" said March.

He still remembered, and Neil despised it. He carried the coffee without drinking it.

"Being shot by Hazel was not my only punishment," said March. "I did two terrible deeds, and I had to correct them. Like a modern Prometheus, I gave mankind fire, but I also made an unnatural man. Like Doctor Frankenstein, I made me an amalgamation, but you were perfect and I loved you."

"I wasn't meant to exist. That's why you killed me."

"I didn't want to." He stopped and turned to Neil and he saw the pain in March's face, the regret. "If you had stayed with me, if you hadn't turned on your creator, I could have protected you. But you failed me. And so I was commanded to kill you."

"Commanded by whom?"

"Always the cleverest, my Neil. Always asking questions, even when you were first made. I was commanded by one of the Seven."

"You have a boss?"

"Not a boss, as such, no. Did you think the Twelve just appeared out of nowhere?"

"None of you will ever tell us. September, Julius, Red Fawn and June are all so cagey about it."

"They would be."

"So what are you? Watchers of some kind, I know that. And who are the Seven? And who are above them?"

"The Three." March was amused now, and Neil felt some kind of trap closing.

"Why come and force me to talk to you?"

"Force? I cannot force you to do anything. Not anymore. You're here on your own."

"If that's the case, then I'll say good-bye. Thank you for the coffee."

"No, wait." March reached out and touched Neil's arm. "I want to explain everything to you. Not that you'll remember. You won't. Things are being turned back to their original factory settings, so to speak. I told you that I made two mistakes. One was making you, and I corrected that."

"And yet here I stand."

"I owe your wife my thanks for that. But leaving that aside, I couldn't correct my second mistake, the mistake I made in giving the blue fluid to Oren McCullen. I couldn't kill Seamus, and now I'm being so closely watched that I can't if I wanted to. So they've pulled out the big guns."

"The modern Prometheus must be punished."

"They're beyond punishment now. The time rips are too big, the instabilities too great. When that girl, Astrid, used Seamus's machine to augment her natural talents and tear a hole to the Library in the void, something changed. It was a trigger. A catalyst. Like a tear in fabric. Once you get a tear started, it inevitably continues. And now, it's too late."

"What are they going to do? What are *you* going to do?"

"As I said, turn it back to its original factory settings. As it was in the beginning, so it ever shall be."

"Seal off the worlds? Close them off from each other? Can you do that?"

"I can, with help. Not on my own, though. It's the only way. This way, McCullen won't get the blue fluid, the machines will never rip holes and the worlds will continue on, just as they ought to have done from the start."

It was too much, the thought too momentous to process in a moment. Everything would reset. Hazel and Seamus would be in their home world with their steam-powered creations. Astrid, Sister and Elliot would be in theirs, the world of living ships and multiple gods and sidhe and people who could also be animals. Felicia would be in her world of ordinary things.

"Which world is mine?" asked Neil. "Which is my home world?"

"The one with me."

"And I'll be enslaved again."

"By necessity. You'll never meet Elliot from the Time Corps on that train and you'll never leave me. If you stay in my employ, you will be safe. I won't have to kill you again."

"When do you planning on doing this? How long do we have?"

March glanced at his watch. "A few minutes."

Neil didn't wait, but dropped his coffee and took off running.

Everything depended on the time machines. March was right. Neil understood that now. There were too many time loops already. Their friendships created time loops. The existence of the time machines themselves were time loops, as Seamus had never figured out how to create the blue fluid. Neil had thought, had hoped, that they would untangle the mess at some point. After all, everyone lived, some married, life continued in all the worlds.

Now he knew differently.

Without the machines, Seamus would never create an accidental time rip, and Felicia would never be in an omnibus accident. She'd never meet Seamus. She never would convince him to take in Hazel, the street child, as his ward.

He tore up the street, past the cars and pedestrians, never running out of breath, never slowing. He might be enslaved again, he might be a killer again, but today, now, he would use his abilities as he chose. For a few minutes, he was still free.

In this world, the hub world, where Astrid, Elliot and Sister originated, things would be a little more stable. Without the machines, Sister and Astrid would still have been swapped at birth. The Unseelie and Seelie would still do as they pleased. Astrid could still free Sister from Unseelie. But Astrid would be trapped in the void. Without Elliot to travel in time and make her little cold iron owl bell and to ring it and lead her home, she'd be lost in the void forever.

Pangur Ban, the white cat, would never meet Astrid because Elliot would never ask the cat to look after his younger cousin. Her kittens, Frieda and Diego, would never be born.

Yukiko would live on in America, never meeting the Time Corps.

He didn't know what would happen to the raven, Huginn.

But there was one other thing hanging behind all these thoughts. He would be a golem again, a killer unable to exercise his own free will. The thought grew huge and then slipped in among the others, less important, less urgent. He didn't matter now. Elliot and Hazel mattered.

He tore around the corner, racing to the house where

the two had gone. They were saying good-bye to a woman who closed the screen door. The moment they registered his appearance, they first looked surprised, then terrified. He couldn't see himself, but the faces of the two he loved best told him enough.

He explained everything.

"We have to get home," said Hazel. "We have to tell the Professor."

"Not enough time. It'll be any moment now."

"My ship! It can't exist in my home world. What will happen to it? What will happen to my crew?"

"The ship will have to stay here," said Neil.

"Elliot!" she said. "I give it to you. I give you Skidbladnir, to own as captain. It's yours."

"I don't want it. I can't."

"Accept it!"

He paused, then he said he did, but Neil knew how reluctant he was to do it. The ship's ownership was governed by ancient laws. It could be bought, sold, stolen or bartered. It could travel in many worlds, but Hazel's wasn't one of them.

Elliot dialed his phone to speak with Astrid, but she didn't answer. Neil knew it was futile, that she was still be trapped in the void, but he didn't stop Elliot. There was nothing any of them could do.

Hazel took Neil's hand.

"Don't let go," she said. "Whatever happens, just don't let go."

"You'll be all right. You'll be with the Professor. Find him."

"I'll already know him. I met him when I used to dress as a boy and run errands for him. But if Felicia hadn't come ..."

Tears welled in her eyes and he pulled her to him.

"I can't go back," she said, a hitch in her voice. "I can't go back there. Without you to save me from my uncle, I'll be trapped. Oh God, Neil. Don't let them take me. Don't make me have to live my life all over again."

She was crying now and he kissed the top of her head, her cheeks, her mouth.

"Just hang on to me," she said. "Don't let go, no matter what. You're strong enough. Just don't let go."

She wrapped her arms around him and he held her. Elliot wrapped his arms around them both, but lightly. He understood, even if Hazel did not.

"I don't want to go back," whispered Hazel.

The sun went dark. Everything went dark. He grabbed Hazel harder, her small form fragile. He could kill her with his grip, and he held her tight enough to hurt her, but not break her ribs. Sound vanished and all sensation disappeared. There was no feeling of air around him or breath moving in and out of his lungs, no rub of clothing on his skin or the press of his feet on the sidewalk. No feeling of Hazel. Then, even his ability to process these thoughts vanished and he fell into the black.

CHAPTER 8

THE OCEAN AIR WAS BRACING and cold on Elliot's cheeks as he shouted an order to the monkey crew to raise the red and white striped sail. The carved dragon head prow of the ship turned northwest, away from Alexandria, Egypt, where he and Sister and the crew had just delivered a hundred bolts of fine sidhe fabric. It was so fine, it was nearly liquid to the touch and came in colors both bright and subtle. Fairy cloth. Sister had wanted some to make a dress, but of course, she couldn't have any. To do anything less than to completely fulfill a promise to the Seelie was about as terrible an idea as one could have.

They sailed away from Alexandria, and Elliot felt better the farther they got. He didn't like the city, and he couldn't say why. The sleek metal lighthouse winked at him in the distance and he rested his hand on the gunwale and looked deep into the water where dolphins occasionally accompanied them. There were none today.

Sister came up from below decks, barefoot and with her blonde hair flying wild and loose in the wind, like a fairy girl. She was Astrid's duplicate, and as his cousin had not returned after saving the world from the Wild Hunt, Sister had taken over her identity. Of course, tongueless and mute as she was, it was hard for her to fit in. She had come to this world illiterate and deeply troubled, but she was intelligent and was learning quickly.

"I had a bad dream," she signed. "I dreamed of terrible

things and beautiful ones too."

"Not surprising."

"Do you have dreams? I dreamed that you said you had dreams that could tell the future. Dreams of memories that hadn't happened yet."

He had never told her any such thing, but every word was true. But his dreams, strange as they were, always came to nothing. They predicted mundane events with no meaning. They were distractions, useless distractions.

Sister held out her mobile phone. "I have a text from Yukiko."

Yukiko, the fox woman who had helped Astrid to get Sister out of captivity had kept in touch with Sister, texting back and forth since Sister could not speak. It had helped Sister learn to read, and had given her someone other than Elliot who helped her feel like she belonged in this world.

Yukiko had not answered any of Elliot's calls, most likely because she felt guilty that she had survived the trip back from Unseelie and Astrid had not. Or, if Astrid had, she hadn't returned to this world. There was no telling. The Seelie, Santiago and Yukiko all had no idea of her whereabouts. Neither did Red Fawn or any of the other strange people who spent much of their time near the Luna Park boardwalk. Astrid was simply gone.

"Are you having strange dreams?" Yukiko's text said.

Elliot sighed and turned to Sister. "I think it's a coincidence. Everyone has dreams and some of them are weird. Simple as that."

"But why would she wonder about it? Why ask me?"

"Because she's checking up on you. You've had such bad nightmares since you came back."

"No. There's more to it. I can tell. The dreams aren't making me cry at night any more. I'm doing better." She turned away, texting Yukiko back.

With luck, they could get back to California in a few

weeks, stopping a few times to take on supplies. The Seelie paid well and he would have enough to give a good amount to his mother. It might even give her the chance to move to a different apartment, or maybe start saving toward a down payment on a modest townhouse. Elliot hated her current boyfriend and wished she'd leave him. But there were factors, always factors. Money was only one.

He glanced at the position of the sun. It was late afternoon, sometime between three and four, maybe. He asked Sister to check the phone to tell him what time it was. She did.

"I need a watch," he muttered, and a small digital clock appeared in the lower edge of his vision. He stepped back involuntarily.

"What the hell is that?"

Sister touched his arm and looked up at him, worried. He waved his hand in front of his face, noting the position of the clock and its movement as he turned his head.

"I have a clock in my eye. I can see it."

She glanced at the phone. "Is it like a phone?"

"No. A phone doesn't make things happen in front of your eyes."

Nothing did that. Sure, there was always talk about the latest wearable technological development, but he owned nothing like the experimental scientific devices found in the technology magazines. Aside from his phone and computer in his quarters, he led a simple life.

"I told you things were weird," she signed.

"Clock on," he said, testing it. "Clock off."

"Do you think the Seelie put that into you?" signed Sister.

"It doesn't seem like something they'd do. They're not technologically savvy."

"But it is strange, like I said. What have you been dreaming about?"

He did have one memory of a dream. It was a woman, a short freckled woman with brown eyes and hair in a braid.

She was looking up at him, upset. And she said he had to take something from her. But her hands were empty. Still, she was insistent. He had to take something from her.

As he thought of it, the memory partially solidified. It was like waking, with reality becoming clearer each moment. It had something to do with the ship. But Skidbladnir had been in his family for generations. The Van Dorns had always owned it. They were descendants of Vikings. That's right. That was how things were. Why had it taken him so long to recall it?

Once, the Seelie had poisoned him with something that made him see time slips more clearly. Perhaps his slow memory had something to do with that.

But no. He knew better. His dreams might be strange, but the little digital clock in his eye was real.

Sister got a look on her face, one he had seen so often on Astrid's face, a look of determination and deep thought.

"Too much is wrong," she signed, glancing around the quarters they shared as if something out of place might give her a clue. "We should find out what."

Elliot did not disagree.

CHAPTER 9

NEIL GREY HAD KNOWN, ALWAYS known, that he was alone in the world. He remembered foster parents, a few teachers, a few friends from school, but he knew none of them now. They were only memories, small and fleeting.

He sat alone in a train car in 1857, heading south through Louisiana to New Orleans, watching the world speed by the window as it had done so often before. Through glass and metal cities far in the future, through towns nearer his time of birth in the twentieth century, even in underground tunnels in cities around the world, always the world sped by. Or he sped through it.

He had no home, no family, no friends, no purpose other than working for Mr. March. And even that was now in question. He had left March, wondering if some of the killings he had committed were of genuinely bad people. He had questions, ones March had been reticent to answer.

His pocket held a folded paper with the address of a woman in New Orleans, one September Wilde. When he reached the city, he could leave a letter with her, and she would notify March that Neil no longer wished to work for him.

That meant that he would be trapped here, in this world, in this time. The Civil War hadn't started yet, but it wouldn't be long. He might be conscripted. He might have to kill people.

Maybe he could find work on a ship. He could sail to Europe and get work there and avoid the war here. He could go to California and farm. The gold rush was over, but there would be other jobs. He only needed to make sure never to remove his shoes in front of anyone, as the people in this world of steam power and war had a prominent big toe, like an ape, and he had narrow, ordinary feet.

The train pulled into the New Orleans station and he stepped out. The platform bustled with people, all of them with a destination, with a purpose. A raggedy man on the far end of the platform played a scuffed violin, his case open in front of him. He did not play particularly well, but now and then, he would play a particular measure and Neil would feel something move inside him. He listened for a few moments.

He wished he could create beauty. Paintings or sculpture or music or poetry, he loved them all, but could only duplicate and imitate. He listened for a minute, tossed a coin into the open case and left the violinist to find the address on the piece of paper. Mr. March was waiting on the sidewalk just outside the station, thin and pale, elderly but vibrant.

"I was wrong," March said, without preamble. "I will explain everything to you. I promise."

March reached out his hand and Neil paused before taking it. The man pulled him into another place, another time, this one closer to his home time. They had traveled this way many times before.

In front of an isolated house sat two automobiles. He guessed by their models that they had arrived close to the early 2020s. Maybe a little earlier.

"I have the proof you wanted," said March. "For all three of them."

Neil had killed more than three people, but the last three had bothered him the most. One was a Mr. Andrew Dubois, supposed child molester in the 1850s. Another was a nightclub owner in 1982 Las Vegas, and the third was a scientist in 2032.

March took him from the desert heat outside into the house of glass and chrome, an expensive home that was sleek and modern but with enough wooden accents and soft furnishings that it did not feel cold. Inside, Neil admired the few paintings on the walls and a well-placed white and gold sculpture on the entryway table.

"Where are we?" he asked. The living room windows were large, almost floor to ceiling, and let in the hard, bright desert sunlight.

"Palm Springs. Do you like it?"

"Do you live here?"

"I do. And you can stay here as well, if you like. I have plenty of room."

March took him to another room with a computer and showed him everything, from genetic evidence linking the nightclub owner to the killings of the Las Vegas showgirls to the future horrors the scientist's technologies would one day become. The molester was more difficult to prove, but March provided him with an interview of an old woman, the daughter of a neighbor, who named him as a sexual deviant from her youth who harmed a few vulnerable children.

"How do I know if all of this is true?" asked Neil.

"Do you think I made these things up? That I created them?"

"You can travel in time and between worlds. You can falsify information."

"I haven't lied to you, Neil. I never have. I've kept information from you because our working relationship is based on trust. You trust me to take you from world to world and to deposit you in the correct place and retrieve you after. Have you ever wondered if I'd leave you?"

"No."

"Then don't wonder now. I hope this information puts

your mind at rest."

It did, mostly.

"You are my strong right arm," said March. "And as such, you are entitled to know what we do, the ideals we work for. None of this is random. We have a glorious purpose, you and I. Perhaps I have been selfish not to share it with you. Would you like to know?"

"I would."

"Then come with me. Because there are those who would wish to stop us, to leave mankind enslaved. It is our responsibility, our duty, to free them from lies and give them the truth. Come and I will show you."

Freedom was beautiful. So was truth. While he could never create beauty on his own, he thought, perhaps, he could defend it.

CHAPTER 10

ASTRID STEPPED THROUGH HER DOOR from the boardwalk office and into the human version of Luna Park and checked the time on her phone. Immediately, her phone tried to synchronize with its network and she shoved it into her pocket while it did so. The park was emptying out, the sun was low in the sky, and she was hungry. She made a Door to her apartment in New York, and the moment she stepped through, she saw she had made a mistake. This wasn't her apartment, but someone else's. She had never made such an error, but she was distracted and jumpy from her visit with the Seelie.

She stepped back through a Door, into the hallway of her building and checked the number on the door. It was hers. She pulled her key from her purse and slipped it into the lock, but it wouldn't open. She made a Door inside and stepped through, only to find that she had not made a mistake with her first Door after all. The apartment was no longer hers.

She returned to the hallway, not eager to be discovered by whoever lived there now, and she pulled out her phone, trying to decide between calling Jeff, Yelbeghen or Elliot. But then she spotted the date.

October 25th.

She had left on October 17th.

Damn the Seelie! They must have done this on purpose, another way of demonstrating their power. Oh, sure, we can force you to lose time. We can do it to your friends and family. We can hurt those you love without truly hurting them. And then we can really hurt them. We can also make you gone long enough for someone else to take your apartment. But why would the landlord rent out her place if she was only gone for eight days? Her rent was paid up for the month.

She had no voice mail and no texts. Odd. But where were the calls from the other psychopomps? She had left her post for more than a week. Surely they wondered where she was. They would have to free all the souls she did not, which meant extra work. All of them kept an eye on each other, though they lived continents apart. Not even Jeff had called her, and he kept tabs on everyone.

And why hadn't Elliot called her? He usually checked in with her regularly. Maybe he was on a mission for the Time Corps.

If the Seelie were up to tricks with time, then she knew the person she ought to speak to. She made a Door to Yelbeghen's island.

The instant she stepped through, she knew he would feel her arrival. She opened the front door without knocking, and Yelbeghen rushed down the stairs and took her hands in his.

She watched as his eyes ran over her, his nostrils dilating slightly as he took in her scent. The set of his shoulders, the way he turned his head and the slight lifting of his chin were reptilian. She forgot sometimes what he was, mistaking his mask of humanity for the real being beneath. She also knew that only distraction and emotional upset would make him forget his human mannerisms, even for a moment.

"I'm fine," she said. "The Seelie just played a trick with time to intimidate me. But I'm okay."

"I'm not certain about that," he said. "Something has happened, but I can't tell what it is. I was hoping you could."

"What sort of thing?"

"Things are off. They're wrong. And I have no idea what that means. It's simply a feeling. I came back from some business in the void, and the smells here were not the same. And there are other things too."

"Someone else is living in my apartment. And I don't have any messages on my phone. The psychopomps haven't called me. Neither has Elliot, but I think he's on a mission."

"You may wish to check."

She tried to call the Time Corps safe house, but the phone had no connection. Thought it registered the date and time and her contact list was intact, the phone no longer worked. The service was disconnected.

"I'm going to LA," she said. "You shouldn't come."

"Are you ashamed of me?"

"I just don't know if you'll get along with everyone. Some of them might be able to tell what you are. Your kind are not popular."

He shrugged, but she could see that he didn't like the situation. He dropped into a chair, stretched his legs out in front of him and crossed them at the ankles.

"I'll wait here."

She made a Door to the Time Corps safe house in Los Angeles, and when Julius saw her, he went pale and rose from the sofa where he had been talking with Santiago, the Coyote.

"I wanted to check on everyone," Astrid said. "Is everyone all right?"

"Ah, the Door girl returns," said Santiago with a wide, delighted smile. "Been a while. Julius, this is that girl from the boardwalk that your sister was palling around with a few years ago."

Julius studied her, then touched his beard. The shock she had seen on his face was not the look of happy surprise.

"It seems I've forgotten your name," said Santiago. He

hadn't moved from his sprawled position with his feet on the coffee table.

"It's me, Astrid. I'm not Sister. Is that what you mean?"

She tried to make sense of it. Why would he not know her name?

"She's the Door that Red Fawn spoke about," said Santiago to Julius.

"If you know who I am," she said, turning to Santiago, "then tell me what's going on. I've been in the Seelie world for a little over a week, and now people don't remember me."

"Oh, sweetheart," he said, putting his feet on the floor and leaning forward. "You weren't there for a week. You were there for, let me see," he counted on his fingers. "Four years or so."

She asked the year and he told her.

"A week then," she said. "I left this year. I left on October 17th of this year."

"Being in Seelie messes with your time sense. Happens to the best of us, believe me. But, wait a moment. I thought you got stuck in the void. The Wild Hunt came, and you led them away. From what your brother said afterward, I thought it was the void, not the Seelie world."

"He's not my brother, he's my cousin, Elliot. Where is he?"

"I don't know where he is now. Why would I?"

"Because this is the Time Corps safe house. Because he lives here!"

Santiago seemed to have an idea. "The Seelie might have done things to your mind. They do that. Do you remember your address? I'll drive you home."

"I'm not crazy, and I need to find my cousin. Is he at his trailer on the beach? He lived there before joining the Time Corps."

"Last I heard, he was sailing that crazy Viking ship of his. Your little twin was with him. He comes into my territory now and then, so I hear things. Last I heard was a few months ago. But I don't know where he is now."

Sister shouldn't be with Elliot. She should be safe in Hazel and Seamus's home world. Safe from the Seelie and their threats. Julius was still looking at Astrid, and she felt something from him she had never felt before. Normally he was jovial and thoughtful, sometimes distant and distracted. Now, he was calculating, thinking over something, and it involved her.

"I'm going to find my cousin," she said, happy to get away from him. Something about his look made her feel like a game piece on a board. She made a Door to the beach where Elliot had once lived, found his trailer and knocked. A different man now occupied the place, and she apologized for disturbing him.

She needed to locate Elliot. She did it all the time with the other psychopomps. They could find each other so easily. She searched for Elliot in her mind, imagining him on the deck of Skidbladnir. Something flickered inside and she followed the thought. Reaching out, she touched something like a thread. She felt it and followed it the way Jeff had taught her. Then she thought of Sister, and the two of them together. There. She thought she had it. She made a Door, glanced through to make sure it was the right ship, and stepped through.

The moment she came on deck, three of the monkey crew leapt away and one called out a warning to the others. Elliot was near the prow and he turned.

It took a moment for him to realize that she wasn't Sister, and the moment he did, he froze. "I thought you died."

"I'm back, but something happened. Something happened with time."

He moved toward her slowly, then pulled her into a hard embrace. It was only after a few moments that she heard his sniff and realized he was crying.

"God, Elliot, I'm fine. It was only a week. I was in the

Seelie world."

"I thought you were in the void. All these years ... and we couldn't have a funeral because Sister needed your name and no one else knew you were dead."

He hugged her again and she let him. Then Sister came from below decks, let out a cry and embraced her. She held the two of them until Elliot asked how she had gotten out of the void.

"I was never trapped there, that's how. Something is wrong. Something happened with time. People don't remember things correctly. The Time Corps safe house doesn't exist. It's just Santiago and Julius there now."

"I told you," signed Sister to Elliot. "Something is wrong."

"What is the Time Corps?" said Elliot.

They talked, and Astrid began to understand more fully. It wasn't simply that time had changed or that the Seelie had played a trick on her mind or the minds of others. The entire world had changed, and she hadn't changed with it.

Yelbeghen knew though. He understood. She promised Elliot she'd find him again. She'd have to get some money from Yelbeghen and have her phone service reconnected, then they could talk by phone. She made a Door to Yelbeghen's island.

The drake was still in his living room chair, apparently napping. She knew he was only waiting, sitting perfectly still. It was his way.

"Do you remember the Time Corps?" she asked.

He opened his eyes slowly and said he did.

"No one else does. You said you were in the void. I think something happened while we were gone. Everyone thinks I was stuck in the void, that I never got out."

"And how did you get out?"

"Elliot rang this little owl bell. He traveled in time and created it and he rang it and it led me home."

She wanted the little object. It repelled the Seelie, and

right now, it would be a talisman and a comfort. She had owned the thing since she was an infant and it had always stood sentinel near her bed.

"I don't think the bell exists anymore," said Yelbeghen. "And I think you're lucky that you exist at all."

CHAPTER 11

FELICIA SANCHEZ KISSED HER NEPHEW good-bye, hugged her sister and got into her rental car. She leaned back against the headrest. Everyone had hope now. Things might just be all right. Even though her nephew, Nathan, had a rare form of bone cancer, Felicia had located a specialist in Brazil who performed pioneering work with an experimental treatment.

The specialist was working closely with Nathan's doctors now, and Felicia would continue to monitor things. Even though Nathan lived in Los Angeles and Felicia was a resident at Tulane Medical Center in New Orleans, she would keep an eye on everything. It didn't matter that no one in her family had much money; she would ensure Nathan got the best treatment. She would ask her colleagues at the hospital, she would research things herself. Her nephew would survive.

It was lunchtime, and even though she had skipped breakfast, she wasn't hungry. Even the thought of stopping at her favorite sandwich shop was not appealing. It must be nerves and travel. She had flown in on a plane to Los Angeles yesterday and would be returning home tomorrow morning. Travel was stressful and could affect appetite. Jet lag must be taking its toll too, because she was exhausted.

She drove to her parents' house where she was staying in her old bedroom. She closed her bedroom door, stretched out on top of the covers and fell asleep immediately, then woke to a darkened bedroom and her mother knocking softly on the door.

"I'll be out in a minute," she called, her heart still beating hard from her dream.

There had been a girl, a tongueless girl. Felicia knew that the poor thing had been mutilated without seeing the inside of her mouth. She had been playing with two striped tabby kittens. Though the girl did not speak, the kittens did. There was another girl identical to her and other strange people. People who were animals. Animals who could speak. The whole thing was a mad muddle.

But that wasn't what made her heart beat hard and her body break out in a hot sweat. There had been a man, a dark-haired man whom she had never seen before. He looked at her with a knowing look, one that made her insides flutter, and leaned toward her. His hair, curly and wild, brushed her lips as he breathed words into her ear, his breath warm and his voice low, with an accent she couldn't remember, only that it was beautiful and lilting. Then he was naked, as was she, and there was no sight, no images, only the press of his body against hers and the feel of him in the dark.

Felicia got up, went to the bathroom and ran a comb through her tangled hair. Everyone had erotic dreams now and then. It was normal. Nothing to worry about, she reminded herself. But she wasn't ashamed of it, exactly. Shame wasn't the emotion pooling in her stomach. It was something else, sadness and happiness mixed, as if she had lost something that made her happy.

A small earthquake shook the house, and she stepped into the door frame of the bathroom, leaning back against it. She called out to her mother to make sure she was all right, and her mother called back that she was. The quake passed, and Felicia headed to the kitchen, pausing to straighten a few curios that had moved a bit on the living room shelves.

Nathan would live. Her family would not bury a tiny body in a tiny casket. Her parents were alive and well, her siblings were fine, and she was in the process of achieving her dream of being a doctor. The scent of lasagna wafted from the kitchen, and though the thought of eating it was unappealing, there was comfort in the familiar smell.

Everything was fine. There was no logical reason for her to feel this keen sense of loss, of something missing. No reason at all.

CHAPTER 12

"**S**EAMUS, YOU WILL BE THE death of me."

Seamus glanced at Oren McCullen, then at the items surrounding his colleague in their shared university laboratory, the devices and wires, the open set of chemicals left out on the table, the leftover lunch plate from the day before.

"There's nothing there that'll kill you," said Seamus, "save that flask of liquid there. It's an experiment. Now, careful. Don't tip it."

Oren handed him the flask. "Not that," he said. "This."

Seamus took the proffered paper and looked it over.

"Why are you reading through these old papers? We have other things to occupy us."

"Those are the plans for the peroxide engine. But look, you wrote this note here, but it's incorrect. I think we should go over it again."

"Why? We went over it a thousand times years ago. It's useful, but a silver catalyst is too expensive to be viable."

"But even so," said Oren. "Didn't you ever get the feeling that we're missing something? That if we only looked again, it would make sense?"

"I live with that feeling daily, my friend."

"We need a better catalyst. With that, the engines could power machines. Such machines as we could only imagine."

"I can imagine a great deal," said Seamus.

"As can I."

Seamus sighed. "That's as may be, but I need your

mind on our work, not sifting through the dust of some old and abandoned project."

"I suppose," said Oren, setting the paper aside. But Seamus saw that he set it on top of his current reading pile.

When they left to eat supper, it was already late. They each had their own houses, but they often dined together. For nearly twenty years they had done so. They had been cellmates in Ireland together, had escaped together and had built a life together in New Orleans teaching at the university and patenting their inventions.

They hailed a hansom cab and passed the shops, a club, then later a pub and a brothel as they rode through a different section of town. The lights glowed warmly behind pulled curtains upstairs.

"Sometimes I think it would be a fine thing to have a wife," said Oren. "Someone at home."

"It wouldn't be fair to any woman to marry either of us. Not with our pasts. We couldn't even tell them our real last names."

It had been so many years since he had heard his own surname, Doyle, that it seemed like the name of another man. Perhaps it was. He was thirty-eight now. Twenty years had passed since he had killed a man. Twenty years since his mother had watched him taken away in irons.

They stopped at their club and ate, Oren going over the peroxide engine notes, Seamus sitting and thinking dark thoughts about his home, his family and his empty Garden District house. But no, he needed to fight against this melancholy turn of mind. There was no sense in dwelling on that which he could not change.

It was nearly ten o'clock when he saw Oren off at the door and decided to walk a few blocks to clear his mind. He knew which sorts of businesses lay ahead, but he had no plans to visit them. He could walk straight past. Just as he walked past the bar without going in, just as he could walk past a gambling den. He touched his hat at a woman leaning against a door frame.

A cat ran past, a stripped tabby, and he paused, a memory coming to him. He had a dream about a cat like that, speaking with him. But the cat was also Oren, discussing his notes. And it was also a little girl, sitting on a stool with her hands under her thighs, swinging her feet.

There were other things in his dream, machines and wonders, strange people. And there was a woman in the dream, a brown-skinned woman with dark hair and eyes the color of rich cognac. He remembered her scent, faint and sweet, almost edible, and the feel of the skin of her shoulders under his hands.

He thought about going back to the pub for a drink, or maybe going home and opening a new bottle of scotch before reading in front of the fire. But that wouldn't help any, he knew. He had spent enough nights trying to quell the pensive thoughts that were always lying in wait. They were like crows sitting in a tree, waiting for something to die.

A steam carriage clattered past, its wheels loud on the cobblestones. It splashed through a puddle and turned the corner. One horse-drawn trap passed, but otherwise the street was empty. The shops were closed and it was too late for business and decent people to be out, but still too early for those who operated in darkness. The pubs and brothels were open, yes, but they wouldn't be busy until later.

He thought of his brothers and sisters, now all grown, mothers and fathers, husbands and wives. And he thought of his parents, now gray-headed or possibly dead. They thought he was dead, and he had to leave it that way. He could never contact them again. He was a shadow, with no family and few friends, the product of a life lived under a false name and identity.

Ah, but this was too much. He knew where these

thoughts led, and how they could pull him into a dark interior place that he would not escape for days. He knew one way to drown out the thoughts and the endless chatter of his mind. Turning down the next street, he saw the building with the front door propped open. Faint piano music drifted out into the street.

He had patronized the establishment a number of times before, and as he entered he found a petite woman playing the piano. Her music was playful and light, something for the early patrons who might stay a few hours.

She finished the piece and smiled at him, a genuine smile, not the one her profession required. She rose and came to him and he greeted her by name. They were old friends. He had known Hazel since she was a girl and had dressed as a boy to run errands for him.

CHAPTER 13

ELLIOT PARKED THE CAR IN the hospital parking lot and turned to Sister.

"You can stay here if you want."

"Astrid called us both," she signed. "I'm coming."

Elliot almost told her that Astrid needed him, not her. Astrid insisted that he could sense things that even she could not, time slips and anomalies. He seriously doubted that he could be so useful, but he had to admit that in a world where he captained a monkey-crewed living dragon ship and found a clock in his eye, anything was possible.

"If you get scared, you can come back and wait in the car," he said.

"I'm not so fragile. I just have nightmares. I read something about soldiers having bad dreams. It doesn't mean they are weak."

"I didn't mean that."

"I know. You are trying to protect. It's what you do."

That wasn't true either, but he wasn't in any mood to have a deep conversation in the parking lot. There was work to do. They headed toward the entrance where Astrid was already waiting. She glanced at Sister but must have seen something in her face that brooked no argument, because she simply led them into the lobby.

"Hold my hands and don't let go," said Astrid. "They have security, but I can get past."

Each of them took one of her outstretched hands and they passed the various checkpoints unnoticed by the staff. Astrid knew where she was going, and when they came to a locked door, Astrid simply made a Door through it. Elliot knew that the living weren't strictly allowed to use her Doors, but the ones she made only transported them a few inches, so perhaps they didn't count. At this point, maybe Astrid didn't care. They took an elevator to the Intensive Care Unit on the fifth floor, and she led them down a corridor.

"I come here now and then," she said. "Lots of people die in hospitals. But this past week, I've found seven old geists trapped here. Seven. In the four years I've been doing this job, I've found maybe a handful, so this is unusual."

"Have you talked to the other psychopomps?"

"Jeff didn't know who I was. None of them did. I never came back from the void, so I never became a psychopomp."

"Then why are you doing this?"

"Because it's my job. The souls need us to free them or they suffer. I talked to Jeff, explained things as best I could. They're happy to have another on the team, even if I am a little old to be starting. But that's not the issue. I want to you check this area and tell me if there are any time slips."

He looked around, but it was an ordinary hospital corridor.

"What am I looking for?"

"Anything. The paint might change color, or the pattern of the tile, our clothes, anything weird."

"Nothing," he said.

She looked at the walls, as if daring them to change, then she took them a few doors down.

"Now, keep quiet for this part," she said, still holding their hands. "I can do what I like and not be seen by the living, but they might actually hear you if you talk. I haven't done this before with humans, only with another Door. But if things get bad, I can get us out."

Elliot glanced at Sister, but her jaw was set and her

posture straight. She was ready.

Astrid took them into a room where a woman in her fifties was sleeping, oxygen tubes in her nostrils and an IV tube running into the vein on the back of her hand.

"Up there," said Astrid, jerking her head toward the upper corner of the room.

Elliot saw nothing. Then, he felt a cool puff of air and something like silver cobwebs wavered in the light. It formed into a torso, a neck, a head and a face.

Sister signed something, but with one hand clutching Astrid's, Elliot couldn't make it out. He knew what she meant. The back of the person's head was embedded in the wall, as was its entire body from the waist down. Only the front part of the poor thing's torso was exposed to the room. He couldn't tell if it was male or female, old or young. The thing was more a representation of a human being than an actual one. The facial features were distorted, blank holes for eyes, a mouth that opened and closed as if speaking, then rounded into a circle of pain and closed. It writhed, arching its back, and the area around its waist and head crackled with electricity, white and sharp. Its mouth contorted in a scream and its eyes squeezed shut.

Astrid's voice shook. "Can you hear it?"

"No."

"You don't want to. Can you sense anything in here?"

Elliot studied the room, from the patterned privacy curtain surrounding the woman's bed to the generic artwork on the walls to the view of the city outside.

"It's all fine. No changes."

Astrid looked disappointed. "I was hoping there was something else. Some answer that made sense. I can't free it. I tried everything. I can't physically tear it out of the wall."

"Have you called Jeff?"

"I'll call him once you leave. Are you sure there's nothing here?"

"Certain."

They left, and Astrid called Jeff from the parking lot.

"I only have a minute before Jeff gets here," she said to Elliot after hanging up. "But I thought of something. In my past, the one I remember, you were drugged by the Seelie and started seeing things. Furnishings, landmarks, paintings, things like that were changing right before your eyes. That's how everyone knew you could sense time slips. It became useful when you were trapped in the Library too. But when you lived in that trailer on the beach, before you joined the Time Corps and before the Wild Hunt came through, you slipped sideways into a slightly different version of our world and the Time Corps came to fetch you. That idea bothered me. First, I thought the worlds were distinct. How could one world have another slightly different one attached? And second, how did you get out of that attached world without the Time Corps?"

He thought about it, and as he did, his memories solidified. It felt strange, as if they were being created just as he needed them, like a line of writing that was only a few words ahead of those he was reading.

"I remember being drugged, I remember the mural in a falafel shop changing while I was on a date with Yukiko. But I remember just being in my trailer afterward."

She looked deep in thought, puzzling together the pieces of the world she knew, one that conflicted with his own. He knew she wasn't crazy and neither was he.

"I just wish the Time Corps was here," she said. "The only ones of us in this world are the ones originally from here."

A small earthquake shook the ground, and a nearby car alarm went off.

"Just an aftershock from the one this morning," Elliot said to Sister, who put her hand to the ground.

"No, I don't think it is," said Astrid. "This whole place is unstable. Void wyrms or geists or sidhe, it's coming together here. This place, right at the border of ocean and land, where the tectonic plates touch, the whole San Andreas fault line, it's all one great big instability. It attracts things. Always has."

The way she said it made her seem so much older, as if she understood things now that he could not. His younger cousin was now someone strange to him.

Sister looked up at the hospital, toward the place with the trapped geist. "What was that light around the soul? It looked like lightning."

"Yeah, it did," said Astrid. "But it's not. That's the light from the place the dead souls go. That wasn't just a soul stuck in our world. It was one half in our world and half in the next. Like it was trapped trying to push through. But instead of going from our world to the afterlife, it was coming the other way."

CHAPTER 14

FELICIA SAT ON THE EDGE of her bathtub back at her apartment in New Orleans. The kitchen timer on the bathroom counter went off and she checked the home pregnancy test. She double-checked it, tossed it into the bathroom trash, walked into her bedroom and burst into tears.

A baby. My God, how was that even possible? She knew how, of course, but she hadn't slept with anyone in—in how long? A long time. Certainly not in the last six months.

"Are you okay? What happened?" asked Doug, her housemate. She had forgotten to close her bedroom door.

"I don't know. I'm just—I'm pregnant."

It took a few moments for it to sink in, and she watched him move from surprise to confusion to something resembling a practiced look of neutrality.

"Are you going to keep it?" he asked tentatively.

She paused, remembering her dreams. Over the last few weeks, she had filled the notebook on her bedside table with recollections of them. People, events, even maps of places she had never been before.

"Yeah, I'm going to keep it," she said.

He sat beside her on the bed. She knew he was trying to be helpful, but how could he? There was nothing anyone could do. She was alone in this.

"Did you, uh, tell the father yet?" he asked.

"I don't know who he is."

Her eyes welled with tears again, and Doug put his arm

around her shoulders.

"It's okay," he said. "You'll be okay."

It was a stupid thing to say. She wasn't going to die from a baby. She wouldn't lose her honor or anything. This wasn't 1950. She'd have her job and life would go on, even if her parents were disappointed in her. She'd have food, shelter, a job, daycare.

The only thing she wouldn't have was a father for her child.

Doug handed her a tissue from her nightstand and she blew her nose.

"Do you have any ideas about him?" he said gently.

"No. I don't remember anything. I haven't slept with anyone in a long time."

"Were you out? Maybe someone slipped you something and you were unconscious." He stood and walked over and pulled down her wall calendar. "When was it?"

"Right around the first week in February if I count from my last period."

He flipped back to that month and read her schedule. "Did you go out that week?"

"I never go out. Or, rarely. You know that."

"Yeah, I know."

Her few free evenings were spent sleeping or studying. Going out with friends was rare, and going to a place where a man could slip her a drug was rarer still.

"When are you due?" he asked.

She got up and flipped through the calendar. "If I count forty weeks, then ... the end of October," she said.

"You have time then. You can call some numbers. There are places that help you buy diapers and baby clothes and stuff. And won't you be done with your residency by then?"

"Yeah, I finish in June," she said. But the logistics of raising a child were not the worst thing on her mind.

Maybe she was going crazy. She was missing a chunk of memory and was plagued by strange dreams. A coyote who was a man and a fox who was a woman, a talking raven, the dark-haired Irish man and the young girl who was his daughter but wasn't.

And his feet. She remembered the man's feet, apelike and dexterous. When they lay in bed together, he would wrap that warm, strong foot around hers, like holding hands. It was the finest feeling in the world.

The windows rattled and their apartment shook. Doug got a terrified look and grabbed the desk.

"It's okay. Just an earthquake," Felicia said. "See, it's already over."

"That's really weird. We don't get earthquakes in New Orleans," he said. "Maybe you brought them back from LA with you."

CHAPTER 15

"**I** WAS JUST THINKING ABOUT YOU," Hazel said to Seamus.

"Nothing too terrible, I hope."

"Oh, nothing like that. Would you like to sit inside?"

She gestured to an adjoining room where men often sat and talked with the ladies before heading upstairs. Due to the early hour, it was currently empty. He accepted her invitation and sat on a burgundy settee with carved woodwork legs. Hazel brought him a small snifter of brandy and sat beside him, arranging her skirts in a utilitarian fashion, not to display her ankle or show herself to her best advantage, but to be comfortable.

"The owner of the Delta Belle isn't too fond of you these days," she said.

"I won a good deal of money on his riverboat."

"A little too much, Professor. You should be more careful."

"I didn't cheat."

"You count cards."

"Which isn't cheating. It's not my business that the other men can't be troubled to learn to do the same."

She sighed. "I'm only trying to look out for you. It would be a shame to make an enemy out of someone like that."

"Have you been out on the Delta Belle again? Or did you learn this here?"

"I go out on the boats when I get the chance. You know I love to be moving."

"Fast horses and fast carriages, that's you. But a riverboat is hardly fast."

"It's faster than sitting here," she glanced around the room, at the heavy curtains, the chairs and tables that were showing their age, the fading silk flowers in a vase on the mantelpiece. Her gaze lingered on a painting of a generic landscape with a horse and rider galloping over green hills.

He wanted to ask her why she didn't leave the city, but he knew. A street child had grown into a woman of the streets and there was nothing he or anyone else could do about it. Since he had known her when she was a child, he never could bring himself to pay for her services. As the years had passed, he was glad of it. This way they could be friends.

"I had a dream about a ship," said Hazel. "You were in the dream, but you were in your laboratory, cursing and banging around, burning some odd thing or other. And there was a monkey who talked, and cats who did as well."

"A talking cat?"

"Isn't that a mad notion? A striped tabby cat, sitting with you talking about your inventions. And a monkey in a vest on this old ship, the sort with a dragon head, like in books."

"What else did you dream?"

"Ah, it was silly, the whole of it. But I thought you might be diverted."

He knew she wasn't telling the truth. The tightness at the corners of her mouth, the way she unconsciously stroked the outer edge of her thumb with her ring finger. There was more.

"Was there a machine?" he asked, watching her. "One that could take us places?"

She looked at him now, her rouged lips parting in surprise.

"Yes. Yes, there was. How did you know?"

"And there were glass-fronted slates, but with pictures that moved. Like daguerreotypes, come to life."

"And metal ships in the sky," she said, staring at that ugly painting again. "Ah, but we can't waste time on dreams, can we, Professor? You and I must live in the real world, not in the one of fancy. Would you like to see Bernice?" she asked, slipping out of her thoughts and looking at him with weary eyes. She was doing business now, their chat was over.

Bernice was his favorite lady. Well, one of them anyway. She was an auburn-haired beauty, rounded and soft with a low, hearty laugh. And she laughed often.

"Do you have anyone darker? From Mexico or Spain, perhaps?" He watched her response, the wary, frightened look that came and passed.

"You know who she is!" he said. "The woman in all my dreams. The woman with the dark skin and topaz eyes. You dreamed of her too."

"We don't have any Mexicans or Spaniards here," she said, rising. "I'm sure Bernice—"

"Forget Bernice! Don't you find it strange that the two of us would dream of the strangest things at the same time?"

"They're only dreams," she said. "And dreams are nothing more than the mind amusing itself. It feeds us little bits of beauty and goodness so we don't go mad or lose hope."

He touched her bare shoulder, and she visibly stiffened.

"You played violin in the dream," he said. "You used to play violin when you were a girl."

"That was a long time ago. The instrument was broken."

"Did you dream about that too?"

She turned away, and he did not try to see her face. He knew she needed a few moments, and he gave them to her. It wasn't that she didn't play violin any more, it was the entirety of her existence that pained her. From the front room came the sound of voices, and someone else took up playing the piano. The person was not as fine a player as Hazel was, but few people were.

"There was a house too," she said at last. "One here in New Orleans, in our ordinary world. A white house with blue trim, and a black woman lived there."

"I remember," he said, though the memory was vague.

"She lived among the white people, but not as a servant. I always thought it strange."

"If it isn't Seamus Connor!" cried Bernice, spying him through the doorway. She glided in, a swirl of pale green fabric and perfume, her pinked cheeks bright against her powdered white skin. "Oh, but I've missed you."

He bowed over her hand, winking, and she laughed her low, pleasant laugh. From the corner of his eye, he saw Hazel step back, then slip out another door, toward the back of the brothel.

The next morning, he found his housekeeper, Mrs. Washington, in the kitchen.

"I'll have your breakfast ready in a minute or two, Professor," she said.

"I'm not hungry," he said, then realized that she was already cooking and that it was rude to refuse to eat. "But I will be soon, I'm certain. I came down to ask you a question."

"And what's that, then?" She put the kettle on the stove and checked the fire underneath.

"Have you had strange dreams lately?"

"No stranger than usual," she said, then grew alarmed. "Did I talk in my sleep? But how could you hear that from way off in your room?"

"No, no. I was only curious. I've heard of people having odd dreams."

"Your friend Oren?"

"No, other friends."

"And you? Are you having them?" she asked.

"A few, yes."

"I think a little less drink, fewer late nights and a good meal now and then ought to cure that. A troubled mind leads to troubled dreams."

"I'm not troubled."

She raised an eyebrow, which would be an impertinence from any other servant, especially a black one addressing a white employer. But she had been in Seamus's employ long enough that she could be forthright.

"Have you heard of a black woman here in the city?" he asked. "A woman who lives in a white neighborhood? She has a white house with blue trim."

"What? Has something happened to her?"

"You know her?"

"I know of her, but I don't know her personally. Her name is September Wilde."

The name meant something. It was a part of something bigger, a piece of a set of information, but he couldn't remember what.

CHAPTER 16

ASTRID STEPPED THROUGH THE DOOR into the small bookshop in Nebraska and immediately went to the employee break room at the back. The shop's owner, Jeff, took the full coffeepot from the machine and filled three cups.

"It's bad, Jeff," said Astrid. "Something very wrong is happening."

Gopan, who appeared as an eight-year-old Indian boy, but was really much older, took a doughnut from the box at the center of the table and munched it thoughtfully, listening.

"There are always a few geists missed," said Jeff. "Our work is more an art than a science."

"It's more than that. It's not just the number, it's the age of the geists. You said the one at the hospital was more than ten years old. And it was coming through from the afterlife."

"We don't know that for sure. Besides, geists get stuck."

He handed her a coffee cup and set one in front of Gopan.

"Why only three cups?" she asked. "Aren't Graciela and Robin coming?"

Jeff drew a deep breath and pulled out a chair, but failed to sit down. He leaned on the back of the chair.

"They aren't coming. They've been asked not to come."

"Asked by whom?" asked Gopan.

"Our higher-up."

As naturally occurring beings, the psychopomps did not have a strict hierarchy or follow orders. But as the eldest, Jeff was nominally in charge, followed by Gopan. But aside from the five of them, there was another living psychopomp, a person who was very old. Astrid had heard Jeff speak of him, but had never met him herself. He was inhuman, she was sure, but she knew no more.

"Why can't they come?" asked Astrid.

Jeff lowered himself into the chair, but he looked like he wanted to jump out of it again.

"He asked them not to come again. Ever. They'll be working directly with him."

"Will they still be doing their jobs?" asked Gopan. "Are they still clearing out souls?"

"I'm not sure yet what they're doing, only that November doesn't want them to come any more."

Gopan met Astrid's eyes and they exchanged a wordless moment of understanding. Jeff had never spoken the name of the man with whom he occasionally consulted. While to Gopan, November was just an unusual name, to Astrid it meant more.

"Why Robin and Graciela?" Astrid asked.

"Because they're loyal. And let's face it, obedient," said Jeff. She had never heard him so weary before.

He was referring to Graciela and Robin's aspects, a black Belgian sheepdog and a black terrier respectively. Black dogs were traditional psychopomp aspects, just as her owl was. Gopan's aspect of a child was more unusual, and Astrid still didn't know Jeff's aspect. It was considered rude to ask, as a person's aspect revealed key parts of their personality and way of viewing the world.

Though Astrid considered them all friends, or had, back when they knew her, Graciela and Robin had a special bond. They were kindred spirits. It was no surprise that where one went, the other did as well.

"I've run across far more trapped spirits than usual as

well," said Gopan. "It's not just Astrid's newbie jitters."

Gopan might not believe that she had been on the job for years, and might think she was more than a little crazy, but at least he seemed to agree with her on that point.

"Perhaps it's because two-fifths of us seem to be off duty," said Jeff. "It's all in the numbers."

"No, Jeff," said Gopan gently. "There really is something wrong."

Jeff took off his glasses and cleaned them, then slid them back on.

"I've heard a few things," he said. "Like twitches on a web. More stories of hauntings and seeing the dead. I chalked it up to the Internet. People are more in communication with each other than ever before. Stories travel farther."

"But what if they're not stories?" said Gopan.

Jeff took a sip of his coffee. "I don't know."

"Doors open between worlds," said Astrid. "And our Doors are no different, other than they're one-way and go to death. But what if they are more permeable than we thought? What if a Door didn't close all the way? Or what if death isn't as well sealed as we always thought?"

"Please, Astrid," said Jeff. "No more about that geist and this multiple worlds thing."

"I know you think I'm crazy, but think about it. You know this November person, and if I'm right, he's one of twelve people. The Twelve. Not human, right? So you already know that there are other types of beings. Why not other worlds? And what if things got stuck between the worlds?"

"Or stuck coming through from one to the other," said Gopan.

"Exactly. That's what I saw at the hospital."

"The dead don't come back," said Jeff. "They can get stuck here after they die, but once they go through, they stay dead."

"How do you know for sure?" asked Gopan. "None of us

can be sure, not really."

"Fine. I'll see what I can learn." said Jeff. "If there's trouble of some kind, we'll find out."

But Astrid wondered if it was already too late for that.

CHAPTER 17

NEIL GREY MADE A SANDWICH for himself in Mr. March's kitchen, took a swim in the heated outdoor pool, showered and went into town for a street fair featuring local artists. He spoke to no one and only paused to study two items: a particularly compelling drawing of a pumpkin on a table and a blue and green handblown glass bowl. He bought a bag of popcorn and stopped in the bookshop for something to read before heading home.

It was a pleasant way to spend the afternoon after a morning spent stalking and killing a man. The man had been guilty, of course. They all were. March was never wrong about these things. Neil did not feel bad for questioning March's word before, but now that he was willing to provide Neil with any evidence he required for a target, Neil found himself at peace.

For now, he was alone, but March would return home after dinner. Neil turned on the sound system, one he was certain had cost several thousand dollars, and sat back on the leather sofa, listening to Vivaldi, then Handel, then Couperin and Scarlatti. The Baroque composers were always his favorites, and March kept a respectable collection.

Later that evening, March appeared in the living room. It didn't startle Neil, as he was used to his boss's method of travel. But he was shocked by the way March looked. It was nothing anyone else might notice. One had to know March to see that the circles under his eyes were darker than usual and his face was gaunt. He looked exhausted and older.

"What happened?" Neil asked, rising from the sofa and following March into the kitchen.

"Things are getting worse," said March. "A conflict is coming. A war." March ladled leftover tomato soup into a bowl and microwaved it.

"I don't understand."

"No, you wouldn't. I've shielded you as best I could. This place, here, in this time, is safe. It's protected, in a sense. But soon, nowhere will be safe. Tell me, have you been sleeping well? Unusual dreams?"

It was an odd question, but not an overly personal one.

"I'm fine," Neil said. He had never been troubled by bad dreams.

March looked at him as if ascertaining if he was telling the truth. Satisfied, he turned back to his meal preparations.

"Why will there be a war?" asked Neil. "Who is fighting?"

March sighed. "Those who want to inhibit human freedom. You know I am not human, correct?"

"Yes."

"Of course you do. But though I am not, I consider humans my kin. My brothers and sisters. I watch out for them. I fight for them. You, along with me, fight for them. Our work together is to remove the small hindrances here and there that ultimately inhibit human freedom. The people we remove are wicked, and ultimately add to the enslavement of the human race, though in small ways. But the tiny pieces add up to a larger whole. I've worked so hard, especially recently, but things are not as they ought to be. Something did not go as planned. Those who want to inhibit human freedom have a thumb on the scale."

"Who are they?"

"Oh, the usual sorts. Ones like me. Ones different from me. Ones who like restrictions on things. There are those who have false notions of peace through enslavement.

They want ignorance and the binding of the human will. I and those like me desire to give humans knowledge of good and of evil. Then they can choose for themselves. And we want them to be free to do so."

"All people desire freedom. Freedom and goodness."

March touched his shoulder, and Neil was struck by how much smaller the man seemed now. Then March cut two slices of bread from a loaf Neil had baked the day before and spread butter on them. He handed a slice to Neil.

"Goodness, as you say, is a human desire. But the defining of goodness is something best left to the individual people themselves. Morality and immorality cannot be defined externally."

"But there are universally accepted rules of behavior. They differ culturally, but they exist. Do not kill. Do not steal. Do not lie."

"And yet you kill. You steal things like identification chips to do so. And do you not lie to get near your targets? I know you do."

"But my actions are in service to a greater good. They are enacting justice."

"Indeed they are."

"And thus, they are in alignment with goodness. They adhere to the idea of an objective good."

March stopped chewing for a moment and looked at him, his eyes sharp and penetrating. "There is no objective good."

"But isn't freedom a good? If you fight for it, then you must believe it is a good."

"It is, perhaps, the only one. All other notions are false. Good is relative. So is truth. Once you move beyond the idea of good and evil, true and false, virtue and vice, there is a sharper clarity of thought that comes. Only complete freedom of action and will and conscience must exist. Nothing else will do."

Neil put on the kettle to boil water for tea.

"But isn't discriminating between freedom and enslavement the same thing as naming them as good and evil? You are placing a higher value on one than the other."

"I am. And I am not ashamed of the contradiction. I tolerate it because of humanity. Struggling, stinking, stupid humanity. The poor things have little interest in bettering themselves, but I work for them all the same."

"People aren't so bad. You do them an injustice."

"You are no more human than I am."

Neil turned and found March watching him. He had known he was not human, though this was the first time March had said as much. As the years had passed, Neil had wondered about his place in the world. He wondered about his extraordinary strength, his speed, his ability to go nearly unnoticed, as if people didn't really see him.

"What am I?" he asked.

"The question the clay asks the potter," said March with a fond smile. "You are what you were made to be. A man of earth. A man of strength and cunning and loyalty. You are a golem."

For a moment, Neil thought he meant it metaphorically, but then he understood.

"I made you," said March.

"Is that why my memories are so few?"

"I believe so. But do not trouble yourself. You are more a human than even I would have anticipated."

"Humans love beauty and art and music."

"They do," said March. "And they can be curious and loyal and creative."

"I am not creative. I cannot make things."

"And for that I am sorry. I had never thought to give you that gift. It never entered my mind that you would desire it."

Neil felt a keen pain, one that he knew would fade a little now, and then come back sharper later, when he had time to think about it. He could never create. The desire to create beauty, that painful longing for it, permeated all of humanity. It wasn't just books and paintings and music, it was more. The creation of inventions, dances, machines and games, culinary delights and knitted caps, poems and mathematical formulas. All of them were outside his reach. He could not create them, only imitate what already was.

"I wish I were human."

"Said the wooden boy. But no. You are better than humanity. You are different, and better."

"You say that because you love me."

"I say it because I see you. And I see them. I see the people, hungry for affection and doing such stupid things to get it. I see them watching mindless television to drown out the monotony of their self-created misery. I see the young people at the clubs, sweating and drinking, laughing and gyrating in the mindless pursuit of pleasure. You are different. You seek beauty for its own sake."

"They seek beauty too, I think. They seek delight in each other's forms and in the pulsing of the music and the taste of the wine. It is not merely the pursuit of pleasure. It may begin as something low and base, but there is more to it. Each man who enters the brothel is in search of God. I read that somewhere. They seek the higher beauty."

"No. That is not so. You see them as similar to yourself. They are not. Don't forget that. You are free in a way they may never be. We work for their benefit, but it is hard work and fraught with disappointment. You are not a product of your era, because you have no era. You have no home world, no home time."

"I have memories of a time and place. I remember things from long ago."

"But they are not your memories. They were collected from others. You have chosen your own path. The humans, they accept the moral axioms of their day. You are free of such limits. You set your own course."

Neil wasn't so sure, but he wasn't prepared to argue the point with March. He prepared the tea.

March looked a little better now, less haggard and weary. He was still thin, but had some color in his skin now.

"It's time you knew something," said March. "I want you to understand. Heaven's war is fought on earth. It seems to always be thus. In such a war, there are soldiers. And you were not the only golem I created."

CHAPTER 18

ANOTHER EARTHQUAKE RATTLED THE HOSPITAL building, the second that day. Felicia watched the lights flicker while she held open her locker door.

"We have backup generators," said one of the nurses who was coming on shift just as Felicia was leaving for the day. "Don't worry about the patients."

By the time she got to her car and turned on the radio, the local news had reported on the quake. She knew that by the time she got home, the local seismographic results would report that the epicenter was under the hospital. Then, if another quake came later that night, it would be under her apartment.

She drove home and opened the door to find her housemate, Doug, sitting on the living room floor, playing a video game. The aroma of lentil soup filled the room. It was late April, and with her lack of appetite, she had lost almost eight pounds. Her obstetrician said she needed to eat and Doug had taken up the job of cooking healthy food for her and insisting she eat them.

"Did you feel the earthquake?" she asked.

"Yeah, but the news said that they're so small that they're not going to cause structural damage to any buildings." He didn't look away from his video game. "But the last few have been stronger."

She thought of her home in Los Angeles, of the seismic reinforcements that the buildings were required to have. Even the freeways were required to withstand minor earthquakes. But New Orleans was not like Los Angeles. The buildings of brick and stone would crumble and people would die. She imagined the older buildings, the historic homes, the places downtown, like St. Louis Cathedral.

She imagined it destroyed, and then remembered that she had dreamed just such a thing. The walls crumbling, the roof falling in, the dust rising and the people fleeing. That part of town called to her and terrified her for no rational reason. The image of the destruction was clear in her mind, but it had not come from an earthquake. There had been a giant, terrible machine.

"I have to go somewhere," she said.

"You need to eat."

"I'll eat when I get back. I've been having dreams about Jackson Square, about bad things happening there, and about drowning. I know why I dream about Los Angeles, since that's home. But there's something about the cathedral that is bugging me."

"They're just dreams. Everyone has bad dreams."

She had told him about her dreams, about the Irish man and the other weird things, but naturally, he had dismissed it. Any sane person would. But no one else she knew had such dreams, such vivid, soul-wrenching dreams, and hers had only started recently, with the baby.

"I'll be back in an hour," she said.

"Fine, if it'll give you peace of mind. Maybe seeing the place will help stop your nightmares. Personally, I think it's a combination of anxiety and stress. My mom told me she had weird dreams when she was pregnant with me."

"You told your mom about my dreams?"

"I was worried about you. I think maybe this is happening because you don't know who the baby's father is. Your subconscious is telling you something."

She was about to retort that he wasn't her mother, but she held her tongue. He was trying to help. For the years they had been housemates, he had been a good friend, and now with her pregnancy, he was attempting to help her. It was cloying and irritating and a kindness she knew better than to rebuff.

How could she tell him that the dreams were more than just irritations? Over the last few weeks, she had filled a journal with them, and unlike ordinary dreams, they were remarkably consistent. The same people and places came to her over and over again, and one of those places was Jackson Square.

She drove to the square, parked and walked out toward the Mississippi River, dark brown under the low yellow lights of the streetlamps. She paused on the pavement, unable to bring herself to move any closer. The water felt like it was pulling her, sucking her down into its depths, closing over her face, filling her nose and mouth with the foul-tasting cold, blocking her ears until all that existed was the freezing water and the dark and the watery sound pounding in her ears. The river enclosed her, like a fist, like a tomb.

A few passersby exclaimed in surprise as a gentle earthquake shook the buildings. St. Louis Cathedral rose over the square, white and old, its clock face ticking away the minutes.

It was a Thursday night and the shops and restaurants were sparsely occupied. The square itself was empty. She headed toward the center, toward the statue of Andrew Jackson seated on his rearing horse.

The cathedral was whole, unlike in her dreams where it was partially destroyed. The river was silent and peaceful, not a place of terror and death. Maybe this was what going crazy felt like, as if reality was disturbed, but only she could see it.

Another earthquake came and she paused, not wanting to lose her balance as the ground moved. Ten yards to her right the air moved, like heat rising off of the pavement in summer. And then there was something else, a black hole opening, like a great wound in the air, and a thing beyond it. A great creature, like a serpent, white and eyeless, appeared, and a strong wind struck her from behind. She almost regained her footing when the wind grew stronger, like a hurricane, and threw her to the ground. She slid forward, toward the thing, and braced herself, digging her toes and fingers into the earth, pressing her body low as bits of loose plant life and garbage flew past her, some of it striking her and clinging to her hair and body.

A man appeared near the rip, in front of the terrifying, hungry white thing which now opened a mouth, a great, wet, red mouth. He was a dark-skinned man with broad shoulders and a sturdy build, like a workman. He spoke a word she could not hear and the white monster vanished, the air ceased to shimmer near it and the terrible wind stopped. The rip was closed and the monster was gone.

Void wyrm.

The word came to her mind then, the word for that terrible thing that pulled the world toward it. And another memory, a man, a small, older white man in a suit. He had something to do with the holes.

The sturdy man was watching her now and she felt a surge of fear, like he was a predatory thing, like he had been looking for her. He walked toward her, not in any hurry, just observing her as she rose and brushed herself off.

Part of her wanted to flee, but the stronger part wanted to know what the monster was and how he had closed the hole. The stronger part won and she looked him in the eye, drawing herself up straight.

"Who are you?" she asked him, then thought of a better question. "What are you?"

"I was about to ask you the same thing."

CHAPTER 19

SEAMUS STOOD AT HIS FRONT door, astonished at the temerity of the woman on his doorstep. For a person of her social standing to call upon him at his Garden District home, his respectable home, was unconscionable.

"Miss Dubois," he said. "I hardly think—"

"I know that you don't think, which is why I came," said Hazel. "You ignored both of the notes I sent," said Hazel.

"I didn't think it was appropriate—"

She gave him a knowing look and raised an eyebrow. She had never stood in judgment of him for visiting her establishment, any more than he had been unkind to her for her profession. Both of them understood the world all too well for that. But his friend Oren was upstairs, going through a box of Seamus's old notes on the peroxide engine, and though Oren knew of Hazel, he hadn't seen her since she was a young girl. He did not know her occupation.

If it hadn't been for his long-standing friendship with Hazel, he would have shut the door in her face.

"I suppose it's best if you come in," he muttered.

"Right. No sense in letting the neighbors see me."

She entered and followed him into the front parlor. She was dressed modestly, and if no one recognized her, she could pass for an ordinary middle-class woman. Still, to have a single female caller, one not related to him, might cause tongues to wag.

"You read the notes I sent, I trust?" she said.

"Of course. I was simply surprised that you were

suddenly interested in visiting September Wilde. It seemed earlier as though you were reluctant to discuss the dreams."

"I thought about it, and I changed my mind. It's simply too coincidental, and these dreams are different than ordinary ones. I remember them too well. They're too vivid." She paused. "They keep coming, every night. And they trouble me."

He knew what she meant.

"Now, why didn't you answer my letters?" she asked.

"I was considering it. I do plan on visiting this September Wilde at some point."

"Why not today?"

"I was going to go alone."

"What about McCullen? Does he have the dreams?"

"No, not like ours. His ideas are as mad as they ever were, but no different than usual. And he says he has been sleeping well."

"I think we should go today," she said.

"I'm not sure it would do us any good."

"And you call yourself a scientist. A man of curiosity and exploration. And yet you hesitate to explore this path and pay a call on the one woman we both know might have answers for us."

He couldn't tell her exactly why he didn't want to visit Miss Wilde. He was curious, true, and he was only moderately concerned with looking like a fool. After all, he and Miss Wilde operated in entirely different social spheres, and she could do him no harm. But what if he learned something about the woman in his dreams? And then there was the machine, the one that let him travel to strange places. The thought of the thing caused a lump to form in his stomach.

But he was, at heart, a scientist. Hazel was right on that point. And a scientist must face facts and evidence, disregarding personal preferences, comfort and expectations. She was now watching him with a steady gaze, waiting in that infuriating way that females had when they knew that you were about to agree with them but wanted to make it seem like it was your own idea.

Oren came downstairs with a box of papers. He stopped at the door, noticing Hazel. Seamus made introductions, hoping that Oren might think this was merely a social call between old friends. He put the box down and took a seat.

"If you won't go today," said Hazel to Seamus, "I'll ask around for her address and go without you. But I'd prefer it if you accompanied me."

"Go where?" asked Oren.

"Seamus and I are having odd dreams, and we were discussing visiting someone who might know something of it."

Seamus was surprised at her direct answer, but Oren was his closest friend, and he had no reason to keep anything from him.

"A lady asks you to accompany her on a social call, and you refuse?" said Oren. "Seamus, that's hardly gentlemanly."

"I hadn't exactly refused," he said, and Hazel stood up, waiting expectantly for him to accompany her. "Very well," Seamus muttered. "I'll get my hat."

Half an hour later, they had obtained Miss Wilde's address from Mrs. Washington and took a hired carriage. Miss Wilde's house was a modest and unremarkable home in the middle of an entirely white neighborhood. Seamus rang the bell and a black woman answered. He recognized her immediately from his dreams, with her long face, close-cropped gray hair and silver spectacles.

For an instant, one fleeting instant, he thought she recognized him as well, but then she was looking at him with an expression of polite interest.

"Are you Miss Wilde?" he asked.

"I am."

"Then you are the woman we are looking to speak with. This is Miss Dubois and Mr. McCullen, and I am Mr. Connor."

She invited them inside, offered them seats in her front room and without asking, brought them each a thick slice of banana bread with walnuts. At first, Seamus didn't want it. He wanted answers, not meaningless hospitality. But the banana bread had a lovely aroma, and Hazel seemed to be enjoying hers, so he took a bite. It was every bit as good as it looked, and he immediately felt the tension and anxiety drain from him.

"How can I help you?" asked Miss Wilde, taking a seat across from them.

"I will go directly to the point," said Seamus. "Miss Dubois and I are having dreams, strange dreams that are the same. And they involve you. Both of us dreamed of you."

"I don't believe we've met before. Have we?"

A white cat sitting on the windowsill behind Miss Wilde opened its eyes to look at them, then closed them and resumed its silent meditation.

"No, we haven't. But, the dreams ..." He felt ridiculous, and Miss Wilde's pitying look didn't help matters. He was at a woman's house, asking about dreams.

"And you?" she said, looking at Oren.

"I'm curious. That's all."

Miss Wilde got a thoughtful look, as if she didn't entirely believe him.

"You aren't fooling us," said Hazel gently. "We know that you know something, Miss Wilde. You're one of those people who watch. You observe things. And you know things."

Miss Wilde's attention was now fixed on Hazel, as if she were the most interesting thing in all of creation.

"We remember people we've never met," said Seamus. "Places we've never been. Inventions and machines, strange creatures, all manner of things. And our dreams line up precisely with one another."

"A coincidence," said Miss Wilde.

"It's not, and you know it," said Hazel. "Now tell us."

"There's nothing to tell."

"What about the machines?" said Seamus, and Oren perked up. "There were machines that could do amazing things. Powerful machines."

Miss Wilde glanced at Oren, and Seamus knew he was not mistaken. For an instant, there had been fear in her look.

"Mr. McCullen has been working on one of the machines," Seamus said. If she was frightened of something, let him use that knowledge. "Both of us have. We're trying to make one, and we're getting close. You would be amazed at what we can do. We are just on the verge of it."

Miss Wilde stood then, and though it was a clear signal that she was dismissing them and ending their visit, he could tell she was internally composing herself. For a black woman to do anything other than be gracious and accommodating to white guests might be dangerous, not only socially, but physically as well if anyone got word of it. He wondered again at her place in this neighborhood, how she stayed without trouble.

"I'm sorry I cannot be of further help," she said. "But I can pack up some fresh cookies for you to have later."

The three of them rose, and Oren accepted a stack of cookies tied in a fresh, clean handkerchief. They donned their hats and coats and walked down the street, toward a busier area where they could hire a carriage. They passed an unoccupied house with a low brick wall out front and a decaying swing hanging from a large oak tree.

"Pardon me," said a woman's voice, and Seamus turned toward the front yard, but no one was there.

"I'm right here," she said again, and Hazel was the first to spot her. A white cat, the same one that had been on

Miss Wilde's windowsill, leapt from the yard up onto the wall. "May I have a word?"

"Of course," said Hazel.

Seamus couldn't speak, and after a few moments, the shock wore off and he wondered at how easily Hazel had answered the animal, as if she were used to the notion. Oren remained speechless. The cat introduced herself as Pangur Ban.

"I too have had dreams," said the cat. "And I can tell you that September is a good sort of person. She isn't trying to be rude to you, though you seem to have upset her greatly. But she is constrained in what she can do and what she can tell you. All of her siblings are, in one way or another. She won't answer my questions either."

"What do you know about the dreams?" asked Hazel.

"Little," said the cat. "As I said, I have had them as well. I thought I was the only one. I too remember machines, and they were important, somehow. They were, I think, dangerous. I think September fears them."

"They let us travel to other places," said Seamus. "They made doors. Rips. Did you dream of that?"

"I have. And I also know that there are other kinds of doors, natural and unnatural. September's siblings cannot all create these rips, but a few of them can."

"They can make these rips?" asked Oren with a look that Seamus had never seen before. Usually, he was self-assured under stress, or he kept a carefully neutral expression. But now, he was hopeful, desperate even. "And could a person step through one?"

Pangur Ban regarded Oren. "The Twelve are nearly impossible to find. You would have more luck trying to make a rip with your terrible machine."

"You said Miss Wilde had siblings," said Seamus. "Are they the Twelve?"

"They are. Some are kind, some cruel. Some are a little of each. September is one of the kind ones. The others you might not wish to meet. But kind or cruel, each can do different things. Some can open and close these rips. One can change people's moods with music. Another can create small illusions. September herself is excellent at negotiation. You enjoyed the banana bread, I presume? Well, she works through her cooking. She calms people when they're agitated. That is how she can live in this neighborhood in peace."

"And the Twelve watch?" asked Hazel. "I knew they were watchers or guardians of some kind. I dreamed that."

"They are. They are guarding things. When a castle is under attack or when a person guards another person, where do they stand?"

"At the point where the attack might come," said Oren.

"At the places where an enemy would enter," said the cat. "The gates, the entrances, the places that are weakest. At the doors. Guards stand at the doors."

"Then these dreams about going to other worlds, they mean something?" asked Hazel.

"I know they are important, but not how," said Pangur Ban. "Frankly, the four of us here are very small and weak. We are just little mortal beings, living out our lives. I can't see why we're having the dreams when we are so utterly powerless to do anything about them. The world is full of terrible things, and we can do nothing. But I suppose this world has always been the devil's playground. We can only make our way as best we can."

CHAPTER 20

"**I** MUST SAY, I'M GLAD YOU'VE decided not to kill me," said Yelbeghen.

Astrid shoved her hands into her jacket pockets. "Of course not. I'm not going to kill a good friend for the Seelie or for anyone else."

"A good friend?"

"A person. Anyone. Friend or not."

But as she said it, she felt her skin grow warm and her pulse quicken. He regarded her for a few moments longer than was comfortable.

"You could do it easily. You could just create a Door to death and push me through."

"Or I could make it under your feet. I think I could even bend it around you if you tried to escape."

"Indeed," he said, apparently not too disturbed by the idea. "Both of us could. I couldn't send you to death, of course, but to somewhere else unpleasant."

"You won't."

"Of course not. I do not delight in death. But I do delight in new things. In fact, I've acquired some new fish. Would you like to see them?"

She said she would, and he took her downstairs to the basement, then through a long, concrete tunnel where their footsteps echoed and the walls dripped with condensation. After walking for a few minutes, the tunnel opened up under a giant curved glass dome that rose twelve feet over their heads. They were under water, beneath Yelbeghen's small lake. Sunlight sparkled down through the green water, creating undulating strings of light on the floor and over both of their faces. Creatures, some ordinary and some strange, swam past. A pair of pale white fish with long filmy tails, like bridal veils, passed, and a group of ducks paddled overhead. One dove down to snatch a beakfull of water plants.

Astrid stole a glance at Yelbeghen and found him rapt with delight, the smallest smile on his face. It vanished the instant he realized he was being observed.

"The new fish are shy," he said. "And they may not come this way for a while."

"I have a question. Actually, a few questions."

"Ask."

"Have you found out anything about why the world changed?"

"I haven't. You and I seem to be the only ones aware of it. Well, there may be others, but I wouldn't know how to find them."

A school of tiny pale green fish swam past, turned and darted back the way they had come.

"I was thinking," said Astrid. "Was the ship Skidbladnir a dragon once?"

"Did she tell you that?"

"No, but no other ship I've ever heard of is alive, and she's a dragon, so I thought you might know about her."

"Yes, I do. And yes, she was a drake. She never will be again."

"What happened to her?"

"She committed a crime and was punished. Now she is bought and sold, traded and stolen, forever belonging to others. She went mad for a while, but when she regained sanity, such as it was, she accepted her fate."

"Is that why you wanted to buy her?"

"She is old and deserves the protection of someone who will look after her. We're family, in a way."

"I thought you only wanted her because she was rare."

"Well, that too. I won't deny it. I would still like to talk to your cousin about acquiring her. I would pay him a great sum."

"She only belongs to him temporarily. I want to find Captain Hazel Dubois. She's the ship's rightful owner."

"So says the young woman who chastises me for keeping living things here. You stand there and tell me that Skidbladnir has an owner, even after knowing she is alive and was once free?"

"No, not like that. It's only ... she belongs with Hazel. Don't you think she'd be happier sailing the seas than puttering around the shores of your island?"

"Perhaps someone ought to ask her."

They stood in silence for a long while, and a group of the new fish eventually swam by, glowing orange and gold, their long, sinuous bodies snaking through the water with grace and strength. Wherever they had come from, this was their home now. They did not seem to mind their captivity.

"If I asked you for a favor," she said, "would you grant it?"

"It depends on what it is."

"Free your servants. Let anyone who wants to leave the island go."

"What makes you think I already haven't?"

"Because most of the people and things that were here when I first started visiting you are still here. You've even added to your collection."

From the ox with ninety-nine horns to the living statues, the sprites in the garden to the elderly manticore that lived in a cave on the far end of the island, most things were as they always had been.

He looked up again at the lake for a long while before answering.

"Two years ago I allowed anyone to leave who wished to. I would not keep an unwilling person or being."

"And me?"

"I thought you enjoyed our visits."

"I do, but if I asked you to free me, would you?"

"You are nearly halfway through our agreement of ten years of dinners with me. If I freed you, would you return to me willingly?"

She looked up, thinking. Yelbeghen was her friend, and she would visit him in his home. She thought about having him over to her apartment, once she had one. Their friendship existed in this place, this remote place, and might not be the same in the ordinary world. But then, the thought of not seeing him burned in her. It would be a loss, a bigger one than she would have thought. The idea of his loss hurt.

A large fish passed overhead, something carnivorous with protruding lower teeth and yellow eyes. It cast a shadow that darkened the room.

"No, you are not free," he said before she could answer, and he turned back and walked down the tunnel.

After dinner, she gave him her latest drawing, a picture of the elderly manticore. He was a red lion with a scorpion's tail and a man's face, an old man's face, marked by age and experience. The manticore was shy and she had only seen him once, so she didn't think it was a particularly accurate portrait. But that wasn't why she had drawn it. The old creature fascinated her, and she wanted to spend time with him, even if only through a drawing.

Yelbeghen studied it silently, nothing in his expression giving her any insight into his thoughts.

"He's Asian, not white," he said. "You drew his face as a white man."

"I only saw him once, and not up close. I know it's not a true portrait."

"Obviously. But the way you treat the tail, upraised, as if he were about to sting, why?"

"I thought it was more interesting than if he had it low

behind him. It gives some movement to the image."

He set it down on the table. "It's derivative. Your treatment of the subject is unoriginal. It looks like a drawing from a fairy-tale book."

"All art is derivative. Every artist draws from her influences, and I draw from mine. It's nothing to be ashamed of. I read a lot of fairy-tale books as a girl, and the manticore is a fairy-tale creature."

"Well, who of us isn't, one way or another?"

He was still testy from their exchange in the room beneath the lake. She took the picture, put it back into its protective folder and set it beside her purse.

"It's a good drawing," he said at last. "You have talent, accuracy and feeling. But it's not your own feeling. The way you draw is imitative, not simply derivative. You're an artistic chameleon. I suppose it's how you've always survived. Silent, watching, observing, processing. But beneath that, you are a real thing in a false world. And until you can be what you are, you will never be whole and complete."

"If you mean my body, I'll never know what I originally looked like. I'm a changeling, and I can't help it. I'll always be a copy of Sister. I even took the name intended for her."

"There's that, even though it wasn't voluntary. But even your owl aspect is a copy of that little cold iron bell you owned for so long. Under the assumed human form, past the owl and the unchosen psychopomp job, what are you? Because your human form and your owl form aren't your real shape any more than his human one is mine. You are as formless and as shapeless as the void itself. And you are afraid to show yourself."

"To you?" she said, angry at the turn of the conversation. She wasn't hiding or a chameleon, she was simply herself. She had never pretended to be anything else. Who was he to say otherwise?

"Especially to me."

"That's ridiculous. I've come here for years, talked with you, eaten with you, walked with you. I've never lied to you. And if I have to say it, yes, we are friends. Good friends, I suppose. I've been nothing but myself, though you seem to relish the idea of hiding behind false forms. And if you want to talk about being a chameleon, then why do you always appear human to me?"

"That's simple. I'm large and frightening."

"And I'm not easily scared."

He smiled then. "That you are not. But come, let's not quarrel. We can have our dessert on the upstairs balcony."

"I have another question," she said, tossing her napkin on the table.

"You have but to ask."

"Gerard said that Yelbeghen isn't your name. It's the type of drake you are."

"That's true."

"What is your name? Your real name?"

"Sevilen."

How quickly he had given it, and she felt guilty for never having asked before. But she hadn't known that she was calling him by the wrong name. All this time, and it had been as if he called her "Door" instead of by her name. She knew that by some ancient laws, giving a person one's name from one's own mouth gave the person power over you. She didn't know if this were true, nor did she have any desire for power over Sevilen.

He stood by the doorway, watching her.

"What?" she said. "I don't have any other name. Just Astrid."

"I was only waiting for you to walk with me."

CHAPTER 21

SEAMUS TOSSED OREN A SPANNER and then turned back to tinker with the inside of King Herod's detached head. He popped out an eyeball and worked at the screws holding it together.

This year's Christmas automaton display at St. Louis Cathedral would be the crowning event of the day. Well, aside from Christmas Mass, he reminded himself. For all his faults, and he knew he had many, he was no faithless heathen. He would make the automaton show as fine and beautiful as he was able. It was only October and they still had months to go, but he knew better than most that mechanical things often went wrong at the last moment.

During the Civil War, the automaton displays had been banned by occupying Union forces. But now, the conquered people needed something to lift their spirits, and though Seamus had been no supporter of slavery, he had developed an affection for his adopted city and its people.

The cluttered room where they worked was upstairs in the cathedral, near storage rooms and a few quiet areas where the brothers who maintained the place performed any work that required an undisturbed space.

Brother Joe hurried into their workroom, obviously flustered. "There are policemen here," he said. "They're looking for two men, but I don't think it's you two."

Seamus glanced at Oren, but his friend had already donned his look of serene assurance that allowed him to gain the confidence of others and allay their suspicions. Seamus kept working at Herod's eye, not allowing his look or movement to betray the terror knotting inside him.

"They're looking for a Seamus Doyle and an Oren McCabe. I explained that you weren't those men, but they insisted."

The officers appeared behind Brother Joe and he stepped aside, his round face the picture of fear and concern. He knew, thought Seamus. He must have doubts about their identities or he wouldn't be so frightened.

Oren tried to explain to the officers that they were Oren McCullen and Seamus Connor, but the officers were not convinced.

"We are under orders to bring you in. You can explain everything to the sergeant," one said, and the two of them were escorted outside, where a police wagon waited on a street beside the cathedral.

As Seamus was loaded inside, he thought he saw something at the center of Jackson Square, a movement of the air, as if it was wavering. But then the wagon door slammed shut, and he and Oren sat in the dark, trapped, just as they had been so long ago.

It had only been a matter of time, and twenty years was a good number of years on the run. They would be shipped back to Ireland where they would either be executed or imprisoned. In their youth, they had been sentenced to transport to Tasmania, but that practice was now outlawed. Death or prison were the only possible outcomes.

"We'll get out," said Oren softly. "We'll find a way. We did it once, and we'll do it again."

"I'm wondering how they found us. How did they know where we were? We've managed to evade them for so long, working in plain sight at the university. How did they find us?"

"It hardly matters," said Oren. "I don't plan on remaining a captive."

After a short ride, they were taken from the wagon and their paperwork was filed. Old physical descriptions of them from their prison days still matched. The date of their appearance in New Orleans coincided with their escape. There had been no mistake.

That evening, they sat across from each other in a cell. They did not speak, and Seamus knew that Oren was formulating their escape. For his part, he couldn't tear his mind from wondering how they had been caught.

"The officer said it was an anonymous informant," Seamus said. "I can't imagine who that would be."

"That girl Hazel Dubois?" said Oren. "For a price, she might do it, friend or no."

"She never knew I was a convict."

"She's a doxy. She can read men like a book."

"She's not a mind reader. It wasn't her."

It had to be someone with something to gain. But who? There was no one at the university who desired their positions. They were both professors of physics and mechanics, neither of them with extraordinary wealth or social position. All they had were their classes, their books and their inventions.

The inventions. The machines. Who would be unhappy about those? Ah, but the white cat had said that September Wilde was unhappy, that she feared the creation of the machines.

"It was September Wilde," said Seamus. "She didn't want us working on that machine. She was afraid."

Oren looked up at that. "Afraid enough to have us arrested?"

"We won't be making any machines that way. Remember what the cat said? She said the watchers stood at the doors. And Hazel said September Wilde was one of these watchers. She knows things others do not, perhaps she knew we were convicts. If we had dreams about her, somehow she might know about us. There's no doubt that she wanted to stop us from making the time machine."

"The one from your dreams that lets you travel to the world of the flying airplanes?" asked Oren.

Seamus had never heard the word before. Airplane. What an odd name for the flying machines in his dreams.

"Is that what they're called?" asked a woman in the doorway. It was Hazel, and she walked up to the bars, clutching her handbag. She opened it, pulled out a pad of paper and a pencil and handed them to Seamus.

"Write to your bank, your solicitor, whoever you think can help. I'm going to get you out. But hurry. They said I could only talk with you for a minute."

"How were you allowed in at all?"

"I know my clientele. Now hurry."

He understood. One of the officers must be a customer of hers, and she had either used her wiles to charm him, or she had threatened him with exposure.

He took the pencil and began to write, not to his solicitor, but to his housekeeper. Mrs. Washington knew what to do. He had not been idle these twenty years. He had money set aside and could hire a lawyer, but not until he reached Ireland. He wrote down his full birth name and the town in which his family lived, his parents, siblings, everything. He looked at the list of names and a little flame of hope sparked within him. He might go to prison, but he might also see his family again.

"You said airplanes," said Hazel to Oren.

"Airplanes, yes. That is the proper name for the flying machines. And the screens with the moving pictures are called televisions. I heard of one being displayed at the World Fair in 1936."

Seamus stopped writing. Nineteen thirty-six. Oren looked at the floor and clasped his hands between his knees.

"I came through to this world through one of those doors that the cat spoke of." As he spoke, his voice regained its

Irish accent, the one he so assiduously tried to lose but which came back when he was upset or emotional. "I was praying at a temple of Epona, one of our gods, and the air moved around me and I found myself here. I stepped through time, and I could never get back. That's why I was interested in the doors. That's why I'm so curious about your dreams of a time machine now."

"I saw the air move like that at Jackson Square," said Seamus. "It shimmered just as we were forced into the wagon."

A look of longing crossed Oren's face, and Seamus felt for his old friend. To be far from home was painful, and Oren must be the farthest of all.

"The machine is not real," said Seamus. "I have no idea how to even begin to make one."

"Neither do I," said Oren. "I just want to go home. I killed an Englishman here in this world, and I've paid for it. Now I just want to go home."

"You said you were at a temple of Epona," said Hazel. "I read about her. She's an old pagan god. Her worship has been over for centuries. How could you pray to her and yet still know about 1936?"

"In my world, the old gods did not die out. Your Christ god did not take hold in the same way as here."

"Another world," breathed Hazel. "Not just another time."

"I believe so," said Oren. "Our gods are not so different though. Do not look at me like that, Seamus. Epona was good and kind. She escorted the souls of the dead into the afterlife. Like an angel."

Seamus was less concerned with theology and more with the idea that another world was possible.

"A rip at this temple," Seamus said. "Do you remember where it was?"

"Precisely. In this world, it's a cloister for an order of your Catholic nuns."

Another question appeared in his mind. If September

Wilde had been the one to turn them in, then perhaps it was not to prevent them from making a machine, but to force them to go to Ireland, where the rip at the cloister would be. But that meant that they'd have to get out of prison.

Perhaps he was analyzing this too much. How many doors into other worlds were there, and how far did September Wilde's knowledge reach? Whether September Wilde wanted them in Ireland or not, Seamus did not like being manipulated, and he didn't like being forced. He and Oren would follow their own path, regardless of the plans of the strange woman.

"Are you finished?" asked Hazel, gesturing to the pad of paper in Seamus's hand. He gave it to her.

"Take it to Mrs. Washington. She'll know what to do."

"She knows what you are?" asked Oren.

"She's the only one. I had to trust someone. And today, I'm glad I did."

Oren didn't look pleased, but at the moment, Mrs. Washington could possibly save their lives.

"I'll do everything I can, Professor," said Hazel, and she touched his hand through the bars. Her fingers were cold.

"Oren and I are both of us murderers," he said. "They're right about that. We're both guilty of killing men. We've run from prison and built a life on lies. Neither of us went to any fancy university for our degrees. We're frauds. Murdering frauds. Why would you want to help us?"

"I wasn't always what I am now," she said, looking down at her dress which was perfectly ordinary. But he knew she was looking past the dress.

"In my dreams, you took care of me," she said. "I was your ward. I lived with you and you were kind to me. You treated me as if I were your own daughter."

CHAPTER 22

"RECORD!" ELLIOT SHOUTED, AND A small light appeared at the corner of his vision, indicating that his eye implant was recording.

He dropped to the deck as a winged, legless dragon soared past overhead. It turned, made another pass over them, but did not burn anything. Then it twisted in the air, the sunlight gleaming on its bronze scales and headed toward the west, toward land, its feathered wings beating slowly, the feathers around its head bright in the sunlight.

The sky was blue now, but a moment before, it had been orange. Was it because of the dragon? The sky darkened to a deep purple and thunder rumbled so loudly he could feel it in his chest.

Sister took his arm and tried to pull him up, but he grabbed her and pulled her down beside him.

"See that?" he pointed into the distance. "See where the dragon went? Look what's coming now."

"It's nothing," signed Sister.

"See the black dots? Those are the slaugh, the Wild Hunt."

"No, it's not," she signed, pulling away from him and standing up. "You're seeing things that aren't there."

He looked again, but the Wild Hunt must have diverted their course, for the sky was clear once more.

"I saw it," he said.

"I heard you record it. Play it back," Sister signed.

He did, and saw only a blue sky, clear and empty.

Sister texted someone on her phone, and Elliot stood and took a look at the monkey crew. They were working as if nothing had happened, as if no dragon had just threatened their lives. Mr. Escobar, the first mate, was watching him, but then glanced away.

"Again?" Elliot said, understanding at last. Sister gave him a sympathetic look. She signed something to Mr. Escobar and he gave a sharp nod, then shouted orders to the crew.

Astrid appeared on deck a moment later, and Elliot watched as she looked him over, assessing his condition.

"Stop it. I'm fine now, but it happened again."

"They're getting worse," signed Sister. "The crew is worried."

Elliot knew what happened on a ship when the crew lost faith in their captain. Though Skidbladnir's monkeys were good and loyal, they were not stupid. They would not follow a mad captain.

"We should go to your quarters," said Astrid. "Somewhere quiet."

Elliot knew that it wasn't quiet they needed, but privacy. The crew did not need to hear their discussion. They went below decks, to the captain's quarters that Sister and Elliot shared. Elliot sank down into his plush reading chair. Astrid pulled up the desk chair and Sister sat on the floor.

"I can't tell when it's not real," said Elliot. "I suppose that's the nature of being crazy, right?"

Astrid didn't say anything. She wouldn't lie to him, he knew. But he also knew it was hard for her to be unkind to him, even to tell the truth.

"I know what's happening," he said. "I know I'm going insane. I'm fine now, and I can tell now, but not when it's happening."

"You're sensing time slips. It's what you do. You were never crazy before. Was it the walking Egyptian statues and the void wyrms again?"

"No. A dragon and the Wild Hunt."

"A dragon? You've never encountered a dragon before."

"I've never encountered any of those things before."

She didn't argue with him, but he already knew what she would have said. She had memories of a different past, one where he had been imprisoned in a terrible library, one where he worked with the Time Corps.

"What did the dragon look like?"

"It was metallic. Bronze. Long neck. Feathered wings. No legs, like a snake."

"And it attacked you?"

"No," he said, surprised. "It just looked at us. I was so sure it was going to burn us, but it didn't. It just looked at us, circled around and flew off."

Astrid got a faraway look, as she always did when deep in thought.

"I'm not too surprised you see the past. Sister dreams of her other past too. But since you sense time slips, I think you might be able to see into the future."

"A dragon in my future?"

"It's possible. Anything is possible, right?"

Sister was looking at them with wide eyes.

"Not all of the things I see are bad," said Elliot. "I saw a beautiful woman reading. She had these silvery markings on her face. And the sky is sometimes pale orange or lavender or dark blue. Once it was a gold so bright it hurt to look at."

"The orange and the purple are the Seelie and Unseelie skies," said Astrid. "But even if you see nice things, most of them are bad. Monsters and rips in the sky. The void wyrms. Terrible things."

They sat in silence, and Elliot knew what had to happen. "I have to give up the ship," he said. "I can't captain like this. Sister, you should be captain. The crew understands your signing. You can do it."

She shook her head. "No, I can't be in charge of all those monkeys. I wouldn't know what to do."

"Astrid?" he looked to his cousin.

"I can't be a captain and leave the ship at a moment's notice to do psychopomp jobs. Besides, I don't want to live at sea. But there's another option, one to think about. Yelbeghen would take care of the ship. He would pay you well, and you can split the gold among the crew. You could let the crew off on their home island in the Gulf of Mexico, and Skidbladnir could live in the waters around Yelbeghen's island."

Elliot wanted to say no, that it wasn't fair to the crew or the ship. But what other choice did they have? He needed to think it through, when he was calmer and wasn't still pulsing with adrenaline from facing death, even an imagined one.

"Do you think it's Yelbeghen I saw?" asked Elliot.

"I don't know what he looks like as a dragon."

"You said you have been dining with him for years, and you've never seen him?"

"He's sort of shy about it."

He knew her look, the longing, wistful look, the little sideways glance, and then her attempt to hide it. She shoved her hands into her coat pockets, which meant she was withdrawing, concealing herself.

"You like him," he said, not bothering to hide the accusation in his tone. "You really like him. He forces you to eat with him. He collects people. He's not even human."

"Neither am I."

"Oh, come on. You're more human than he is. You're not a monster."

"He's not a monster. He can be kind."

"It's called Stockholm syndrome. You were like that with your mother too, defending her even after she tortured and abused you."

He saw the anguish on her face and knew immediately

he had been too harsh. The subject of her mother needed
to be broached delicately, and he had been too blunt and
hurt her.

"I'm sorry," he said, though he really wasn't. "I just
hate when you don't think you deserve better. You take
scraps when you deserve a meal. Fulfill your obligation to
the drake, but don't let him make you think he actually
cares about you."

She was looking at the floor now, shutting herself away
from him, but he knew her thoughts.

"He can't care about you. He's not a man, no matter
what he looks like. He's not your friend."

"I don't have real friends, Elliot. My friends from art
school are fine, but they can't ever know what I am. Same
with the guys I dated. The only friends I can be myself
with are the psychopomps who don't remember me and
the Time Corps who are in another world. So what else do
I have, really?"

"You have us," said Elliot.

Sister looked from one of them to the other and then
signed her agreement.

But Elliot understood what Astrid meant all too well.
She was right about being alone. He didn't know how much
Sister understood, but if he knew anything about her, it
was that in her forced silence, she was always listening
and watching.

Sister stood up. "I'll be acting captain until we get
home. We have one more delivery before we can go back
to Los Angeles." She left to speak with Mr. Escobar, and
Astrid poured a glass of water from a jug.

"I'll stay as long as I can," she said.

Elliot climbed into his hammock, hating his uselessness
and helplessness. A deep anger burned in him at the
thought of being dependent, of needing others, especially
his cousins, to watch after him, like a child.

He read for a while, then dozed off. He woke to the

sound of Astrid pushing back the desk chair and coming toward him.

Her skin was mostly gone and what was left hung from her form in dried slivers. Her short blonde hair was patchy with white, as if her skull had been out in the sun too long. She held a cup in her hand and said, "Drink."

"I can't," he said. "I see you wrong. I see you dead."

The skeleton stopped and her head tipped to the side, regarding him with her dark eye sockets filled with rotted flesh, the remnants of eyes. He felt the world spin, gently, so gently, around him. It was like a mother, holding him and twirling to soft music. The piano played in his mind, and he heard a person's steps, the gentle thud of feet on the floor, the swish of the shoe soles, the tinkling of the notes.

Then Astrid changed, her eyes became a sharp, clear gold, unmoving in their sockets, like a reptile, but the pupils of the eyes, instead of being shiny with moisture were dull black. They pulled at him, and he knew the sensation, the thread of his mind being pulled, unraveling, the pull of the void.

"You never should have come through the mirror," he said. "You've touched the mirror, and you know what it is to see yourself there, your hand touching your own hand. We all felt the cold glass, but it's not the truth, not really. We touch our own hand, not the glass.

"You and Sister are the same person, or you should have been before you came through. See, she was there, trying to protect you. You thought it was you saving her, but it was the other way round. She was pushing you back when you touched your hand to the glass. She was trying to save you, to keep you from the world, the terrible world, to keep you from coming through the mirror. It was a hell there. Both of you knew it, but you knew opposite sides of it. And she tried to save you, to push you away.

"That's why none of us had duplicates in the other

worlds. Our twins saved us. They pushed hard so we couldn't go through the mirror. Except yours." He sighed. "Except yours."

She set the cup on the bolted-down table beside his hammock and left. He didn't understand why she wouldn't answer him. He was only trying to help.

CHAPTER 23

"I'VE SEEN MANY VOID WYRMS in my time," said the strange man to Felicia. "And that one was after you specifically. Now, why is that?"

Felicia watched as he looked her over again, paying special attention to her hands and feet and then took a few steps to view her from behind. She turned with him, unwilling to be looked over and too wary of him to turn her back.

"How did you close the hole?" she asked. "What did you do?"

"Were you in Los Angeles recently?"

"A few weeks ago."

"Yeah," he sighed. "And I suppose you've been in the hospital recently?"

"I work there."

"It makes no sense. You're not special. You're not unusual. You're just ... nothing."

"You're too kind. But tell me how you did it."

"But that's just it," he said. "There's no reason for it to be happening."

"What is it that's happening, exactly?"

"You noticed the earthquakes, right?"

"I think they're following me."

"Yup. Now, what's your name?"

"Felicia Sanchez. Yours?"

He appeared to be deep in thought. "Doesn't ring any bells. Do you go by any other names?"

"No."

"Janeiro."

It took her a moment to realize that he was giving her his name.

"You're related to that other man who can make the rips, right?" she asked.

"What man would that be?"

"He's short and pale. I don't remember his name."

She felt the memory inside, part of her dream. Perhaps the name was in her dream journal, but she doubted it. She had read and reread it enough times to have it memorized.

Janeiro spun around, throwing an arm in front of her as if an attacker was coming. A moment later, another rip opened, a terrible void wyrm head pushing forward. Janeiro said a word, and then said it again, more forcefully.

She tried to remember the word. It was short, or maybe it was a few syllables long. And the beginning sound was a hard consonant. Or was it something softer? She wanted to write it down, but already, the word was gone.

The rip closed.

"They're hungry, and you're attracting them," he said.

"Why? What do they want with me?"

"An excellent question. We should leave New Orleans immediately. It's an unstable place, and you're only making it worse."

"I'm not going anywhere with you."

"I understand. You are wary of a strange man, and that's sensible. But honestly, you saw the void wyrm, you know the earthquakes are following you, and you know I can close the rips. There are not many others who can do that, and the ones I know of won't help you. So think about it."

He crossed his arms and watched her, as if she was going to make the decision on the spot.

"Where would we go?"

"Lots of places. There are more stable areas, and I can

feel the rips just before they happen. I can keep you safe."

"Why? Why not let them eat me? Then they won't come any more, right?"

He tipped his head to one side. "What a strange thing to say. First, there's no guarantee that your death would stop them from coming. Second, I want to know why they're after you specifically. Call me curious. And third, I'm one of the kinder of my sort of being. If you know my brother, the pale man, then you know that not all of us are so charitable. I am obligated to help you, and I want to."

"What are you? You and your brother?"

"Fair enough. I'll tell you, but we need to get away from Jackson Square. The whole city is a big instability, but this place especially."

"I'm not getting in a car with you."

"I don't even own one."

They walked along the river, and Felicia tried not to look at the water too often. In saner times, she would never consider Janeiro's offer, but here she was, thinking about it, wanting to satisfy her curiosity about her dreams and the rips, and more than anything, to keep her baby safe from those terrible void wyrms. He walked beside her, his rubber-soled work boots silent on the pavement, his windbreaker buttoned up to his throat.

"Will the wyrms come for me until they eat me?"

"Most likely. Wherever you go, it'll become unstable. So we'd have to keep moving."

"Where?"

"Other times, other worlds, anywhere we like. I'd pick, of course, since you wouldn't know where to go."

"For how long? I mean, I can't just run forever."

"Until we figure out why you're attracting them."

She knew already why she was attracting them, and she didn't want to tell Janeiro. But whatever sort of thing he was, he was her only hope of understanding anything. Her only hope of keeping her baby safe.

A rip opened at the riverbank, and this time Janeiro had to shout the word four times to make it close.

"It's getting harder to close the rips," he said.

She made her decision, for her child's sake.

"I'm pregnant."

He pressed his palm to his forehead and muttered a string of profanities. "They didn't know, did they?" he said. "They couldn't have known. Or maybe they did." He looked at her with narrowed eyes. "Do you remember the worlds splitting?"

She said she didn't, but then another earthquake shook the city, and a rip appeared on the sidewalk ahead. Janeiro closed it and took her arm. An instant later, they were in a forest, redwoods soaring overhead and a chilly bite in the air. The place was quiet but for the wind in the leaves and the harsh sound of a distant bird.

"I don't want anyone to get hurt," he said. "I can still take you back."

"This place is safe?"

"For now."

"Then tell me everything," she said.

"You first. How did you know about my brother?"

He led her along a narrow path, like a deer path, overgrown in places and invisible in others, and as they walked, she told him everything about the dreams. In return, he told her that there were many worlds, and that she had known a man who made a machine that allowed people to traverse the worlds. This man was her husband. But they were from different worlds originally, so when the worlds were again sealed off from one another, they were separated.

"They couldn't have known you were pregnant, or they'd have removed the child."

Fear seized her. "They won't remove it now, will they?"

"No. It's too late now."

"And who are the 'they' you talk about? Who did this?"

"My brother and some that helped him. It was agreed upon by the various higher-ups." He waved his hand as if indicating the air itself.

"And the dreams?"

"Now that's where it gets interesting. Because from what you say, it sounds like someone on my side is interfering." He said it with a delighted smile, like a little boy. "I don't think that was supposed to happen."

"Someone is giving us the dreams?"

"Looks like it. Usually it's a little more subtle, or a one-time thing. But hey, it's not my job, so who am I to judge how it's done?"

"Who?"

"I'm not sure, but I have my suspicions. No one you would know. Just tell me what else you dream about, and we'll see if it's any use to us."

They arrived at a small cabin in a clearing, its roof coated in moss. Janeiro opened the door and let her inside.

"It has plumbing and electricity. We're in your future. We can stay here awhile."

"I have a life back home. Family. Friends. Work."

"You can go back now and then. Visit people for short periods. You can schedule doctor visits. You won't be stranded. I can see how you might be worried about being stuck far from home. But you can get back, I promise."

"Tell me about the Twelve," she said.

He took a seat and clomped his boots up onto the coffee table. "Do you know in a war, there are more than two sides, right? It's always like that. In this war, there are those who are good, those who are evil, and those who are neutral."

"And you claim to be good."

"In an objective sense, yes. I follow the dictates of a moral code that claims superiority over the alternative. I have three siblings who do the same. Julius, September and May, who now goes by Red Fawn. Then there are four who are more situationally ethical. They don't choose sides, but we can work with them from time to time. June Yee, November and Augustus are three of those. And then there are the other four, those who operate by a different code entirely. They think themselves free of rules and orders, but they're not. My brother March is the pale man you remember.

"Each side has one member who can open and close rips. There's me, March and November. November is neutral, more or less, but he also has another function. But between you and me, neutrality in a war is the same as helping the enemy. My better siblings and I disagree on that point, however. But we're watchers, guards, observers, depending on what's needed."

"And your higher-ups?"

"The Seven, the Five, the Three, the One, though it's debated whether the last two are the same thing. There are many others. So many. Multitudes. 'We are legion' as the saying goes."

After a while, Janeiro said it would be safe for her to return to her apartment to pick up her things. She left a note for Doug, called her mother and called work to tell them she wasn't going to come in the next day. Then she told Janeiro how she needed to get medical leave from work, keep up to date on her bills and keep her life as normal as possible.

"Once the baby is born, I want to go back to a normal life."

"We'll do our best. I've called some of my siblings to talk about the situation. We'll figure out how to keep you both safe."

He took her back to the cabin, and in the silence of the forest, relief engulfed her. For the first time since she saw the lines on her pregnancy test and the earthquakes started, she felt like things might just turn out all right.

CHAPTER 24

IN THE BRIG, DEEP IN the damp hold of the cargo ship that was serving double duty as prisoner transport, Seamus passed the time. He whistled old tunes, tried to figure out a way to escape and played endless games of solitaire with an old deck of cards that was missing the queen of diamonds and the four of clubs.

"Play a hand with me," said Seamus.

"You count cards," said Oren.

"I won't this time."

"Yes you will. You can't stop yourself."

Seamus shuffled the cards and laid out another round of solitaire while Oren returned to his thoughts. Throughout the voyage, his friend had remained completely silent for hours, only speaking to discuss ideas about the time rips and possible mathematical possibilities, to whisper an idea in Gaelic on a plan for escape once they reached land or to mutter profanities about the English. He had revealed to Seamus his part in the Irish Republican Army in the twentieth century. Now, faced with punishment for his murder of an Englishman in this world, the embers of Oren's hatred had burst into full flame.

"Do you hear that?" asked Oren when the guard brought in their evening rations.

Oren was speaking in English, which meant he wanted the guard to understand. They were headed to an Irish prison and would be docking in Clonakilty in Southern Ireland first to unload the two of them. Then the ship would sail on to Bristol, England, with its cargo. The crew was made up of Englishmen, which meant Seamus always feared that Oren would lose his tongue and say something unfortunate.

"Do you mean the terrible sound the engine is making?" said Seamus, catching on.

"Yes," said Oren. "It's been running hot ever since we got on, and it's only getting worse."

"I know just what it needs," said Seamus. He and Oren went through a few quick ideas, acting as if they didn't notice the guard pausing to listen.

"Of course, I'd have to look at it," said Oren. "We fixed things like that in our sleep, didn't we, Seamus?"

"That we did. That we did."

The guard left and Oren sighed. "I know they have our records up there. They know we were good with machines. We had enough patents between the two of us to impress anyone."

On the second day, the steam engine sounded worse, and Seamus noted that the crew slowed it periodically to allow it to cool. On the third day, they shut down the engine for two hours, ran it for two, then shut it down again for two. On the fourth day, when they ran it at all, they ran it low, which meant traveling at only half speed. And on the fifth day, Oren sat in his bunk facing the door, his arms crossed, waiting.

The ship's engineer came in, frustrated and pink-faced, the cell key in hand.

"Only one of you," was all he said. "And if you try anything, I'll shoot you dead where you stand."

"Of course," said Oren, standing. Seamus didn't try to take his place. Oren had gotten them out of prison once, and though Seamus might be a cheat at cards and a skilled liar, they both knew that Oren possessed the more cunning mind.

Seamus listened to the engine as it shut off. Oren

worked for more than three hours and returned just before supper. The engineer locked him back in his cell, his manner more relaxed but far from pleased. It couldn't be flattering to ask the prisoners for help. Seamus would be surprised if he kept his job at all once the voyage was over.

Late that night, Seamus heard Oren whisper his name.

"I'm awake," he whispered back.

"We're a few days from shore," Oren whispered in Gaelic. "I learned that when I was up there. They'll need me again tomorrow. I made certain of it."

"Sabotage?"

"Just a little. But I have more in store. There are three engines, a primary and two secondary. Things will happen."

"What?"

"Let's see first if my little plan worked. I loosened two of the nuts on a critical portion of the engine. The attached parts will be clattering by noon tomorrow."

Sure enough, by lunchtime the engine was shut down once more, and once again, Oren was summoned from their cell. When he returned, a guard was in the room, and Seamus only looked up from his solitaire game with feigned mild interest.

"Soon," muttered Oren in Gaelic under his breath when he returned.

When the engine exploded, Seamus grabbed the edge of his bunk. The guard tore out of the room to see what had happened, and Seamus turned to Oren, who reached into his left sock.

"What did you do?" asked Seamus.

"I can rig an explosive, Seamus. It's not the first time."

"But an explosion like that—people will have died."

"Most likely. But it's kill or be killed, my brother."

He held up a key. "The engineer is not experienced in working in close quarters with a pickpocket."

"I didn't know you could do that."

Oren reached through the bars and fit the key into the

lock. "Didn't know I was born in 1927 either, did you?"

They ran up the stairs, and when Seamus lurched to a halt and pressed his back against the wall to avoid a passing crew member, Oren fell in beside him. Their guard chose that moment to return, and Oren didn't make a sound as he struck the man. Seamus slammed him against the wall while Oren took his revolver. Oren then knocked his feet out from under him, grabbed his head and slammed it against the steps again and again until the man quit struggling.

"Christ, Oren," said Seamus, louder than he ought to. The suddenness and savagery of it chilled him. They dragged the man to the cell, and Oren hauled him onto the bunk and threw a blanket over him, then closed the cell door. The man was still breathing.

"Let's go."

Seamus wanted to leap into the first lifeboat they found, but Oren pointed to another one at the end of the row.

"That one. But first, we untie these."

The second engine exploded then, and they ducked behind some tied-down crates to avoid detection as frantic crew members raced past. Oren gave Seamus a wink. At the other end of the ship, men screamed for the ship's physician, and black smoke poured into the sky. They were in the middle of the sea with no land in sight. There was no water or food on the rescue boats, and he and Oren were about to leave the only safe place there was.

"Help me lower them all," said Oren, and the two of them untied all but one of the rescue boats. There were only five in total, and Oren put bullet holes in the bottoms of four of them, aiming carefully to do the most damage to each.

They hid again as two men came by, and Seamus heard them discussing a great hole in the ship's hull. Seamus glanced at Oren who had the look of a very satisfied cat. Once the men were out of sight, Oren sprang up and leapt into the rescue boat, unfastening the tie while Seamus climbed in. Oren lowered them down. When the boat reached the water and Oren unfastened the last rope, Seamus put the oars in the sculls and started rowing. The sun was setting, and if anyone looked into the water, there would be no cover of darkness to hide them.

A third explosion rocked the ship.

"It'll sink, if I'm half the saboteur I hope I am," said Oren. "And all those stinking English whores' sons will be food for the creatures of the deep."

"They were just doing their jobs."

"Yes, doing their jobs hauling Irish prisoners. They ought to leave us to our own countrymen."

Seamus kept rowing as hard as he could, unwilling to waste any effort in arguing with Oren. They were free, and if they could reach land alive, they just might remain so.

"We're only a few miles from shore, I think," said Oren, but Seamus knew he wasn't certain.

The smoke from the ship was thicker now, and if he looked closely, he thought he saw the ship listing to starboard. Men were gathering at the railing, pointing at the rescue boats now all either sunk or barely afloat.

The men spotted the two of them, and one of the men ran off and then returned to raise a rifle.

"Down!" yelled Oren, and Seamus flattened himself on the bottom of the boat, Oren lying on top of him.

The man missed, and as the man reloaded his rifle, Seamus again took to rowing, pulling as hard as he could until his arms and back felt like they were on fire.

Oren aimed for the man who held the rifle. He fired and missed, then cursed.

"They're too far away," he said.

They were farther out now, but the man with the rifle took another shot. He missed, and Oren offered to take the oars. He was older than Seamus, but still a vigorous man, and Seamus was wearing out.

The man with the rifle fired again, and the moment Seamus heard the crack, Oren jerked and dropped the oars. A red blotch appeared and spread on his stomach, and Oren put his hand to it, swearing an oath of anger more than of pain.

"You have to row," said Oren. "Help me move."

Seamus helped him from his seat, easing his friend to the bottom of the boat where he could lie mostly concealed. He took the oars again. The ship was listing hard to starboard now.

"It'll take hours," said Oren.

"It looks partly sunk already."

"I meant for me to die."

"You're not going to die. We're going to get to shore. We get to land and find you a doctor."

Oren nodded slowly, like a drowsy man trying to stay awake. A few minutes later, he said he was cold, and Seamus spread his jacket over him, the same one he was wearing when he was arrested at the cathedral. It was dirty and smelly, but he was glad to have it to offer. It didn't seem to help. Oren tried to put pressure on the wound on the front of his body, and Seamus wadded up Oren's jacket so he could lie on it, putting pressure on the exit wound, but still Oren shivered as the bottom of the boat grew dark with his blood.

"The doorway, the cloister, is in Fintona, south of Omagh. That's where the air shimmered that day. The sisters were kind to me. They fed me and gave me a bit of money for a room in town."

Seamus knew the place. He knew it well. He had grown up close by.

The cargo ship was invisible now, and the column of thick black smoke had dissipated into the sky. Whether that meant they were too far to see it or it had sunk, Seamus could not know.

Once the stars appeared, he found the North Star and

adjusted course a little, singing an old rowing song he had learned from a friend of his brothers, long ago in Ireland.

"Tell me about your home," said Seamus. "Tell me about the machines."

Oren tried. He must have known what Seamus was doing, attempting to keep him conscious, and he told him of radios and telephones and electric lighting. He spoke also of machine guns and bomber planes, tanks and atomic bombs that could destroy an entire city.

Seamus rowed until he was forced to stop. His arms felt like those of a rubber doll, and he knelt beside Oren, pulling back his shirt to examine the wound, a shredded, bloody mass of torn flesh. He was no doctor, but he knew it was bad. They were still nowhere near land, and Oren had lost so much blood.

"You'll be all right," said Oren.

"I'm not worried about myself."

"If I had to die, I'm glad it was by your side. You've been a good friend to me, Seamus."

"Don't talk like that."

"Promise me something."

"Anything."

"Don't bury me. Don't waste the time. You are on the run, and you won't have me to look after you. Put me in the water. Then take the revolver, get to shore and run home. There's a good boy." He let out a long breath. "Now, say a prayer for me."

Seamus began the Ave, but Oren stopped him with a lifted hand. "No, one of mine. Like this."

He said a prayer to Epona, asking for a peaceful death and a walk at her side to the land beyond. Seamus repeated it, not caring if it was blasphemous or if God would count the pagan prayer as a grave sin. He made Oren as comfortable as he could and took the oars again.

He knelt by Oren's side when the dawn sky lightened and then burned yellow and the life left his friend. And not knowing what else to say, he said the prayer to Epona once more as he knelt and lifted Oren's body.

He was unwieldy, heavy and covered in blood. Seamus was ashamed to give his friend such a burial, but he would not break his promise. Oren was, if anything, a practical man, even to the point of brutality. He would waste no sentiment on the manner of his burial.

As he pushed his friend overboard, sea water splashed Seamus's face, stinging his eyes and getting in his mouth. The cold sea wind blew, and he watched as Oren's white face vanished beneath the greenish water that clouded dark with the blood from his body and clothing.

He took the oars again, breathing the little prayer under his breath as he wept and rowed.

CHAPTER 25

NEIL GREY AND HIS BROTHER golems sat in March's living room, listening as their creator explained things to them. There was a conflict, there were those who would restrict free choice, and the golems were soldiers who would fight to give the human race their freedom.

There were six golems, seven including Neil, and they spanned the human spectrum in skin tone and ethnicity. Neil thought it made perfect sense, as each of them could remain invisible to strangers in various countries and time periods. Each of them was as forgettable and unremarkable in appearance as he was.

He studied them as they listened to March, and he wondered about the internal workings of their minds. He knew that he was the eldest brother, but did that mean that the others could create beautiful and original things? Did March correct that error in their makeup? Or had he simply wanted strong, cunning foot soldiers?

"It's time to go," said March, but instead of taking each of them by the arm as he usually did with Neil, he made a Door and stood aside as each golem stepped through. Neil tried to be unobtrusive as he peered through before stepping through, while his brothers appeared to simply trust their creator and went through without hesitation.

Neil stepped into in parklike area in a city. It was evening and Neil knew by the cars that they were about fifteen years into the twenty-first century. The license plates indicated California. The air was cool and moist and had a tang to it which meant they were near the ocean.

"Portsmouth Square, San Francisco," said one of his brothers, and Neil studied the place as they walked through behind March. They were in the center of Chinatown, and he longed to explore, but they had a serious job to do.

He paused at the statue of the Goddess of Democracy, studying the figure. She was dark and angular, blocky, but strong and graceful at the same time. She was sturdy. She held a torch aloft with both hands and her hair blew out sideways from her head, like a flame. He wondered at the person who made it, the many people who viewed it. The woman symbolized an important truth, something beyond the idea of the political system of self-governance. Something more important.

"It's coming," said March, touching his arm, and he turned to follow his brothers. They were a strange group, and if searched, they would produce seven Glocks in shoulder holsters, seven bowie knives and seven guns that shot tiny electronic tracking devices that March could use to track void wyrms or drakes through time. But even unarmed, the golems were one of the more deadly groups of beings on the planet.

An earthquake hit, and the golems crouched instinctively, bracing themselves. It was not a strong earthquake, and when it ended, the void wyrm appeared though its rip. Three of his brothers leapt forward to latch hold of it while the others circled around the sides.

As golems, they were immune to the pulling effect that the void wyrms used to draw their prey. The air blew around them, hunks of dirt and stray leaves flew into the rip, but they were not affected. Neil knew his job, but as the eldest, he had always been assigned to killing people instead of void wyrms. His brothers had more experience with the strange creatures, and he hung back to watch, preparing to help them if they required it.

The golems pulled out their bowie knives, and Neil watched as some of them held the void wyrm immobile and the others slit its throat. Or it must have been its throat since it was on the underside of the thing. One of his brothers hacked at the top half of the head. The thing shook and screamed and tried to pull back, but the golems were too strong, the ones on the ground bracing themselves to keep the creature from pulling back into its hole. Neil knew that each of them could fight off multiple men, and with six of them, the wyrm was simply outmatched.

The void wyrm's blood flowed over the golems' hands and knives, pooling in a pale bluish puddle that glowed faintly and wet the soles of their shoes and splashed on the legs of their pants. Neil wanted to turn away. The thrashing desperation of the creature touched him, and he steeled himself. He killed people, though he almost always did it with poison or a quick gunshot. He did not like suffering.

"This is what you must do," said Mr. March from beside him.

"I know you said they are bad, that they rip holes, but why not simply close the holes?"

"I used to be able to. Me and the others who could help. But now, with things as they are, we cannot keep up. There are simply too many unstable places that attract them, and each void wyrm can make many rips. By exterminating them, we reduce their number, thereby reducing the number of rips they can create."

"Why do they come? What do they want here?"

"They are attracted to instabilities. And they come because they are hungry."

"Why not eat in the void?"

"It's empty. Surely you know that."

He did. But what sort of creature existed in a place where it could not feed?

"Will we kill them all?" he asked.

"I hope so."

"That's extinction, isn't it? Genocide."

"It's survival. It's necessary to keep the world safe."

The void wyrm was now dead, and his brothers pulled back. March made a rip around the body and the pool of pale blood, letting the thing's corpse fall back into the void. Perhaps its brothers and sisters would feed upon it.

The golems returned home with March, where he praised their swiftness, strength and decisive, quick action. They seemed pleased, in a reserved sort of way, and Neil wondered if that was how he appeared to others.

He thought of the void wyrm, bleeding and struggling and dying. It was only trying to eat. That was the most natural thing in the world. It was not a murderer or an inventor of terrible weapons, a rapist or child molester or one who indulged in evil and unnatural practices. The void wyrm was the very opposite, following the most natural urge in the world, to survive.

The brothers ate a meal prepared by March and then went upstairs to their rooms. Neil walked over to the sound system in the living room and played a piano concerto by some modern artist he had never heard of. He imagined her fingers, nimble and slender, dancing on the keys, her heart poured into the music.

"You are a more sensitive creature," said March. "Your brothers are a little different. They are more quick to act and slow to ponder things."

"I thought they might be like me."

"No one is quite like you. And each of them is an individual. Do not forget that. I love each of them as I love you."

Neil wasn't jealous of March's affections. In fact, he felt nothing at all at the idea of having beloved brothers. It made them a family, did it not? But it didn't feel like a family. But how would he know? He could only see other families and imagine the experience.

March left him to his music, and Neil stretched out on the sofa, not bothering to turn on the light as the sun set and the room grew darker.

He thought of the other people he had killed, and the evidence March had shown him. He had trusted that the evidence of their guilt was true, but how could he know for certain? They may very well have been innocent. Something about the void wyrm stirred up discontent in his heart and disturbed the peace of his thoughts. The thing, monstrous as it was, seemed innocent.

He thought of its ugliness, and how the idea of ugliness was only in his mind. To its parent or mate, the creature might be quite beautiful. There were beautiful people with ugly interiors. He knew that. Perhaps this creature was beautiful inside. That was possible. What if killing it was the killing of an innocent? The thought ate at him.

But this was all futile. He was a golem, and a golem obeyed its master. He had read books, and he knew the stories. Golems were made to do a prescribed deed, and then things went wrong and they'd kill someone or do something terrible. Then they would have to be destroyed. They were unnatural things. and the moral lesson to the tale was that mortals should not attempt to imitate nature and natural forces. A man should not take on the power of the gods to create life or to mete out death. But March was no human man.

Besides, those were only stories. He and his brothers were made for good, not evil. They weren't mindless animated hunks of earth, but people. They had minds and hearts, though if they turned on March, they might just be destroyed.

In the end, he supposed he was like all people, trying to do good according to his view of right and wrong. And that made him no different than March or any human being, although March claimed there was no objective right and wrong.

Except for one thing, a thing he saw embodied in the statue of the Goddess of Democracy. Freedom was good. He and March were in agreement upon that point.

CHAPTER 26

"**A**LL HALLOW'S EVE IS TOMORROW night," sighed the drake.

"I know," said Astrid. "I always loved trick-or-treating as a kid, and when I had an apartment, I liked handing out candy."

"The night wasn't always celebrated in that way. I was born in what is now Turkey. It wasn't until much later when I moved north that I learned how the spots where the worlds touch become thinner on that day. Many years passed before the advent of the modern practice of sending children to threaten people and demand candy."

"It's more fun than it sounds."

"Oh, I doubt it. It sounds terribly fun already."

The sun was setting and they left the balcony that faced the western ocean and ate a meal of falafel, hummus, flat bread and goat cheese.

An old man, one Astrid had seen many times before, served them. He had always seemed so shy, and she had never asked his name. Sevilen knew. He knew the names and life histories of everyone on the island. Only a few humans remained, and all of them of their own free will. She knew Sevilen's desire to hoard and collect and his occasional attempts to overcome that hunger. But he still hadn't freed her from her obligation, so she couldn't truly pity him. He might be lonely, but unless she was allowed out of their agreement, he was still using force and obligation to hold her.

"I have another drawing," she said. "I did this one in colored pencil."

She pulled the folder from her bag, but the moment she did so, she wished she hadn't brought the drawing. This one was too personal, too intimate. But maybe this was the drawing he'd accept as fulfillment of that portion of their bargain. Maybe it was *true* enough. She never minded creating art for him, but she wished he'd accept a piece already. The endless rejections, as interesting, educational and kindly as they might be, wore on her. He took the folder and opened it. He did not disguise his surprise.

"What is this?" he asked, though the subject was obvious.

"A dragon. You told me before that you were Turkish, and I looked up dragons from that region and tried to guess what you might look like."

"You think I'm red and gold?"

"I don't know. I just thought they were beautiful colors together."

"Do you think I'm beautiful?"

He looked up at her, and she saw that his question was neither playful or taunting, nor was he flirting. He was genuinely curious.

"I don't know. I just wanted to draw a beautiful dragon."

"You should ask for what you want. You don't do that often enough."

"I don't want anything."

"Obviously you're curious about what I look like. You spent at least a few hours imagining this drawing, yet you've never asked me to show myself to you."

"I didn't think you would. You didn't grant my request for freedom."

His expression changed, and she saw that she had hurt him.

"You ask me to free you as if you don't like coming here. You visit longer than required, you bring me gifts, you say we are friends. And we are more than that as well."

"Friends don't keep each other under any obligation. Friends come to each other because they like each other."

"I am out of practice. I haven't had very many friends."

He didn't have any, is what he meant, but she knew he was too proud to say it.

"Can you show me? Can I see you as a dragon?" she asked.

He hesitated, then said, "Outside, on the beach. I'm rather large."

Sevilen walked behind her, and no sooner had they taken a few steps out on the sand than the men attacked. They poured through a Door, each of them armed with drawn guns and knives in sheaths on their belts. She felt Sevilen rise up behind her in his dragon form, and the men looked up over her head without fear.

"Not the woman," shouted one of the men and they opened fire on Sevilen.

She hit the sand, scrambled away and then turned back. Sevilen was on all fours, a creature more magnificent and more frightening than she had imagined in her drawing.

He was black, but not an ordinary dull black or even a shining, lacquered black. More like hematite, metallic, and his scales shone blue here and there as he turned to attack the men. Their bullets had to have hit him, but she knew that dragon scales were notoriously impervious to damage.

He was as beautiful as he was terrifying. His neck was long and muscular, his head triangular and his silver eyes bright and sharp. His tail was long and mobile and his body was thinner than she would have guessed, more serpentine. When he opened his mouth, his teeth gleamed white and she felt a thrill go through her to be at the side of such a creature.

These attackers had to be men from the Seelie. The Seelie had been the ones who wanted the drake dead, and now they were here to accomplish what Astrid had refused to do.

But now, looking at each one in turn, she recognized one of them. It was he who had commanded the others not to kill the woman.

"Neil!" she yelled. "Stop it. He's my friend!"

Neil glanced at her, clearly confused, and then turned back to Sevilen. The drake inhaled deeply and Astrid scrambled farther back in anticipation of the certain inferno.

"Neil!" she screamed.

She watched as Sevilen paused and studied Neil, knowing what he was and that he and Astrid were friends. And then she understood. Neil didn't know her. They had never met.

Two of the men leapt onto Sevilen's back, long knives drawn. The drake bucked and turned his long neck to grab one and tear him free. The other stabbed him, and finding himself unsuccessful, used the knife to try to pry up a large scale. Sevilen ripped him off as well.

A moment later, Neil and the other men, who must be golems judging from their strength and tenacity, dropped down into the sand, vanishing, but Astrid got a look at the place they went. It was icy and empty. Sevilen had made a Door.

"Golems," said Sevilen. "I can tell that they're just matter with no soul inside."

"Why are golems trying to kill you?"

"Why are they being ordered to, you mean?"

An instant later, another Door appeared and the golems returned. Astrid was not going to sit idly by this time. If the golems were stronger together, then splitting them up would be her goal. She made a Door beneath the feet of the nearest golem and sent him to the Sahara desert. Another she sent to the Rocky Mountains. Sevilen sent the others to places she didn't see. She took special care with Neil, sending him to Los Angeles, to a park near the Time Corps safe house.

"They aren't the ones making the Doors," she said to Sevilen. "It's March. It has to be. He was the one who used to control Neil."

"Then he'll fetch them all and send them back to us again."

The golems reappeared, none the worse for wear. On their personal time lines, it might be a week later. March could take his time in collecting them and letting them rest, traveling through time and space as he pleased.

The old serving man was hurrying down the path from the house, a gun in his hand and a look of pure fury on his face.

"Don't!" cried Sevilen, but the man began firing on the golems. One of them turned and returned fire and the old man fell where he stood.

Sevilen roared in fury and anguish and he opened a Door to the void. All seven golems would have fallen through, but Astrid made another, smaller Door and wrapped it around Neil, sending him back to the Los Angeles park. Maybe, like Elliot and Sister, he might remember a few bits of things that had happened in their shared past if he saw a familiar place.

"Come," Sevilen said. "We'll go to the void. It'll be safer for us. But first I want to bury Ihsan."

Astrid didn't know if they had much time before the next golem attack, but she supposed if they had to, the two of them could simply step through their own Doors to safety. Even golems could not survive in the void, though she and Sevilen could remain there indefinitely.

As Sevilen turned, she noticed a wound on his leg where one of the golems had managed to cut the flesh beneath the scales. His blood was a pale, glowing blue. She knew where she had seen such a substance before.

"Your blood," she said. "Seamus uses it in the

time machines."

He turned toward her, fixing one gleaming eye on her. "Does he now?"

"He doesn't harvest it himself," she said. "He never even knew what it was. He got the original vials of it from his former partner, Oren McCullen. And McCullen got it from March."

"Then March either got it from a drake or from one of our children."

"Your children?"

"You call them void wyrms. They are our young. A stage between egg and full grown. As I told you, we are void creatures."

"But the void wyrms are—they're terrifying. And they try to eat people."

"It's natural for young to be hungry. All babies are."

"Why are they in the void at all? You live here."

"Because most of my kind were banished long ago. There was fighting. There was a war. We lost. A few of us, the more peaceful ones, were allowed to stay. I am among them. But the rest of our kind were sent to another world, a world that could not sustain us all. But as things that can live in the void, we survived. Our children seek out food, like a newborn piglet seeking its mother's teat. Only the teat is a tear between worlds."

"And Seamus made the tears worse. And then I used his machine to go to the Library to save Elliot. That destabilized things even more."

"It did. There are natural Doors like you and I. There are ones that appear for no reason. These are not dangerous. Only the ones made by man are."

He lifted Ihsan's lifeless body with his front claw and clutched him to his chest. He walked beside her on three legs to an area at the far end of the garden that she knew held a small graveyard.

"Ihsan has been with me for many years," said Sevilen.

He set the man to one side, and Astrid knelt to close his eyelids.

"It wasn't Neil who killed him," she said. "It was one of the others." It was important to her that he knew. He began to dig a hole, and Astrid sat back, letting him pile up the damp earth beside the long, narrow hole.

She kept alert for the golems to return, but they did not. Sending six of them to the void had been too simple. She couldn't believe that they were dead, and even if they were, Neil still lived.

"It hardly matters which one killed him," he said. "They act under March's orders. March wants me dead, but why? And why now?"

"Do you think he's working with the Seelie?"

"I doubt it. The Twelve are more concerned with humanity than the sidhe are. But almost everyone would rather that my kind vanish into memory. Do you have a coin to place under his tongue?" he asked.

She told him she didn't.

"No matter," he said. "Ihsan has earned his way to a good afterlife. He will not need a coin to travel. His good deeds will be currency enough."

He placed his friend gently in the grave and filled it with earth. And even though he was in dragon form, she could see the pain in his posture. He said a few words in a language she did not understand, presumably Turkish, and then he turned to her.

"Let me get my clothes and I will change back. Then we will go to the void."

He pushed off the ground and took to the air, covering the distance to the beach in moments. By the time she arrived at the beach, he was again human and clothed.

"I think I can move the entire island to the void," he said. "But it will take me a minute."

"You do not have so long," cried a woman behind them. She was tall and slender with hair so white it was almost transparent. Her skin was an ordinary human shade of medium brown and her eyes were the deep brown of a fawn's. She was accompanied by three identical men who looked like bodyguards.

"You do me an honor to pay me a call," said Sevilen. "I suppose you are only returning my surprise visit to your throne room. Queen Bai, I would like to present my friend Astrid, the Door."

Astrid supposed she ought to curtsy or bow to the Seelie queen, but by the time she thought of it, the queen had looked her up and down and stepped toward her.

"You have failed at your third task," she said.

She was imposing, frightening even, but Astrid was no longer the easily intimidated girl she had once been.

"I won't kill my friend."

"You shall. You will send him into the realm of the dead, and you will do so immediately."

"Is that so? Well, how about, no? Get me a different task. I'm not killing him."

"Your human copy is in this world. So is your cousin. And I believe they no longer have the time machines to allow them to escape us."

Ah, so the Seelie also knew what she and Sevilen knew, that the world had changed.

"Don't you dare," said Astrid. "If you touch one hair—"

"Astrid," Sevilen said, taking her hand and pulling her close. "It will be all right. You can find me."

"But why?" she whispered. "We can fight them."

"Perhaps, but what happens after that? Other Seelie would get to Sister and Elliot."

"We could find them first."

"And take them where? The void? The Seelie will hunt them until death. This way is best."

"Why would you do this? You don't care about Sister and Elliot. You don't love them."

"Not them, no."

He pulled her against his body and kissed her. At first, she was shocked, then concerned with kissing a man in front of the Seelie. But then everyone disappeared and there was only Sevilen, his skin unnaturally warm, smelling like wood smoke and cinnamon. She felt his heart beating very slowly within his chest.

"Find me," he said.

His kiss left a burning, sweet sensation on her mouth with a metallic tang, like blood.

"I can't."

Other Seelie were walking up the beach to join the queen and her entourage, presumably to witness the drake's death.

"My soul is still in my body," Sevilen whispered into her ear. "The worlds are tearing apart. You said the geists are coming from the afterlife to this world. You can open a Door. You can find me."

"It's time," said Queen Bai. "Don't try your tricks like you did with your cousin. If you send the drake to anywhere but death, I will kill your cousin and your human copy slowly."

Astrid obeyed, making a Door to death. Its mirrored surface quivered, then stilled.

"That's it?" asked Sevilen. She could tell he was afraid, and he had every right to be.

"Just step through." Her voice sounded far away, even to herself.

"You are not freed from your obligation," he said. "Dinner fortnightly. And a piece of art."

She watched him as he turned and stepped through. The door contracted and disappeared.

She stood for a moment, then turned to the Seelie.

"Get out."

The queen looked at her, chin high. Astrid took a step toward her.

"I said, get out! You are not welcome here. I have

fulfilled my three tasks, and now I am free of you. I banish you from this island from now until—until forever. This is my home now, and I order you from it."

The queen watched her, perhaps taking her measure, and Astrid met her eyes. All her fury and hatred burned within her and she was sorely tempted to send the whole mass of them straight into the void. Only her fear of what the Seelie would do to the loved ones of the queen's murderer stopped her. The queen turned to her entourage, said a few words, and they walked down the beach. Astrid saw a boat, the modern kind, anchored offshore and three smaller boats pulled up on the sand.

She waited until they had all taken the smaller boats and boarded the larger boat. It sailed away. Then she walked back into the house and paced up and down the halls, through the small rooms that served as galleries and then outside, through the gardens filled with wonders. They did not interest her today, but she needed to walk and think.

How did Sevilen have such confidence in her? It was just like when Elliot had been sentenced to death by the Seelie, and he had asked her to carry out his sentence. He had been so confident that she would figure out a way to save him. She had done so by making a Door to the Library and then later getting him out. He had always known she would get him out, but that was because everyone knew that he'd still be in the Time Corps when he was older.

Now, time had been reset. Everything was happening again, happening twice, but with variations. Neil was a golem again, enslaved to March. And again she was a small, ordinary person up against forces she could neither control nor fully understand.

The whole world was reliving a story, a twice told tale, but this time, there were no older versions of the Time Corps to give them comfort. And none of them could possibly know how the tale would end.

CHAPTER 27

"I T'S A BOY," SAID THE obstetrician, and Felicia leaned forward to view the wriggling blood-covered child, still connected to her by the snaking gray umbilical cord. He was deep pink, and after the nurse suctioned his mouth, he let out a high cry.

She delivered the afterbirth and the staff weighed and examined the baby. Then the nurse murmured something to the obstetrician that Felicia could not understand. He nodded in acknowledgment, and Felicia thought she caught a look of concern pass over his face. He went to examine the baby.

"What is it?" she asked.

"It's his feet," the doctor said, handing her the warm, squirming bundle. "I'll have a specialist come later to look at him. He can discuss options."

She opened the blankets to see that his tiny feet had an exaggerated big toe, almost like an ape. She touched his foot, and his tiny toes curled around her finger with a tight grip. The nurses did their work while she studied her child, and after a long time, they left the two of them alone.

"Like your daddy," she breathed against his little head. He was perfect, and she wouldn't let anyone do a thing to his feet. She held him, studying him, memorizing every detail of him for a long while.

"A Halloween baby," said Janeiro, stepping through one of his Doors. "I'm sure that's lucky somewhere."

"He's already proving lucky. There hasn't been an

earthquake or void wyrm here the entire time. We've run for so long that I'm surprised they aren't here already."

"I've been working overtime to ensure that they stay away. I'm sorry I couldn't be with you when he was born. But I had to stand guard."

"There wasn't time anyway."

Her labor and delivery had been fast, unusually fast for a first pregnancy. Just before labor had started, Janeiro had brought a plate of sugar cookies from his sister September, telling Felicia that they were a gift. She had gladly eaten a few, and afterward had such a feeling of peace and well-being that the beginnings of the labor pains hadn't frightened her at all.

"Was there something in those cookies from your sister?" she asked.

"Nothing harmful, I promise. No drugs. They were just sent to relax you. That speeds up delivery. I didn't want you in one place for too long. You'd both be sitting targets."

"It worked a little too well. There wasn't even time for an epidural. But you should have told me."

"I wasn't sure it would work myself. September's cooking can affect people under normal circumstances, but people dealing with birth and death ... those are a little different. It might not have done anything at all."

"Where are we, anyway? I didn't want to sound like a lunatic by asking the staff."

"Los Angeles. We're in the hub world, as you all used to call it. I made sure your calendar would align, so the child wouldn't be born before it was conceived. I figured that would add stability to his existence. But I couldn't take you to your home world. This place was easier to fortify to keep you safe. My brother helped me."

"March?"

"No, November. He spends a lot of time in this world, so I thought this place was a safer option."

"Have you spoken with your brothers and sisters? You

said yesterday they were close to finding a way to keep the baby safe."

"We've talked. But first, let me look at this little one."

She let him hold the baby, and Janeiro looked him over like a proud uncle, examining his little hands and studying his small, serious pink face.

"Name?"

"Luke Seamus."

Janeiro kissed the baby on the forehead, and Felicia got the distinct feeling that it was some sort of ritual, like a mark of protection.

"What was that?"

"Just a kiss."

But she knew he was lying. She wasn't used to that. Janeiro was a straightforward person, loyal and decent though occasionally too blunt. He'd leave facts out or refuse to answer, but he had never lied to her, not that she knew of.

"I want you to know that the Twelve are more like you humans than anything else," he said. "You think we know things, but we often don't. Some of us chose a side and some didn't, but none of us ever had the full picture. We still don't. We're just foot soldiers. Watchers and guards."

"But you said the Twelve would know how to keep the void wyrms from following us."

"I do."

The way he looked at Luke, with something like sadness, set off every maternal instinct she had.

"Give him back to me." She couldn't keep the strain from her voice.

"Oh, I won't drop him. He's fine." He stepped back, away from the bed.

"I want him now. Give him to me."

She swung her legs over the edge of the bed and grabbed onto her IV pole. The birth had been painful, of course, but now she was glad she hadn't had the epidural. She could move and walk, albeit painfully.

"Janeiro!" she said. "Please."

"The pawns on the board are just that. They don't run the game. And sometimes there's a sacrifice, and a piece is removed from the board."

"You can't hurt him!" she lurched forward, but Janeiro made a Door and appeared across the room.

"I won't. He'll be alive. He'll be safe. But he's hastening the destruction of the worlds."

"He's a baby!"

"I'm sorry. You're not the only mother who made a great sacrifice. I know how it is. 'Thine own soul a sword shall pierce.'"

"Please," she said, moving closer, pretending to feel more pain than she did. Maybe she could get close enough and snatch back the baby. "Please."

"Your sacrifice will save the worlds."

She leapt for him, but the moment her hands reached Luke, he and Janeiro were gone. There was only the empty hospital air, and then she hit the floor hard. The pain in her knees and hands was nothing. Her son was gone.

A cry tore its way from her throat. Gone. He was gone. That man took him, and she had no idea where. Any place. Any time. Any world. Never was a child so lost as her little Luke, and she was helpless to do anything about it.

But no. Not helpless. Not weak. She was something new now. And she understood something she had never understood before. She understood why you never got between a mother animal and her baby. Because the mother will kill you without hesitation. She would never hurt another person, not without very good reason, but for her child she wouldn't hesitate. She would do anything to save him.

She would get Luke back. If it took her until her dying moment, she would get him back. The Twelve, the Five, the One, the Thousand, she would fight them all. She would take on the devil himself, if such a being existed. She'd tear apart all the worlds if she had to.

This was the hub world in Los Angeles. Janeiro had separated her from everyone she knew. Her family would be in her home world, her husband in another, and her son somewhere else, but she was here and she didn't need to open up her dream journal to know what existed in the hub world.

Pulling open the overnight bag she had carried with her through the worlds these many months, she went through a plan in her mind. She wouldn't report Luke missing, as the police couldn't help and talking to them would only waste time. She'd walk out of here, doing her best not to look like a patient, and get him back herself.

She pulled on the comfortable tee shirt and loose pants she had brought for wearing after the birth, then put on socks and sneakers.

Janeiro had been her friend. Her trusted friend. He had saved her and protected her during her pregnancy. His betrayal hurt, and under other circumstances, she might have raged or wept at the pain of it. But now, there was no time for that. Pain and rage would come later, when she had the luxury of the time to feel them. But now, she had to keep a clear head and figure out what to do.

Money. She needed money for a cab. She had some bills in her wallet, but wasn't sure if currency was the same in this world. But gold, that was always worth something. She had gold earrings and could pawn them. She'd walk if she had to. She'd do whatever was necessary.

Before now, she had been a time traveler, a wife, a Civil War nurse, a twenty-first century medical student. She had traveled between worlds, escaped void wyrms and crashed a monstrous machine into the Mississippi River. But now she was Luke's mother.

She zipped up her coat. She might be bleeding and weak, in pain and exhausted, but it didn't matter. Her child needed her.

CHAPTER 28

HAZEL DUBOIS STOOD ON THE deck of the passenger steam ship, leaning as far over the prow railing as she could. This was the closest thing to heaven she could imagine, the wide green sea, dark and filled with living things, the wind, cold and bracing, the sky so high and empty, the feeling of flying over the water's surface.

As a woman traveling alone, she was already an oddity on the ship, so when a gentleman stood beside her and asked her where she was headed, she didn't hesitate to look him in the eye and answer honestly.

"I'm going to meet someone," she said. "And his family."

"Ah," he said, and she knew he thought she was speaking of a suitor or fiancé.

She knew she ought to ask about his destination and feign interest in how he was enjoying his voyage, but she wasn't working and thus had no obligation to entertain a strange man. She was in possession of a good amount of the Professor's money, no one knew who or what she was, and she was not in a position to need anything from anyone. It was a delightfully freeing feeling, almost as good as flying over the water.

After a few more questions, which Hazel answered in the shortest manner possible while still remaining polite, the man gave up. She felt bad for a moment, but she wasn't interested in making social connections. Besides, it wasn't as if she could tell him that her friend was a prisoner and that her first stop in Clonakilty would be at the police station. After that, she would find the Professor's family and figure out what they ought to do.

She had no family of her own, none that she could acknowledge, anyway. But her dreams, like the Professor's, held memories of people. In one particularly strange dream, she saw a man made of stone, lying very still. He was important, but she did not know why. She would never tell the Professor or anyone else, but she also had memories of a man, an ordinary-looking man, but with the sort of face one might fall in love with given time. He was quiet and hung along the edges of things. He had a bravery, a depth that surpassed mere valor and a courageous heart. He was, in short, a good man.

This man knew her secrets. That was the most terrifying thing about him. But it was also the most comforting. Because he knew the things her uncle had done to her in the dark, the things that would ruin her for a marriage to any respectable man. She was a soiled woman, but this man had not thought in those terms. He thought differently and used different language than she was used to, though he was no foreigner. And he saw the ruined places within her as places to pour kindness instead of as damaged parts. He had loved her.

It hurt to think of him. The idea of such a person was too much. People like that didn't exist, not in the real world. One got by on strength and cleverness, playing the hand of cards one was dealt as best as one could. Kind men who loved you didn't exist, not for her. Men wanted the comfort of a woman, her gentle touch, or perhaps a more passionate one. They wanted her heart as food, her kindness as a balm for their own hurts, her body as a soft place to enjoy, if only for a time. They did not concern themselves with the interior of a woman, her true thoughts and deepest heart. And they certainly didn't look unflinchingly upon the darkest and most shameful parts with kindness.

The air was cold now, and her thin shawl was not enough to keep her warm. She turned back, went to her cabin and changed into her nightclothes. She glanced at the trunks full of the Professor's equipment as well as her own smaller trunk. Only one more day at sea and she'd be in Ireland. She had only ever traveled to the towns on the outskirts of New Orleans before, and the strange wide world was both intriguing and frightening. But with money and a bit of boldness, she would make her way. She had too many questions not to, and the Professor was depending on her.

"All aboard were lost," said the man at the police station. "The ship sank. No survivors."

Hazel stared at him. "Are you sure?"

"Of course we're sure. They searched the area extensively. No survivors."

"I see," she said. "Thank you." She turned away, walking out into the street, into the cold, bright light.

The town of Clonakilty was tiny compared to New Orleans, and unlike her city, with its mix of races and languages, everyone here was white and spoke the same language, although with a different accent from her own. Even the air had a different quality.

When she had first stepped off the boat, she had enjoyed the novelty of it. She had come to the police station full of hope, and now the Professor was at the bottom of the sea. So was McCullen, though she was less concerned with him.

She checked into her hotel room where her bags were already waiting. Money could purchase so much, including comfort and ease, but it brought her no satisfaction. Closing the door, she cried. Her friend was gone, she did not know where the cloister was where McCullen had come through, and she had no way of learning why she and the Professor had the same dreams. The people in her dreams, the people who felt like family, were permanently out of reach.

All she had was the address of the Professor's family. In that moment, she made a decision. She would go to them, give them the Professor's solicitor's address, his patent numbers and bank information. She would tell them of his death, his second death, for they had mourned him twenty years ago. She ought to be the one to tell them the terrible news of his real death. If she caught the first train in the morning, she might get to their farm by evening.

She would go to them, and she would tell them about the inventor, the mad Irishman, the clockwork creator, the scholar and the good man he had been. And though they weren't family, they would mourn together.

CHAPTER 29

"THERE ARE REALLY ONLY THREE rules to being a psychopomp," Jeff said to Astrid and held up a finger. "One, get the sticky souls through the Doors. Two, no one but the dead can use our Doors. No free travel for anyone. And three, don't use our ability to pull threads in people's minds on living people, only on the dead."

She stirred a sugar packet into her coffee and glanced at Gopan. He was still eight years old, at least in appearance, but his eyes looked so much older. The back room of Jeff's bookshop seemed emptier now without Graciela and Robin, and all three of them felt their absence. Neither Gopan nor Jeff had heard from either of them, and they were hesitant to just make a Door and pop in at their houses uninvited.

"Well, I've broken all three already," said Astrid. "Besides, I wasn't asking permission. I was informing you."

"I get that," said Jeff. "But understand that you won't come back. This is death, Astrid. We're its servants, not its masters."

"Something is wrong with the world. Something is happening, and we're uniquely suited to finding out what. It's my fault to begin with. I made a Door to the Library to get my cousin out, and you said at the time that using the Professor's machine to amplify my own abilities could lead to bad things happening. So long had passed that I thought we were safe. But the more holes the Time Corps ripped, the worse things got. I think this is the result."

Jeff's mouth tightened at the edges, a sure sign he was furious.

"I know you don't remember the world as it was before," said Astrid. "But I do, and our world was a hub world and it wasn't always sealed off from the others worlds like it is now."

Gopan and Jeff exchanged a look. "You're talking about being a living person and going into death. And all to retrieve the soul of some drake."

"His body too. He went through with both."

"It'll kill you," said Gopan. "No one comes back."

"Not necessarily," she said. "You've seen the increase in sticky geists just like I have. And you know as well as I do that they might be coming through from death to here. Maybe I could do the same."

"It's unnatural," said Jeff. "Emulating something unnatural isn't right."

"I just think the answer is where the geists are. If I can see why the geists are coming through, we might understand why the world changed."

"Do you know how you sound?" said Jeff.

"Yeah, I suppose I do. But at this point, I don't care. I know what I know. I'm not crazy. You know the drakes exist, the Seelie exist, the Twelve exist. Graciela and Robin are gone with little explanation. You've seen the recent geists." She shoved back her chair. "But if you won't help me, then I'll do it on my own."

"Wait," said Gopan. "What do you want us to do?"

She was glad he had offered. She knew she could count on Gopan. "First, give this package to my cousin." She set a box full of her drawings on the table and tossed her phone in with them. "And then I want Jeff to talk to this November person. He's a psychopomp and one of the Twelve. He's a Door. He knows things we don't."

"He won't talk to me. He won't answer my calls," said Jeff. "Now that he's working with Robin and Graciela, he doesn't seem to need us anymore."

Astrid saw the slump of his posture, the weariness that all of them shared. Jeff, out of all the psychopomps, saw his function as a part of the natural world, as a piece of a necessary whole. If November said he was no longer needed, then he had cut a vital piece out of the man. Without a wife or children, the bookshop and his job as psychopomp had been the center of his life.

"Without November helping us, there's nothing for us to do," said Gopan.

"We keep clearing souls," said Jeff. "We don't just leave them. We keep on."

"You two will have to do it without me," said Astrid. "I'm sorry."

"You have a duty to them. You know that," said Jeff.

"I have a duty to the whole world too. The ideas aren't unconnected."

"I can't stop you, can I?"

She put her hand on his shoulder. He might have only known her for a few weeks, but to her, Jeff was an old friend.

"I'll come back if I can," she said. "And if I can't, make sure Elliot and Sister are looked after. Elliot has parents, and I suppose they might help. And in this world, Sister has my name and identity."

How alone they were, she thought. Without the Time Corps, Elliot was just a man teetering on the edge of sanity, and Sister was a shadow girl with no purpose. She owed it to both of them to set things right. Their lives, in a sense, depended upon it.

"I want to go now, while the boundary is soft," she said.

"It won't matter," said Jeff. "Your Doors always work. Hallow's Eve doesn't matter."

"I think the geists are going to be coming through more often as the boundary gets softer. I'll see what I can do from the other side."

She made a Door, watching the mirrored surface become still, like liquid mercury, and reflect her own image back to her. She was plain, if she was honest with herself, and had never been able to quite get her short fair hair to obey her. Her figure was unremarkable, though she had gotten a little curvier as she aged. Still, she had trouble imagining why Sevilen liked her. Loved her. Or had he only said that to manipulate her into retrieving him from death?

No, if there was one thing she knew about him, it was his devotion to the things to which he was attached. And he was without question attached to her. At first, it was only because she was an Unseelie-born Door, a very rare thing. But with time, it had grown into more. She knew that her feelings for him exceeded friendship. She wanted more from him, his heart.

Maybe Elliot was right. Maybe her feelings for Sevilen were just like Stockholm syndrome. Like Beauty and the Beast, though she was certainly no beauty. But sometimes, the captor fell in love with the captive. And didn't maidens ever fall in love with their dragons? Perhaps she and Sevilen were two broken creatures, two things that didn't fit into the world, clinging together through a storm.

Well, storm or no, she had a job to do.

"Luck!" said Gopan just before Astrid stepped through.

For an instant, she saw nothing, and then her vision returned, and the world became blue, then indigo, then colors came into focus and finally shapes. The sky overhead was mostly overcast, but there were gaps in the dark clouds through which she saw the sky. It was a deep, rich purple, mottled blue and black, like a bruise. The land, stretching out around her on all sides, was gray, from the distant mountains to the wide, hilly expanse of land stretching out before her, all rocks and plants and even the earth was drab and ashen.

She turned slowly. She was alone. No birds sang, no insects buzzed, only a gentle wind blew from somewhere in the distance. The air had a heavy scent to it, like ocean air, and she wondered if the breeze was coming from the sea. Why death would have a sea, she could not guess. But if it could have mountains and hills, then perhaps the landscape would contain other familiar things.

She needed to get the lay of the land and couldn't do so from the ground. She changed into her owl aspect, then flew upwards, circling, studying the land near and far with eyes that were so much sharper than they were when she was a human.

The hilly land stretched on for miles in all directions, and she couldn't spot any sea. The only thing breaking up the monotony were the mountains. She studied them, and noted a thin, winding path up one of them. It would take her at least a day if she went on foot, but by air, she could fly there in a few hours, stopping to rest if need be.

It meant leaving her clothing behind, which meant she'd be nude if she changed back into human form. But her jeans, shirt, underclothes and shoes were simply too heavy to carry and make good time. She left her little pile of clothing behind and headed toward the mountains.

After a long while, she caught lightning from the corner of her eye. It flickered behind the clouds now and then, but she didn't fear being hit. She wasn't touching the ground, and thus electricity would not seek her like a lightning rod.

The clouds grew thicker, and the lightning more frequent behind them. None of it struck downward, but illuminated the sky, sometimes blinding her for a moment. A few clouds drifted apart and she caught sight of what was beyond them. Far off, high in the mottled bruise-colored sky, there were people. She knew what they were on sight. Geists.

The sky was cracked in various places. Jagged rips tore the sky and geists gathered, like leeches on a wound. They passed through one another, grasping and clinging, pressing themselves against the cracks, trying to squeeze through. Lightning flashed from the cracks and illuminated the geists, young and old, male and female. Some were unidentifiable, some undulating and shapeless.

So the dead truly were returning through rips from the afterlife. She and the Professor, between the two of them, had damaged the walls between the worlds beyond repair, and now the dead and the living were paying the price.

She flew higher, catching a wind current that propelled her onward with less effort, and from this height, she got a different perspective on the little mountain trail.

At the top stood a closed iron gate, the sort with two sides held together by a heavy latch and an enormous padlock. She could easily fly over it, but so could the geists. In fact, judging by the ones trying to escape, they could fly higher into the sky than she could manage as an owl. The gate had to mean something. It was a boundary, a doorway.

And if she was good at one thing, it was opening doors.

CHAPTER 30

"WAIT HERE," SAID FELICIA TO the cab driver. "I'll be five minutes."

The driver must have wondered about the woman who wanted to drive from the hospital directly to the adult novelty store, but Felicia didn't care. She selected a pair of handcuffs, the sturdiest metal ones they had, even though they were lined with bright green fuzzy material. They would do.

The man at the counter accepted her money, which was a relief. It must be close enough to the currency in this world to suffice. She got back in the cab and gave the driver instructions as they drove, holding her dream journal open in her lap. She knew most of the streets from her dreams, but was unsure on others. They went through two neighborhoods before turning down one last street. She knew the house on sight.

"Pull over here," she said and paid the driver.

She slipped the key to the handcuffs under a rock near the pepper tree out front, then headed for the door. Without bothering to knock, she shoved open the front door. The house was quiet and the living room empty. She found Julius and Santiago, the Coyote, in the kitchen, and while Julius looked like he was seeing a ghost, Santiago merely looked her over, sizing her up.

"Where is Janeiro?" she said. "Call him now."

"I'm sorry, I—" said Julius.

"Stop. I know who he is and I know who you are. Call

him now."

Santiago got a look of amusement, no doubt entertained by the madwoman confronting Julius in his own kitchen.

"How are you even in this world?" Julius asked.

"Because of Janeiro. He was keeping me and my baby safe from the void wyrms, but he took my son. And he's going to give him back."

"Took your son?" asked Santiago. He turned to Julius. "Can you guys do that?"

"Only if absolutely necessary," said the older man.

"That's terrible." Santiago studied Felicia again. "You just gave birth to him, right?"

"Yeah. A few hours ago."

His eyes narrowed in a canine smile. "And here you are, ready to tear out Julius's throat."

"Only if absolutely necessary," she said, smiling without a shred of humor.

Santiago laughed. "A tenacious woman. A fine bitch."

A fierce female might be one of the few things Santiago respected, but she had no time for him.

"Your brother," she said to Julius. "He said you all had discussed this. All the good ones of the Twelve. Or formerly good ones."

"A necessary evil," said Julius.

"Aren't they all?"

She moved toward him slowly, reaching her hand into her bag to grip the handcuffs. Santiago pulled out his phone.

"I'm getting my son back," she said. "Your brother is going to bring him back."

"Impossible."

"No. It's not. He can make Doors anywhere. Don't pretend that he can't. I know all about you."

"He's coming," said Santiago. "So please don't kill Julius. He's one of the few friends I have."

She took her hand from her bag. If they thought she

had a gun, she wouldn't correct them. Julius didn't seem frightened, but as far as she understood, death was not permanent for their kind. It could, however, slow them down.

Santiago, hearing something, raised his head a moment before the front doorbell rang.

CHAPTER 31

SEAMUS COUNTED HIMSELF LUCKY. Not every man could sell a stolen gun and then triple the money at the card tables within an evening. After more than a day at sea, he had rowed ashore near Rosscarbery, southwest of Clonakilty. It was a small town, one where a stranger stood out, but once he had the money from the ship's guard's old revolver and had paid for a meal, it was only a matter of finding a few willing card players. A man with money to spend was welcome in any town, small or large.

He played until late, paid for a room, and in the morning he purchased a used traveling case, a pipe and tobacco, a hat and a set of clothing fit for an ordinary workman. He considered visiting the barber for a shave before deciding against it. A beard served as a disguise. He imagined Oren beside him, telling him to keep his head, to stay unobtrusive. He knew he was an excellent liar, but even so, he could not afford to get clumsy and lose this opportunity for a new life. Oren had paid such a steep price for his freedom.

And indeed, he was free. With a new name, he could go nearly anywhere. He couldn't return to New Orleans or stay in Ireland. Even London would be a foolish choice. But he could go to New York or Boston or any other city far away and make a life for himself. As he was legally dead, he could do anything so long as he remained unrecognized.

Early the next morning, he took the train to Cork, then on to Belfast. Far away, his family was waiting, and he would go to see them. It had been twenty years, and he hadn't even written them a letter. That was by necessity. He could never let them know where he was, lest he risk exposure. This time, it would be different. He was older, perhaps a tad wiser, and he knew the value of people who loved him.

He studied the land as he rode past on the train from Belfast to Ballygawley. It was as it had always been, green and overcast, with a feel so different from other places. Ah, but he had missed this. The great famine was over now, and though certain places reminded him of those dark times so filled with death and suffering, there were other memories as well. He got off in Ballygawley and hired a horse-drawn cab to take him to the edge of town, then paid a cart driver to ride along on the road south to Aughnacloy. The cart driver was glad for the company and relentlessly tried to engage him in conversation. He gave a false name, of course, but just to be on the safe side, he got off the cart two miles from home. There was no sense in giving the police or locals any cause to recognize him.

The wind was cool and rich with the scent of earth and autumn hay. His brothers and father would be bringing in part of the harvest, while his mother and sisters canned and dried a portion of it.

A pair of boys raced across the road, hopped a low rock wall and tore off across a field. So like he and his brothers, they were. And there was the farm of Abigail O'Riordan, the first girl he had ever kissed, and there was the road that led to his friend Peter's house. The two of them had been whipped in school so often for daydreaming or talking that they had decided to run away together and become pirates, robbing the English. Seamus remembered the hundreds of tiny drawings of machines he had made on his slate instead of writing out his sums. For a poor farmer's son with a fifth-grade education, he had not done so poorly for himself. Well, if he didn't count the murder charge and being a hunted man. On the whole, he had avoided death and had made a good life for himself, using what wits he had to do it.

None of it would have happened without Oren. He thought of his friend, of his family in a world so far away. Oren would never reunite with his grieving mother or see his home again. His family would never even know of his death, only know that he had vanished without explanation.

He rounded a low hill, and there stood his house. It looked so much smaller now, from its gray stone walls to its slate roof. The low fence around a small vegetable garden was new and freshly whitewashed. He noted the pots of flowers out front, lovingly tended. He started up the path.

A man was smoking beside the house. He was tall, lean and dark-haired, like Seamus, but younger. Seamus knew him on sight and had to keep himself from rushing forward and crushing his youngest brother in an embrace.

"Good afternoon," the man said, and Seamus read the wariness and suspicion in his tone. Since when did a man coming up the walk elicit such a cold greeting? Sure, he was no fine gentleman, but he was decently dressed in a proper hat, wool trousers and a decent coat.

"Bill, it's me."

He pulled off his hat so his brother could see and watched the blood drain from the man's face. Bill looked him up and down, and unable to deny the evidence of his eyes, swore a colorful oath.

"Now, don't you let Mother hear you, or you'll have a taste of her lye soap."

"They said you were dead."

"And as you can see, they were mistaken. But we ought to go inside. No sense letting the neighbors see."

"The neighbors can't see this far."

Of course they couldn't. He was so used to city life and the constant scrutiny of the ever-present people that saw and remembered all. How refreshing to be far from all of them, back in the country air where a man could have some space to think and live free.

Bill hesitated, then gestured for Seamus to follow him inside.

"Ma!" Bill shouted. "You have to come now. There's another visitor."

"I'm up to my elbows in the dough," cried a woman, and Seamus was startled at the intensity of pain and joy that rose within him at her voice, the voice that had sang to him at night and scolded him and called his name across the fields.

His mother rounded the corner, covered in flour, wiping her hands on a dish rag. She seemed shorter now, and she had certainly grown stouter. Her hair, which had once been as black as his own, was now streaked with gray, and the years showed on her face. She didn't say a word, but her hand flew to her mouth and she shook her head, as if denying what she saw.

"It's me, Ma. I didn't die."

Her look grew sharp then. "I can see that. I'm no fool." Then her face softened, and she burst into tears. She embraced him for a long time, then pulled back to look up at him and take his face between her palms. She kissed him and again crushed him hard against her. "My boy," she whispered. "My boy."

Bill gathered the rest of the family. Only his father, mother, his sister Oonagh and Bill still lived on the farm. All the others had grown and moved out on their own.

His father embraced him and turned aside, his eyes wet. Seamus turned back to kiss his sister while his father collected himself. Seamus listened as his mother chronicled what had happened to each of his siblings, who had married, who had left for the city to find work. None had died since he left, thank God, though his brother's wife had given birth to a stillborn child three years ago. And of course, his sister Branna and her unborn child had died before he had run. Her husband had beaten her, causing her to lose the child, and she had died of her injuries and blood loss soon after. Seamus had been eighteen when he murdered Branna's husband.

"Bill, go to Darragh," said his mother. "Tell him to send word to everyone."

"No, no. I can't be found," said Seamus. "They'll hang me for certain."

He thought his mother might object, but she was a woman of sharp faculties. She hesitated, then nodded once and told Bill to fetch only Darragh, Cathleen and Thomas, the siblings who lived nearby.

His mother grasped Seamus's face and kissed him again. "My angel." She shook her head in disbelief and pulled off her apron, flinging it onto the kitchen table. Oonagh, who had been just a toddler when he had been taken to prison, put it on and set to preparing the evening meal. She was slender and graceful, with the dark hair and clear blue eyes that most of his siblings shared. He wondered if she had any young men who came around to see her, and he decided to ask later to make certain they weren't the scoundrels he knew all young men to be.

"Ah! I forgot!" said his mother. "Bill, when you get to Darragh's, tell him to send Thomas to go up the road to fetch Miss Dubois. She'll be as surprised as we are, I dare say."

"Hazel is here?"

"Of course she is. She came yesterday. Told us you were drowned at sea on that terrible ship. Traveled here from America all on her own, she said. She went out walking an hour ago. Fierce independent, that one. Said she wanted to walk because she loves the wind and wanted to see the world. I told her there was more to the world than our little slice of it, but she said it was good enough for her."

Seamus took a chair in the front room, the finest one

by the look of its shabby brethren, and his sister made a pot of tea while his mother made up a plate of cold beef and bread with mustard, gave it to him and insisted he eat. She took the seat opposite him.

"You're too thin. Did they starve you on the ship?"

"I've always been like this, Ma."

"That you have. Now, I ought to slit your throat with my sharpest kitchen knife for not telling us where you were these twenty years. Twenty years, Seamus."

"I had to stay hidden."

"Just a letter to say you were alive."

"I'm sorry, Ma. Never again, I promise."

"Well, you'll not be leaving our sight. You're staying here."

"I can't. I'll be recognized for sure."

"I don't know about that," said his father. "You're older now. Grow out your beard, start talking like a sensible person instead of rattling on about machines like you used to, and we'll say you're a cousin from down south."

"Someone will know. It only takes one person to recognize me, and then I'm back in irons. I killed a man, and someone will be sure I pay for it."

"That was twenty years ago," said Bill.

"And I escaped not once, but twice. That's a hanging offense."

His mother slapped her thighs and stood up. "We'll think of something. For now, we're just glad you're alive."

Ten minutes later, Hazel opened the door. Her cheeks were bright pink and she was out of breath.

"It's true!" she cried, but stopped herself before embracing him. They were not family, only friends, and it would have been improper. Instead she beamed at him. "I should have known you'd live!"

One by one, his siblings arrived and the house filled with voices and laughing and tears. His sisters did not cease to grasp his hands and kiss his cheeks while his brothers pounded him on the back and put their arms around his shoulders. Amid the din of conversation, it seemed he was never without someone touching him, as if they thought he might evaporate into smoke if they ever let him go.

Nieces and nephews appeared later, after the adults decided upon the name James Doyle and the story that he was a cousin from Cork.

They ate and talked until it was late and the little ones had to go home to bed. Extracting promises from him that he'd stay at least a week, his visiting family left and the house grew quieter. He went outside to smoke, leaning up against the house. A few minutes later, Hazel joined him.

"They won't let me help clean up," she said.

"Of course not. You're company."

"They're good people. You have a kind family."

He heard the tiny hint of pain in her voice. As far as he knew, she had no family. How else did a girl end up living on the streets by age eleven?

"Oren died," he said. "Shot by the English."

"I figured it was something of that sort, but I didn't want to ask in front of everyone."

"He died saving me."

"Which wouldn't have been necessary if September Wilde hadn't turned you over to the police."

"We're not sure it was her."

"Who else could it be? Brother Joe? Mrs. Washington? I've known you for years, and I never knew you were anything other than what you claimed to be. It was her. And if she was afraid of the machines, then I want to know why. I brought some of your equipment from home."

"Truly? Where? Upstairs?"

"Bill put it up in the attic. I wasn't sure what all to bring, but Mrs. Washington and I made our best guess. But now that McCullen is gone, you'll never be able to find that place he came through."

"He told me where it was, more or less. It's in Fintona. Only a few hours ride from here."

"You grew up close to it then."

"It appears so. But I've been thinking. I can't get on a ship to America any time soon. My name and description are still fresh in the minds of the law. If you have my equipment, I think I'll go to the cloister and see what I can learn."

"I'll go with you," she said.

"Now why would you want to be doing that?"

"I have the dreams too, Professor. I want to know what they mean. And it isn't as if I have a life of ease waiting for me back in New Orleans."

An awkward silence passed. Seamus knew they were both thinking the same thing.

"I had your money," she said. "I only took what I needed for a decent voyage. I gave the rest to your parents along with all the information on your patents and such. They didn't care about it. They simply sat there like stone statues, like the life had been pulled right out of them."

"It hasn't been easy for them."

"I suppose not. Still, it must have been good all these years knowing someone loved you."

"Yes, I suppose it was."

They stood for a few minutes before Hazel yawned. "I'm going up to bed."

She was sharing a bed with Oonagh, while Seamus would bunk with Bill. After the dishes were washed, dried and put away, they sat up talking and one by one, went to bed until only Seamus and his mother remained.

"I'm afraid if I go to sleep, I'll wake and this will just be a dream," she said.

"I'm as real as you are. And I'll be here in the morning."

She sighed and took his hand across the table, pressing her lips together and nodding. The floor creaked upstairs.

"Now tell me about Miss Dubois," she said. "She says

she's a friend of yours, but what friend would come all this way across the sea? There's more to it, I'm sure."

"We're friends. Good friends, I suppose."

She sat awhile, waiting for him to go on. When he didn't, she said, "All right, if you want it like that. But if it matters to you, I like her. I sat up talking with her last night, like you and I are talking now. She's a brave girl to come all this way. She's got a bit of wits to her as well. A good mind. If a man wins a lass like that, especially a man like you with your quick brain, always running like a motor, I'd say he could do worse."

Hazel was hardly wifely material, but if his family ever knew why, they would be scandalized. He would never commit so wicked a betrayal as to tell them. Whatever Hazel was, she was his friend. And with Oren gone, she was the only one outside his family who knew who he truly was.

CHAPTER 32

NEIL FROZE AS HE SAW a familiar shimmering at the edge of March's property. But no sooner had it appeared than it was gone. This was the desert, and the air rippling in the heat was not unusual, but Neil knew what he had seen. It was a void wyrm, trying to come through and failing. March's protective fail-safes around the house were working. He took down the box of paper coffee filters and set a pot of coffee to brew.

Void wyrm activity had increased tenfold. Unlike ordinary people, the golems could travel back and meet themselves, forming teams of ten or twenty copies. But even with all seven golems killing void wyrms, they hardly had time to eat or rest. He had only gotten a few hours of sleep. and he knew March would have a new assignment for him any moment now.

The drake on the island in the Mediterranean had escaped them, but he was now gone from the world, according to March. There were others, some in Dubai, a few in New York and some in Singapore. Some of the drakes were more reclusive, preferring isolated Russian mountains or South American jungles, but March would locate them. He had to. The drakes were creatures who could tear holes between worlds. They, and especially their young, the void wyrms, were brutal and hungry things, dangers to humanity and the stability of the worlds.

March came in, still in his pajamas and robe. Neil told him about the void wyrm.

"Not surprising," said March. "Things are getting worse. I had hoped to do better, to save more people. Instead, the void wyrms are still eating people."

"Because they're hungry. Perhaps if we find a way to feed them, they won't come here."

"I've thought of that, but there's nothing we can feed them. I could shove truckfuls of material through a hole into the void, but it would do no good. The drakes will keep breeding, like vermin, and become stronger in number. The only answer is eradication. After breakfast I want to show you something."

The other golems were somewhere near Johannesburg, seeking an old drake who March said had opened a new rip near the city. March finished a cup of black coffee, then took Neil in his car and drove out into the desert.

"I need your advice on something," said March. "I love your brothers, but your mind works in a different way than theirs."

Neil said nothing. March turned from the main highway onto a dirt road, then onto a narrower one and finally onto a path consisting of two worn tire tracks, almost invisible, stretching through the weeds. At last they reached a shed, the old concrete kind that looked like a bomb shelter or an abandoned utility building. March parked and instead of unlocking the padlocked door, took Neil's arm. An instant later, they were in a dark, windowless hallway. Fluorescent lights flickered overhead. It was quiet and still, and Neil knew that they were underground.

"Why not take me here directly from our kitchen?" asked Neil. "Why drive?"

"I want you to be able to find it. In case anything happens to me. Now come."

He led Neil to the end of the hallway, through a door and down a set of metal stairs. They came out into a large room, as large as a warehouse, that was empty but for two enormous cells. One was empty. The other held a drake.

The creature was beautiful, in a way that Neil knew would horrify most of humanity. It was sleek and serpentine, with bronze scales and a long, narrow head and large dark eyes. It had no legs, only great wings, feathered in fiery orange and shining gold and folded back along the length of its body. Matching feathers grew from the back of its skull, forming a sort of spiked headdress. It was curled up, as if to keep warm, at the corner of the cell, but from the moment they entered, it watched them.

"She has been here for weeks," said March. "And she refuses to help us."

"What do you want her to do?"

"To tell me where the other drakes are, the ones that are hidden. And to tell me how to close off the void once and for all."

"Did my brothers catch her?"

"Yes, but I told them not to hurt her. She's old, and I wish to know what she knows."

"And when I refuse to tell you," the drake said, "you punish me with continued captivity. It is torture."

"If you will not help me willingly, I will seek to understand how you think. How all of your kind think. I am studying you. Hunting you one by one is one solution. But understanding your kind deeply will allow me to anticipate their actions. I seek to understand."

"You and your damned brethren are incapable of true understanding. If you think that by keeping me here, you will reveal my true self, you are mistaken."

"Is that so?" said March, approaching the bars of the cage. The drake reared up but kept her lower body coiled. It was not a hostile movement, one of preparation to strike, but was done to put her face on the same level as March's. "You remain silent for so long, and now that I bring my friend with me, you decide to speak. You can say whatever you like in front of him. I simply want to understand what you are, to know your heart as I understand the hearts of men."

"To know your enemy," she said. "I understand. I know men like you. Beings like you. You think that by harming, by keeping a thing like me in a cage, that you will know us. Do you think I will become more myself somehow? A mask will fall away and the true thing I am will be revealed?"

Her tone changed, and Neil knew she was not solely speaking to March.

"All wild things react the same way to a cage," she said. "They try to escape, and they suffer. All things react the same way to torture. They cry out, they recoil in pain, they try to escape. All free things need to be in the cool air or deep in the sea or running over the open land. When tortured by captivity, we do not reveal anything unique. We reveal one thing. We reveal our commonality with all other living things. Our pain at being caged. Isn't that right, golem?"

She turned her head to fix him with her deep, black eyes.

"You understand a cage," she said. "You were made to be a slave."

"I am not a slave," he said, but knew the moment it was out of his mouth that it was untrue. March could compel him to do whatever he pleased. Neil obeyed, but only because disobedience was not an option.

"As you say, golem. But think upon this. Your master, like all torturers, seeks a level of understanding, an unveiling, but he forces the creature to expose its most base needs, not its higher ones. Not its unique ones. When any creature is tortured, its pain and suffering reveal the same things. That is true of you and me. That also is true of the torturer, though he is rarely so self-aware as to understand this. Your master is one such being. He thinks he can unlock understanding. He thinks he will meet the true drake. But that is like raping a woman and thinking you meet the true woman. You are merely harming. That is easy and simple. How much harder to truly know something."

"And will you tell me what you are?" said Neil. "If I wanted to know you?"

She regarded him. "You do not tear apart the rosebud to get it to bloom."

"We do not want our world to be destroyed. March might free you if you helped. The holes in the worlds are causing harm."

"That depends upon your definition of harm," she said. "And you parrot your master's words. You are wondering something. Something deeper."

He was. He wondered about her and her kind, about what they could do and what they were. About all the worlds and why they could not exist peacefully, side by side. He wanted to know more about the drake, her life and experiences. But how much of that was his natural curiosity, his affinity for beauty, the inquisitive nature that March himself had built into him? How much was his own? How much of him was like this drake? A thing unable to be what it was meant to be because it was caged?

"Why don't you make a Door out?" he asked the drake.

"The cage walls are special," said March. "They prevent it. If you were to walk to one and push through it, like she can, she would find herself right back where she started. I created the cage myself. It took a great deal of effort. Aside from that, she receives a chemical mixture in her water that inhibits her ability to make Doors. Otherwise she could make a Door in the floor or around herself."

"Has she tried not to drink?"

"Of course. But the need to survive is too strong."

"If I ever get free, I will kill you," she said to March. Neil studied her, surprised at her tone. She said it softly, without malice or passion, simply stating a fact. Something about it touched him. He did not relish harming living things, though it was so often a necessity, and he did not like a cage.

An earthquake shook the room, causing the overhead lights to sway crazily.

"Those are the birth pains," she said. "A new thing is being born."

"What is it?" asked Neil.

"A new world."

CHAPTER 33

"**A**STRID LEFT THESE FOR YOU," said the small Indian boy who had stepped through a Door onto the deck of Skidbladnir. He handed Elliot a closed box.

"What do you mean, 'left them'? Where is she now?" asked Elliot.

The boy sighed. Sister had ordered the ship to drop anchor near Santa Maria Island, one of the Channel Islands off the coast of Southern California. After Sister had taken on their next shipment from a pair of elderly twin men who did not trust ordinary shipping methods with their fine perfumes, the monkey crew had been allowed a day of shore leave.

"She's alive," said the boy, "but she went to the afterlife this morning. To death. She was trying to save that drake she visits. The Seelie forced her to send him to the afterlife, and she went after him. I'm sorry."

"You guys are going to go get her, right?"

"We can't. It's death."

"But Astrid must have thought she could come back."

"That was her intention. Bring back the drake, find out why the dead are coming through into our world more often and figure out why she thought she had been a psychopomp all this time when we just met her."

"She remembered things differently."

"Right. Look, I need to go."

The boy looked miserable, but Elliot knew from Astrid

that this boy was a grown man. What Elliot was viewing was only his psychopomp aspect.

"Wait, I—"

"I have a job. Someone died just now. There are only two of us doing the job of five, and we're busy."

And with that, he made a Door and was gone. Elliot turned to find Sister right behind him.

"Did you hear?" he asked.

She nodded and took the box, pulling it open. Inside was a stack of drawings, and on top of it all, Astrid's phone.

"We should look at these below deck," said Elliot. "The wind is too strong up here."

They went to their shared quarters and pulled the drawings out one by one, setting them on the desk. There were separate drawings of a Latina woman with a determined expression, a tall, thin white man with wild black hair, a young Asian woman, a raven and a white cat.

"That one," he said, as Sister pulled out a picture of an ordinary-looking man in a long black duster. "I've seen him."

"He was a fighter," she signed. "Astrid told me about each of these people, their names and everything."

She took out the next drawing, this one of a group of people. On the left was a heavyset bespectacled white man with a close-trimmed white beard. He stood beside a black woman, an older Asian woman, another white man with orange and gray hair and slanted green eyes and a gray-haired woman of indeterminate race.

"A few of the Twelve," signed Sister. "Julius, September Wilde, June Yee, Augustus and Red Fawn."

Last, she drew out a picture of a freckled woman with a long brown braid.

"That's Hazel," signed Sister.

"Get Mr. Escobar," said Elliot, forgetting that he was no longer captain. Still, Sister hurried up the stairs and came back with the first mate.

"Do you remember this woman?" Elliot asked, showing him the picture of Hazel.

"I do not."

"Nothing? No dreams about her or anything?"

Escobar said he did not. Sister turned on Astrid's phone and thumbed through the display. "Astrid left us a recording."

They played it. The video was shaky, but her voice was clear. She told them that she would come back, that the cracks where the dead were coming through were real and that she was trying to find out what caused them so she could fix them.

"I hope to find out why the world changed," she said. "The drawings are to help you remember. I love you both."

Then she was gone. Astrid, who had never had the dreams that Sister and he had, was once again lost in another world, one where he could not help her. Sister set down the phone, and Mr. Escobar studied the other drawings.

"You think Astrid was crazy," said Elliot to the monkey.

He looked up. "Yes."

"And me."

"Yes. But Sister is not."

Thunder rumbled, and Sister stiffened in alarm.

"I wish it would rain," said Mr. Escobar as they returned to the deck of the ship. "It just keeps on like this with the clouds and the humidity with no rain. It feels like it's waiting."

Lightning flashed, and Elliot saw the sky split open about a half a mile away. The rip started small, with flashing light behind it, then grew longer, like a zipper opening. Long, thin shapes, like wisps of smoke, came through the hole, some of them forming into something resembling human forms. He grabbed Sister and shoved her behind him as the shapes swooped low, then tore off toward land.

"What do you see?" she asked.

"Spirits. Souls."

The tear was dark with souls crowding through, and then he saw another tear, far in the distance and high up in the sky. He couldn't make out any geists, but something dark was pouring from it, splitting into long, thin streaks as it separated.

"They're everywhere," he said. "They're coming through. Astrid failed."

"It is nothing, Elliot," said Mr. Escobar. "You are having another of your episodes. There are no spirits."

More rips tore open the sky, now behind them, now to starboard. More shapes poured out, and now he heard them, the low howl, like the wind. Thunder crashed, immediately followed by lightning. But still no rain fell.

"They're coming," said Elliot. "The souls of the dead. Coming through the cracks."

"Do you think it is a vision?" Sister signed to Mr. Escobar. "Astrid said that he could feel it when time slipped."

"I think he is a madman. Try to get him to lie down."

Sister took his arm and guided him down to the captain's quarters.

"Lie down awhile," she said.

"You can't hear them, can you?"

"I only hear the thunder and the wind."

"There are just so many. So many souls."

CHAPTER 34

ASTRID FLEW CLOSER TO THE gate at the top of the mountain path, examined it and landed on one of the curling metal flourishes on top. She knew there was more to it than decoration, and a person on foot could scale it with a little effort, so it was hardly functional as a barrier. That meant it had significance. It was important in some other way.

The moment she leaned forward to take off she felt it, the thing holding her back. It was not unlike the sensation of cold iron nearby, a sickening feeling, a painful one, but this was different. It wasn't simply that she was repelled by it, but that she could not physically move farther, even by force.

She was alive, and this place was death, so it was possible that only the dead could pass through the gate. True or not, it would pose no problem for her. She made a Door that opened just above the gate and let her out a few yards away on the other side. Simple.

She paused to rest, landing atop a scraggly bush. The trail on this side of the gate looked more worn, which was odd. It had to mean that people arrived here and then turned back, or the trail on the other side of the gate would look the same. The path on this side twisted down the mountain and then off over a hill. She could not see what was beyond. The sides of the path were lined with tall grass, and a cold wind made the blades whisper together.

"Hush."

She thought she heard something, but the wind gusted harder and grass hissed.

"You hush."

She heard the words clearly now. Had she been human, she would have missed them. They were coming from off in the grass across the path.

"It's one of them. Hold still."

"You hold still. It can't see us."

"It can hear us, and that's just as bad."

It sounded like three separate people, but it was difficult to tell.

"It's no danger. What can it do to us?"

"It can eat us."

"No it can't."

"Chickens eat bits of stone. So do toads. This is an owl. She's ten times as bad."

"They don't eat bark or plants."

"They can claw. Look at those talons."

"Oh, it can't eat us, you beef-witted buffoon."

"Hush now. Look at it. It hears you."

Astrid blinked slowly and turned her head to look into the distance. The whispering voices went silent for a while, and fearing they would slip away, she decided to speak.

"I won't hurt you," she said.

"Lying," whispered one.

"It's just a bird. We're not mice."

"It'll eat us, sure as we sit here."

"Both of you quit your twattling and get back to work."

"What work?"

"I can't remember. But find something useful to do."

Astrid flew over, hovering over the spot where she thought the voices came from. Sitting below in the grass, staring up at her in horror were three small figures, no larger than loaves of bread. They were stout and short-limbed, like babies, with wizened little faces. One was made of brown bark, another of green moss and the third of pale mottled stone.

"Helping me would be a useful thing to do," she said and landed in the grass.

The bark and moss creatures held each other while the stone one stood in front of them.

"Off you go then," it said, making a shooing motion. "Nothing for you here."

"I don't eat stone. Or bark or moss. I'm looking for someone."

She jumped up and took a perch on top of a little stone house, its roof so low and rounded that it blended perfectly into the land.

"We haven't seen no owls come past," said the bark creature.

"She doesn't mean an owl," said the stone one to the moss one. "But someone else with a proper body."

The three creatures exchanged a glance, then huddled together in a knot.

"Too many if you ask me."

"More will come, just watch."

"A regular highway for them."

"Ten years for the one, but less for the other."

"I figured it out. I know what it is."

"And what would you know? How long you been watching this gate?"

"Same amount of time as you, you old slubberdegullion."

"There were a few, but it has been so long —"

"It's listening!"

They all turned to her, but she couldn't disguise that she had been paying close attention.

"Where did they send the one with a body who came through recently?" she asked. "Where is he?"

"We know what you are. You're a Door!" cried the moss creature, pointing at her with a small, thick finger.

"I am. And I'm looking for a dragon, a drake. Have you seen one?"

They glanced at each other.

"He could be anywhere," said the stone one.

"This place is large," said the moss one. "You'd know that if you were here longer."

"I've only just arrived," said Astrid. "That's why I need your help."

"Don't answer it. It'll eat us," said the bark one.

"Oh, by the River, do stop going on about it eating us," said the stone one. "It won't."

"Stop!" said Astrid, and the creatures looked up at her. "Just tell me where the drake might be. Do you know?"

"Across the river," said the bark creature. "Past night's Plutonian shore."

"Everything is across the river," said the stone creature. "It asked."

"All right," Astrid said. "I go across the river. What then?"

"Did you love him?" asked the moss creature. "Is that why you came? There was a singing man once, like you, who came for someone he loved. Don't look back, that's the lesson he learned. You'd do best to heed too. Now, do you love him?"

"I don't know," she said. Then made up her mind. "Yes." There was more to say, but she decided that simplicity was best.

The creatures put their heads together again.

"But I don't know."

"You don't, but we do."

"Bring your lump of a head closer."

"Are you sure we should be helping it?"

"And why not? Might be interesting."

"The cracks in the sky are interesting."

"Not the same thing. Now let me touch your head."

They went silent for a minute, touching one another, and then turned to her in unison.

"Cross the river. Follow the path until it splits and go to the left three times. There's a big valley up over the far hills and sometimes drake spirits like to fly about there."

"What about humans? Where do they go?"

"The same place, but farther on still. It's all the same place here."

"But vast."

"Did you see the drake yourself?" she asked.

"We did. But far off, in the distance. He had a body, we saw. He didn't come through this gate. Now, this gate doesn't open. Not for diggers or flyers or walkers. None can get through. Not anyone."

"I got through."

"We know. We saw. You're a Door. And you said you wouldn't eat us."

"I won't."

She thanked them and took off, crossing the wide, slow river and keeping an eye on the thin path below. There was no sun here, only a dim, ambient light, and she couldn't make Doors to the place on the horizon to speed her trip, or she might lose the path. It took most of the day, at least by her own internal reckoning, for her to reach the third forking of the path.

She soared up and over a high range of hills and paused to rest on the edge of a long, tree-filled valley. She was about a third of the way along the valley, but both edges were so far away that they were difficult to make out. Here and there flitted smoky shapes, long and undulating and slender. Some were clearer than others, forming into sharp bodies with wings and tails while others were more indistinct.

She felt for Sevilen, reaching out with her mind like she had done with Elliot and others. She waited a long while, but felt nothing. She took off, deciding to fly from one end of the valley to the other, starting at the closest end, making Doors here and there to cover more ground quickly.

The closer side of the valley was hilly, and a large lake had formed from hillside runoff. She thought she spied large shapes moving beneath the water, but did not swoop lower for fear something might leap from the water and catch her. The center of the valley was filled with trees and the occasional set of hills, dipping and creating smaller shady vales where drake spirits flew or walked, some glancing up at her as she flew past.

The far end of the valley was rocky, filled with boulders as if there had been a great rock slide long ago. Some of the spirits lay on the rocks, basking, while others slithered into deep crevices between the giant stones at her approach.

Sevilen had not lived in lakes or rock caves, but preferred his house and his island. Perhaps he was far away on an island in the sea she had smelled. Or maybe he lived among the humans. Why hadn't she thought of that?

She searched around the caves, peeping into a few, finding sleeping drakes and angry ones, and some that scuttled back into the darkness. Some were larger than Sevilen and some smaller than she was. She emerged from one cave and blinked to adjust to the light.

A great dark shape was flying toward her. It was solid and bluish black and she knew him on sight. She took off and met him in midair. He turned, and the air current from his wings forced her to angle her wings and adjust her path so she would not be knocked from the sky.

"I heard that an owl was flying about," he said. "I came as quickly as I could."

Astrid tried to make a Door to her world, but the image in the center of it fluctuated between the path she had followed, the valley, the river and the area with the three little creatures. She tried again with the same result.

Sevilen's great eye swiveled toward her, though he did not speak.

"I can only make Doors within this place," she said.

"This purgatorial place or the others?"

"There are others?"

"I haven't seen them, but yes. This one is a place to get prepared for the next one. It's temporary."

She tried again, attempting to make a Door to the place she had entered the afterlife, but failed. It was the gate. She was sure of it. Something about the gate kept her from passing through.

"We're going to take a roundabout way," she said.

Many of the drake spirits were moving toward them now, rising from the trees and poking heads from hidden dens. A few were moving fast, streaking toward them at alarming speed.

"Best hurry," said Sevilen. "I made a few questionable promises. I told a few of the other spirits that if they informed me when an owl or a human woman came into this place, then she would help them return to the world of the living."

"How many did you promise?"

"Not that many. The rest must feel that you are a living rip, like the ones in the sky. They're attracted to it."

"Let's go then," she said and made a Door to the place with the three creatures. The two of them flew through and the little creatures shrieked in terror as the great drake appeared in the air over them. She closed the Door. High above, other spirits turned toward them. More came over the nearby hill, spirits of humans, but also other things, some animal and some unrecognizable.

She made a Door to pass through the gate and Sevilen followed her through.

"The gate ought to hold them," she said as they flew toward the place she had entered the world. If she had come in at that spot, then it was their best bet for getting out. "They can't pass through the gate."

Sevilen did not answer. They flew lower.

"Grab my clothes," she said, and Sevilen reached his great clawed paw and snatched them up and continued flying.

She tried to make a Door, and they had to circle the area three times before she succeeded in creating a Door to Luna Park. Of course it was Luna Park. That place was a borderland, an instability. Naturally it would be the easiest place to come through from this world. She expanded the diameter of the Door and Sevilen flew through.

Before she followed him, she glanced behind her. The spirits had indeed clustered around the gate, obscuring it. But something happened as she watched. The spirits tumbled out, some intertwined, some shooting off toward her on their own.

Through the thick tangle of souls she saw it. She had broken one of the cardinal rules of her kind, that no psychopomp could bring someone back from death. There were consequences for such an act.

The iron gate now hung open.

CHAPTER 35

FELICIA PULLED OUT THE GREEN fuzzy handcuffs, attached one end to her left wrist and yanked open the front door. The instant she recognized Janeiro, she clapped the other end on his right wrist and tightened it down.

"Now, take me to my son," she said.

He shot a dirty look at Santiago. "You didn't tell me she'd be here."

Santiago shrugged with a half grin.

"He didn't like that you stole my baby," said Felicia.

"I doubt he cares too much about that. Now, take these off of me."

"Can't. Don't have the key. You can search my bag."

Julius rummaged halfheartedly through her bag and a few moments later, Janeiro got a strange look. Through their months together, she had seen him happy and sad, thoughtful and excited, but she had never seen that look before. It was a look of fear and surprise.

"A Door just opened at Luna Park," he said. "I have to go."

"Nice try. But no."

"I can't just ignore this. It's an unstable location."

"I told May we never should have allowed her to build that place," said Julius.

"You couldn't have stopped her," said Santiago. "May never would listen to any of us. She was such a wild girl." He got a fond smile. "So very wild. A fast runner too. Liked to make me chase her."

Julius gave him a disgusted look.

"If I don't go, something terrible will happen," said Janeiro. "It's not an ordinary Door that opened."

"Let him go," said Julius to Felicia. "He isn't playing. This is serious."

"And so am I. You want to go? Then take me along. And then we'll go to my son."

"I can't take you. You'll be in danger."

"It didn't bother you to put a newborn baby in danger."

"He's safe. He's been safe for a long time now."

"A long time? What time did you take him to?"

An earthquake rattled through the house, and something small shattered upstairs.

"People may die because you're preventing me from going," he said, looking down at her, now with a concern she thought might be genuine. "You're a doctor. You don't cause death. You're a healer."

"I'm a mother."

"Your child was never meant to exist. With parents from two separate worlds, he couldn't exist. You know that. The void wyrms could sense that he's a living instability, and they followed him, attracted to it like they are to all rips between worlds. The boy will tear apart the worlds. My siblings and I are doing what we can, according to our abilities, but you are trying to stop us."

"So where did you take him if he's so dangerous? And why can't you take me there?"

"You need to tell me where the key is."

"Do you have children?"

"No. We're all siblings."

She wasn't sure who the "we" was, but if the Twelve had other siblings, then she wouldn't be surprised. Nothing could surprise her at this point.

Janeiro's phone rang. It was Red Fawn, and Felicia heard the woman telling Janeiro that the Door that had opened at Luna Park was not from any living world.

"Call November. I can't help," he said and hung up.

Julius looked on the verge of panic. "What if we can't find November?"

"You'll have to," said Janeiro. "I can't work attached to a human like this."

"You can find bolt cutters at the hardware store," said Santiago.

"I thought you were helping me," said Felicia. "Whose side are you on?"

"He's on his own side," said Julius.

"You want to come along with me?" said Janeiro. "You want to see your unnatural child, you selfish woman?" His expression was dark with fury. "Then we'll go visit him."

CHAPTER 36

FOR A WHORE AND A murderer, Seamus thought that he and Hazel made a good pair. Both of them excelled at reading others and used the talent to be near invisible or to get what they required without a fuss.

Today, they required a hired carriage to take them to the town of Fintona. Ordinarily, Seamus would have been content with an open trap or even the back of a cart, but today's ride would be long, and he had a woman along. He knew Hazel would have been perfectly happy in the open air. She would have preferred it. But one had to keep up the appearance of normality, and ordinary women did not wish to become freckled and windblown.

The driver snapped the reins and they rode out, through the town and onto the long road to Fintona. Hazel pulled out a book while Seamus sat with his notebook, working through some calculations that Oren had written down and that Hazel had brought along with countless other note pages and pieces of equipment.

Now that Oren was gone, Seamus often dreamed of him, of their inventions and failures, of their good times and narrow escapes. But there were dreams of a more disturbing nature as well, of a terrible betrayal, of Oren stealing one of Seamus's designs, of a great machine destroying the city of New Orleans. The dreams revealed something about his friend that he did not like to consider: that Oren was a decent man so long as he had no power. But once he had money and opportunity, he might transform into something else.

Seamus felt like a traitor, as if his dreams were defiling the memory of his loyal friend. He didn't want to mention them to Hazel for that very reason. But he ought not to dwell on these thoughts. He had equations to work through before they arrived.

The village of Fintona was small and unremarkable. Seamus paid their driver, and they checked into the town's only inn, posing as cousins. They took their things to their rooms and then crossed the street for lunch.

"We'll have to be canny about this," said Seamus over plates of lamb with greens and potatoes. He pushed the potatoes to one side and cut into the lamb. "We're only going to the cloister to take readings, but we can't go in broad daylight, or we'll be noticed. You can ride all right?"

"Well enough."

"I mean, can you ride like a man? If I were to hire two horses and one was a sidesaddle, they'd notice. They'll both have to have ordinary saddles."

"I can manage. I can put on a pair of your trousers under my dress, cinch them at the waist and be decent."

"Very well. I figure we should go between the times when the nuns are up praying, between Matins at midnight and Lauds at dawn. So long as the sisters are sleeping, we'll be well enough. But tomorrow is All Saint's Day, and neither of us should be seen missing Mass tomorrow morning. People like the innkeeper might notice. You sure you'll be all right with such a late night?"

"Late nights don't bother me," she said, but softly, and he regretted bringing it up. Of course she was used to being up late, but he hadn't thought of her as the sum of her past deeds, and he supposed she didn't think of him in those terms either. Friendships were strange things that way, making reprobate people into ordinary folk.

Late that night, Seamus brought two hired horses around the back of the inn where Hazel waited with an unlit lantern and a few pieces of Seamus's equipment packed into two bags. Seamus took both, figuring Hazel would have enough trouble riding in a dress. But small as she was, she managed to mount on her own, and he saw his own trousers, rolled thick at the bottom, covering her to the top of her sturdy walking boots.

They rode, Seamus stopping to study the little hand-drawn map of the outlying areas around town that a man in a bar had sketched for him. Once he was sure of their path, they rode on.

When they arrived, he found that the cloister was larger than he would have thought, but the great rectangular building must have enclosed not only the women's living quarters, but a garden and a yard for walks or recreation.

"What if the spot is inside the cloister?" asked Hazel.

"It couldn't have been. If Oren had come through there, I don't think the women would have been so keen to feed him and give him a bit of money. They'd have thought he was a burglar."

"Where then?"

They rode closer to the cloister, and Seamus spotted the chapel, a small building with a peaked roof, attached to the far side of the cloister. Behind it rose a number of simple headstones inside a fenced yard.

"He said he was here to pay homage to Epona," said Seamus. "If this place was a temple in his world, perhaps this little chapel might be the spot."

"You're going to break into a church?"

"It's a chapel, and no. I'm going to get some readings nearby."

He tied the horses to the nearest tree and lit the lantern. He got out his equipment and took a few readings here and there and discovered that the oddest signals came from the graveyard.

"I'm sure we'll learn nothing," he said, pulling his remaining equipment from his bag. "But I want to be certain."

"You're only saying that so you won't be disappointed."

He didn't answer, but asked Hazel to open up his notebook and read out some of the numbers for him. He calibrated the handheld machine and checked the tiny electrical power source. He was inordinately proud of the little thing, erratic as it was. It hummed, and he waited for the arm on the dial to stop jerking and steady itself. Hazel set down his book and followed his instructions on taking readings from a second machine, kneeling on the ground while Seamus held his high as he could while still being able to discern the readings.

"You there," called a voice. A young woman wearing a novice's white veil stood at the doorway leading from the cloister to the graveyard.

"Are you grave robbers?" she asked, approaching, and Seamus immediately admired the girl. She was neither afraid nor repulsed, but as calm and firm as could be.

"No, we're not disturbing anyone's grave. We're performing a scientific experiment."

The novice looked over the machinery, the wiring and the open notebook, pages flapping in the night breeze, and must have believed them.

"What sort of experiment?" she asked, drawing closer.

Hazel stood, and Seamus watched as she shook out her skirts and approached the girl, friendly and benign. If the girl went back inside and sent someone to fetch the police, their trip would be for naught.

"It's an experiment involving air currents," said Hazel.

"Why at night?" said the girl. "The air currents are the same during the day."

Ah, so the girl was clever. That made her dangerous to them, but she was also curious, and they could use that to their advantage to delay her.

Hazel must have had the same thought. She said, "The cool air and the moisture from the land interact in a unique way at night, especially late like this. It's complicated, but interesting. Would you like to see?"

The girl hesitated, glanced back at the dark windows of the building, and then nodded.

Yes, they had her, Seamus thought.

As a novice, she would not have taken her perpetual vows and thus could leave the cloister. It would still be an act of disobedience since she did so without permission, and thus a sin, but he was in no place to judge the sins of such a simple girl. His own deeds weighed far heavier on the scales.

"Tighten down these fastenings, if you would," Hazel said to the novice, and the girl knelt to do so.

Good, thought Seamus. Get her to participate in the crime. Now, she was on their side.

"Have you ever seen anything strange around here?" asked Hazel in a conversational tone. "Like the air wavering. Or any people appearing that ought not to?"

"Nothing I can think of, no."

"What about disappearances?" asked Seamus. "Anyone go missing?"

"One of the other novices ran away, but she must have gone somewhere far off, because she didn't go back to her family. We never heard of her again."

A disappearance was interesting, but not conclusive. He powered up the machine and scrambled over to take note of the dials on a larger box he had rigged to take more detailed readings than his smaller handheld device.

Once he had taken note, he cranked up the power on the signal generator, followed by the signal amplification device. The air crackled, like it did during an electrical storm, and he pulled the lantern closer to get a better look at the readings.

"Oh!" cried the novice, and Seamus looked up.

Another nun stood before them, but she was not alive, not physically at least. She was grayer and parts of her elongated and snapped back into shape, as if she was unused to being in that form. She was elderly, but stood straight and strong. She looked straight at them, one by one, and as her gaze fell on Seamus, he involuntarily drew back. The air around her shimmered.

"I know her," breathed the novice. "That's Sister Mary Benedicta. She died of a fever a few months after I entered."

Seamus leapt for the machine to shut it off and flipped the switch, but the ghost still stood there, regarding them. Behind her, another figure appeared, this one less distinct, but most definitely a man.

The novice crossed herself but did not move.

"Shut it off," said Hazel.

"I already have," said Seamus. A third figure came through behind the other two. The figure of Sister Mary Benedicta looked up at the cloister and the chapel.

"Oh, Professor," whispered Hazel. "What have we done?"

CHAPTER 37

NEIL PICKED UP NOTE THAT lay on the kitchen counter. It was from March, telling him that if he was not back by that evening, Neil needed to give fresh water to the captive drake. She would not need to eat for another few days. March included instructions on the location of the drug and the dosage. It should be added to the water tank on the side of the cage and it would dissolve immediately. Simple. March had even left a key.

That night, Neil drove to the tiny building, unlocked the padlock and went down the metal staircase, deep underground. He located the room with the powdered drug, measured out the proper dosage into a little vial and pushed in a rubber stopper.

When he arrived at the side of the cage, the drake slithered up to the bars, enormous and strong. He discovered with surprise that he was genuinely afraid of her.

"Now that March is gone, perhaps we can speak frankly," said the drake.

"What would you like to speak about?"

"Killing him."

Neil couldn't hide his surprise. "I don't want to kill him."

"Perhaps not, but you do wish to be free."

"I am free."

"No more than I am. If March wants you to do something, you do it."

"He explained things to me. How we fight for human

freedom, the freedom to choose one's own path, the only true good."

"And you believed him?"

He could not look into her cold black eyes and lie. Behind those bars, she held no power over him. There was no compulsion for him to speak the truth. But she was correct that they were kin, in a sense, and he would not dishonor their kinship with lies.

"I think about it," he said. "How can a thing like me be good if there is no good and bad? How can rules and obedience be evil if there is no evil?"

"A good question," she said. "One worthy of study. You see, he denies you your freedom. Just as he does with me. According to his own version of good and evil, he is evil."

"He has been kind to me."

"I'm sure he has. Love will make one follow a wicked man. A rogue golem is a dangerous thing, and he does not want you to disobey him. I have met your brothers, some of them, and they are more ... internally malleable than you are."

"I know you want me to free you."

"Of course. I do not hide that fact."

"I won't be tricked."

"I have said nothing tricky, nothing deceptive. You will do what you choose to do. An act of free will."

If he hadn't known better, he would think she was smiling, though her face remained as reptilian and inhuman as ever.

"Do you have a name?" he asked her.

"I do. But I will not give it to you. You may call me Coaxoch if you want a name."

"If March recaptures you, he'll kill you for certain."

"I know. And I might say the same to you. Once you outlive your usefulness, once you disobey, he will kill you."

"Did you really mean it when you said you would kill him if you got free?"

"Yes. But one of the other drakes might do it instead. March has never let any of your brothers come see me alone, so either he trusts you or something happened to him. I doubt he trusts you, not after we talked last time. You were too interested in me. Too curious. Too understanding. He saw it. But then, why not send one of your brothers to drug me? March is up to something and sending you was a risk. So I must conclude that something has happened to him. One of my kind may already have ended his life."

"I think I would know."

"Would you? Do you think you would feel a sense of freedom?" She seemed genuinely interested in the answer.

"I suppose so."

"There's one way to put it to the test. But remember, if you are wrong and he is alive, he might kill you."

"He loves me."

"That will not stop him. He has a higher purpose. Or a lower one, depending on how you classify his type. He wants humans to make their own way, to follow their passions. Without rules. Without restrictions. It is a lovely notion, if you don't know too much about human nature. You and I are inhuman and may have trouble comprehending them. But you are young and I am old. I can tell you, without standards of good and evil, however they are set, man descends into barbarity. Strength gives power and power is kept with violence. It is always so."

"I would not see them enslaved to falsehoods and rules only to keep people docile. Isn't that worse?"

She thought about it. "Perhaps. If complete freedom holds no true goodness, and standards of behavior do not either, then you can pick one was well as the other."

"Then what is goodness?"

"A question I do not think the two of us can address while speaking through bars. Or ever. Our kinds are not natural allies."

A question rose in his mind, and he decided to ask her. "Did you have children? Are any of the void wyrms your own?"

"Not now. My children are grown. But some of their children are still young and live in the void."

"I did not like the idea of killing them. They are hungry babies. I can see that."

"They do not want to destroy your world, only to live and eat, like all young. The drakes don't want your world destroyed either."

"But there are earthquakes and the void wyrms are eating people. March wants to stop this from happening."

"March seeks to be the only thing who can open the Doors between worlds. But already, the worlds are in peril. Either with warrens between them or sealed off from one another, entropy will win out. The events are already in motion, and though March can kill as many drakes as he likes, he cannot stop it. He knows this, I believe."

"What will happen?"

"I am not sure. I cannot see the future."

"If I free you, I will have to run, to hide from March."

"We both will, if I don't kill him immediately. And I will not promise to help you," she said.

"This might be a trick," said Neil. "A trap set by March to test my loyalty."

"It might."

He pulled out the vial of white powder and studied it.

"Tell me about your life before you were here," he said.

"If it will help you," she said, and told him tales of her life in Mexico, of soaring over the land and the sea, of the people who lived in her land, how they honored her and how she watched over them.

"They were a people of laws. They had their gods who demanded certain things and forbade others. It was not always peaceful, but it was stable, in its way. But things changed, as they always do, and the men of you color came. They killed some of the people, enslaved others, married a few. You know how it goes."

"Where did you go?"

"I spent some time in the void, but preferred this world. There are still mountains and forests where I can go, and like most of my kind, I can take human form if I wish. I had kin, at first. Though many were forced to leave, I was not, as I am a peaceful being. Most of the time."

They regarded each other. The moment had come.

He knew. He had known what he would do from the first moment he had seen her curled up in the cage.

He slipped the vial into his coat pocket and walked away.

CHAPTER 38

"YOU KILLED HIM?" CRIED FELICIA.

"No," said Janeiro. "I said we were going to death. The child is alive."

Janeiro took Felicia's upper arm more roughly than necessary and created a Door. She had come with him through many others and had always been able to see where they were going. It was like stepping through a picture frame into another place. But this time, the center of the picture was mirrored. Every instinct in her told her to avoid going through, that it was beyond mere danger. It was annihilation. But Luke was there, and he needed her. She stepped through, Janeiro's hand gripping her arm.

"This isn't heaven," said Janeiro. "Or hell, either."

They stood in a village of cottages and small homes with roofs of both thatch and slate. The buildings were stuccoed in white, wood paneled or walled with brick, but every color was washed out, as if the very air in this place pulled the life out of things. The village looked like a mishmash of architectural styles and eras, with both gaslights and wall torches illuminating the dirt road.

The hills farther off were grayish, though the plants nearer to the town had a little more color. To Felicia, they seemed like aquarium plants, simulations of the real things.

"This way," said Janeiro, pulling her down a narrow road. Gauzy spirits floated here and there, some solid and others less so, a few busy going somewhere while others simply hovered and observed.

"What is this place? Where is my baby?"

Janeiro didn't answer, but dragged her between two buildings, emerging near an open-fronted stall. Inside was an unlit forge and an anvil to one side. Various blacksmithing tools lined the wall.

"Oh, no you don't," she said, understanding what he intended to do to the handcuffs that linked them. "You're taking me to my baby first."

"He's here, but I'm not taking you to him attached to me like this. I have to manage the rip that opened at Luna Park as well as the time tears your husband made. All of you have created a lot of problems."

He muttered something unflattering under his breath as he pulled a large pair of iron shears from the wall with his free hand, spun around and shoved her wrist down on the anvil.

"Hold still. I don't want to accidentally hurt you."

She was about to pull away when a boy of about ten approached. He was better formed than the spirits, and his expression was watchful and intelligent. He had dark, curly hair and golden brown eyes the same shade as her own. He wore a baggy green tee shirt, and as he rounded the edge of the stall, she saw his blue jeans, rolled up at the bottom. His feet were bare. They were his father's feet.

She felt the crack of the metal as the connecting chain between the wrist cuffs broke apart. This boy, his face, his shape, were all known to her and yet so strange. She took in his hands, long-fingered and oddly clean compared to the rest of him, his narrow shoulders, the shape of his mouth, his teeth, including the slightly crooked second incisor, his quick and questioning look between Janeiro and her, and back to Janeiro.

"Hi, Janeiro," the boy said. He looked genuinely happy to see him. "Did you bring me anything?"

"I did, as a matter of fact," said Janeiro. "I brought your mother."

The boy looked her over, interested, but in a detached sort of way. He had not expected this, she knew. He had not asked for her.

"My God, what did you do?" she turned to Janeiro, but he was gone.

"He must have something he has to do," said Luke. "He has to go suddenly sometimes."

"You're Luke," she said, wanting it to be true, but fearing the answer.

"Yes."

He looked more wary now, and she supposed he was reasoning through things. Here she was, recently handcuffed to Janeiro, who Luke seemed to like, looking crazed and disheveled.

She had to keep her head. She couldn't break down or cry or snatch him into an embrace, not if she wanted this child to be comfortable around her. Her fury and pain would have to wait. Luke didn't need to see her despair over their lost years apart.

"Have you always lived here?" she asked.

"Yes."

"Do you have a family?" she said.

"No."

"Then who raised you?"

"Janeiro. But he leaves me alone now that I'm old enough to take care of myself."

She watched as he took the iron shears and reached up high, tiptoeing to hang them back on the wall.

"You're hurt," he said. "I can see by how you stand."

"I just had a baby."

He glanced at her stomach, still swollen, and then at her face.

"Want to come with me? I have a place where I take care of people."

"Sure," she said. She didn't want to stay standing in this blacksmith's stall, and now that she had finally found him, she was intensely curious about him.

"Why did Janeiro bring you?" he asked. "He usually just brings food and clothing and medical supplies."

"I made him bring me. I wanted to find you."

He did not answer or look at her, and she sensed how out of place he would be among ordinary people. A spirit slid past them, and he took her into a long building with several square windows along the side.

It was a hospital, of sorts. A spirit hospital. Beds lined the walls, just as in a medical ward from the nineteenth century, and spirits lay in most of them.

"You can lie down, if you want," he said.

"No. I want to stay with you."

"I have work to do. But you can help. Janeiro told me my mother was a doctor."

She hated Janeiro now, but he had not lied to the boy. She wondered how much Luke knew.

A spirit nearby rolled over in bed, her dark eyes locking on Felicia's face. She pulled her hand from inside her blanket and held it out, palm up.

Luke stepped forward, kneeling beside her. Neither of them spoke, and the boy and the spirit simply looked at one another. Then Luke stood and brought her a glass of water from a nearby jug. She sat up and drank.

"How can they drink?" asked Felicia. "And how can they need medical care?"

"They're thirsty. Or hungry. Or they have a disease or a wound or pain of some kind."

"But why? They're dead."

"This is the place some of the spirits come to when they're dead," he said, moving to the next bed to check on a man's broken arm. "They come here to be healed and to suffer."

"How can it be both?"

"Because this is where justice can be done. Justice before they go on to the final place. These people here, they did bad things, but they were sorry for them. I don't ask them, but sometimes they tell me what they did. That's part of justice too, admitting what they did. They hurt people when they were alive. They beat their spouses or children. They raped or attacked people. Some killed people. Once there was a regiment of men who gave diseased blankets to a village. They came in with terrible sores and fevers."

He relayed this information with perfect serenity, as if recalling the deeds of a villain in a cartoon. He pulled a blanket up over a sleeping man.

"If they are so bad, then why do you help them?" she asked.

"That's part of justice too. See, they did bad things and they know that they deserve punishment, to even the scales before they're judged. So they accept the punishment, see? But also they have me to help them, and that makes them better faster, but it also hurts them inside. Because they get kindness where they dealt out cruelty, and that hurts them, but it does good too."

He looked up at her, and she knew he was evaluating her reaction.

"You're doing a good thing," she said. He looked away and moved on. "Who taught you to do this?"

"Janeiro."

"Did you ever want to go back to the regular world? The world of the living people?"

"I asked about it, but Janeiro says I can't. He says it will hurt people."

He turned to look into the eyes of another spirit, and there was something about him, something familiar. It wasn't his resemblance to his father or to her, as he was his own unique mixture of them both. His mouth was her mother's, his ears were unfamiliar, perhaps coming from his father's side. It was something else, something in the set of his jaw, his look as he tried to figure out what

227

his patient required. She had seen him before. She was certain of it.

A great rumbling began far in the distance, then grew closer and shook the building violently. She instinctively put her arms around Luke, pulling him down to the floor. A water basin crashed to the floor, and a great cry went up among the spirits.

The shaking stopped and Luke stood, then reached to gently take her hand. She thought her heart might burst with the tenderness of the little gesture. She wanted to embrace him, to kiss his cheeks and hold him forever.

"The trumpet!" a spirit in the nearby bed yelled. "It sounds!"

But Felicia had heard nothing. The other spirits took up the cry, rising from their beds and hobbling toward the door, some dragging themselves along the floor. "The last day! It's time!"

Luke led her through the spirits and outside where they saw spirits running, walking, gliding and flying. All headed in one direction. In the distance, lightning split the mottled purplish sky.

"I've never seen that before," said Luke.

"It's open!" murmured a nearby spirit. "The door opened. It's time."

"What's happening?" asked Felicia, still holding his hand.

"They think it's the final judgment."

"And is it?"

He looked up at her, uncertain. He was so young, and she thought that no child should have to wonder about such a thing. But she was even more lost than he was. Two lost souls in the realm of the dead.

Other spirits appeared in the distance, clearly inhuman. Luke saw her watching them.

"I stay mostly in the area for people. But there are other places with other types of things."

The human spirits crowded past, and Felicia was reminded of something, of animals fleeing a forest fire.

"I think we ought to go with them," she said. "If it's a way to get out of here, it might take us home."

CHAPTER 39

SEAMUS WATCHED AS THE SPIRITS continued to come through into the cloister graveyard, one by one, and then in groups.

He turned on the machine again, trying to reverse what he had done to close the opening, but he had no success. The rip opened wider, revealing a blotchy purple sky spiked with occasional lightning. And still the souls came.

The novice crossed herself and pulled at Hazel's arm. "We should go. We should fetch the priest."

"I don't think it will help," said Hazel.

"I'm going to wake the sisters. We'll send someone into town for the priest. Hold a moment. Are those your horses?"

Hazel said they were, then knelt to help Seamus reset the machine.

Without another word, the sister ran and untied the larger animal, Seamus's mount, then leapt onto it. Seamus thought she must have been a farm girl with experience with her father's plow horse, or perhaps the daughter of a landowner with a stable, for she handled the animal expertly, turning it and riding it at a full gallop, her woolen stockinged legs gripping its sides and her habit flying out behind her.

"A lass like that is wasted in a place like this," said Seamus, twisting the knob to crank the power level up to maximum.

"Maybe she's not," said Hazel. "The outside world isn't so kind to women as to men."

They watched a group of spirits as they drifted away, in the direction of town, while another group came through, this one including people in clothing from centuries ago.

"It's not working," said Seamus in exasperation. "I can't get it to work, and I don't have time to recalculate the numbers."

"I don't think we can do anything, Professor. And it's getting worse."

The rip now was nearly as high as the cloister walls and was widening as well. They gathered up the machinery and hurried away. Now the spirits were coming through in groups of ten to fifteen, and though most were either thoughtful or confused, a few appeared angry and shrieked at the sky or shouted unintelligibly at one another. Their clothing became increasingly stranger, with women in trousers and some people wearing less than a typical person's underclothes.

"We should go," said Hazel, but halfheartedly. She craned her neck to see beyond the spirits who crowded and pushed through. Seamus understood her conflicting desires to run away or to see what was through the rip.

"You're welcome to go," he said. "But I want to see what this is. Oren said that in his world, this place was a temple for that goddess who walked with the dead, that he came through a shimmering doorway. And the air now at the edges of the rip is just like he described, just like the shimmering I saw at Jackson Square back home."

A line of spirits tore past them, and Seamus put his arm out to shield Hazel, but he needn't have as she leapt back, as nimble as a goat. Seamus hopped up on the low wall that surrounded the graveyard, getting a good look beyond the spirits. Hazel maneuvered her skirts and scrambled up beside him.

"My God," she breathed. They could see clearly through the tear now, into the land beyond. "It's hell."

Seamus wasn't sure what it was, but though it wasn't

231

any kind of paradise, it didn't look like a place of eternal torment either.

In the distance stood an open iron gate at the top of a mountain pass. Souls crowded thick near it, pushing through, some climbing over each other. They poured down the mountain and raced across a wide gray field, straight toward the rip. Lightning flashed, blinding him momentarily. It had come from a place very close to the tear, but inside the other world. A great freezing wind picked up, whether from this side or the other, he could not say. It came from all directions, as if converging upon this very spot, and it whipped their hair and clothing. The air smelt of electricity and a coming storm.

A pack of souls screamed past, and Seamus lost his balance. Hazel grabbed him just as another group ripped into them, passing through them. The sensation was terrible, like an icy wind that pierced clothing and froze flesh, but internal, as if the very marrow of his bones was freezing and hardening into stone. The souls grew thicker as the main body of approaching souls was now arriving at the rip, screaming and howling, flying and running, some in joy and some in madness.

Hazel leapt down on the far side of the wall and pulled him with her. Together they huddled with their backs against the stones, sometimes touched by the passing souls and sometimes narrowly avoided. Their remaining horse shied and screamed, bucking and eventually pulling free of its tie and racing into the distance. Seamus managed to crawl out to pull his equipment together and stow it in his bag, and twice they tried to run, but both times the souls were too thick, crowding the road, the fields and the graveyard.

Now and then there would be a space between souls and he could look up at the cloister where he saw the terrified faces of the nuns, disembodied pale ovals, peering down through the windows.

He and Hazel huddled together until dawn, and as the sun rose, his hopes died, for he had wondered if the souls might fear sunlight and the light of day. They were undeterred, though he noticed that there were fewer and fewer as time passed.

Despite Hazel's objections, Seamus hopped back onto the wall. The line of souls had dwindled down to a trickle. But why? If they so clearly desired to escape that drab place, then why stop now? Surely there were more souls than just the few thousand they had witnessed.

A quarter of an hour later, he was able to walk up to the rip. A few souls still meandered toward the rip in the other world, but that wasn't what caught his eye. A hundred yards away, coming across the field toward the rip, were two figures. They were solid, colorful and fully alive. The shorter one, a boy, he did not know. The woman he knew from his dreams.

"Professor!" shouted Hazel as he got close enough to the rip for the shimmering air to envelop him.

"It's her," he called out to Hazel. "The woman from my dream. Can you see her?" Hazel joined him just as a great dark shape filled the air over the distant mountain. It swept over the gate, moving faster than anything he had ever seen and down toward the pair on the ground. The woman moved to shield the child, and Seamus stepped forward. Two spirits slid past him and he saw other spirits coming now, inhuman, some large and some small. The large shape passed the woman and child, but another one, this one lumbering and huge, like a living thing of plants and earth, strode toward the pair.

"They're alive," he said to Hazel. "And they're trying to get to us. We have to get them out."

"No, no we don't. They're coming this way, see?"

They were, but at a painfully slow pace. The lumbering thing stopped in front of them, and they appeared to be speaking with it. He watched as the woman pushed the child behind her, protecting him.

"You stay here," he said to Hazel and leapt through the door, running across the land, dodging approaching spirits, watching as the creature raised its vaporous arm, and the woman and child turned and fled.

The creature must not have wanted them too badly, as it turned toward him, toward the rip. The woman and child turned back, and they were close enough now for him to know for certain that he had never seen the boy before, but the woman's face was well known to him. And from her look, his own was just as familiar to her.

"Professor!" called a voice far behind him, and he turned to see Hazel, his equipment bag over her shoulder and her skirts gathered in her hand, running toward them. The area behind her was empty, and it looked like no more spirits were traveling through the rip. He could still see the top of the cloister wall and the sky of his world beyond, though they were small and distant.

He raced toward the woman and child. "It's you," said the woman to Seamus once they had reached one another.

"I've never seen the spirits so upset," said the boy.

"Come with me," said Seamus. "I'll get you out."

He turned back. Was the rip smaller now, or was it his imagination? No, for as he watched, it contracted. He yelled for Hazel to go back, but even as she turned, it pulled closed, snapping shut like an eye.

Seamus tried his machine, but to no avail.

The boy, Luke, insisted that his mother sit and rest. She was pale and clearly exhausted. Her story was even more strange than her clothing and speech, a story that included being married to him, which Seamus found believable, and of giving birth to a child who was stolen away and kept in this land for ten years by one of the Twelve.

As he tried the machine again and again, attempting to

recreate the rip with known coordinates, the four of them traded information, going over what they knew, where they had been and what they remembered. Something resembling the swapped tales of asylum inmates emerged.

"We should go back home to my rooms," said Luke. "This place is dangerous for us. The dead are fascinated by us, and some are not so friendly."

"I saw as much," said Seamus, but the area was now empty. One of the halves of the gate at the top of the mountain hung crookedly, half ripped from its hinges. The other half lay on the ground.

Hazel was still fiddling with his machine, trying various combinations of settings and power levels. It had been hours, but she was a stubborn thing and had decided upon randomly trying varying settings based on luck and desperate prayer.

"Pack everything up," he said. "We'll try again from Luke's safe place."

"I think I'm close," she said.

He helped Felicia to her feet. Hazel tried the machine again, and after a moment, the air shimmered for an instant but did not form a complete doorway. Seamus leapt to study the readings, then worked to adjust the machines, making tiny changes and studying the results each time. Hazel giving him instructions on what she had done, while he argued with her at the impossibility of it.

"This way!" Hazel turned a knob, changing the settings to ones that would never work. That was precisely why he had not tried them. The air shimmered and Felicia moved forward.

"No, don't go near it!"

"I think it won't open any farther for us," Felicia said. "I think we can step through when it's like this. I think I've done it before."

"We don't know where it goes."

"What do your readings say?"

"I can't make much of them. They're similar to the ones

from my world, but not quite the same."

"We could all go," said Felicia.

"I have to stay here," said Luke. "Janeiro said."

"Janeiro stole you and hid you," said Felicia. "You belong in the world of the living, not the dead. Besides, Seamus here can close the rips that the void wyrms come through. I'm not leaving you here."

"I'll go first," said Hazel, and before Seamus could react, she leapt up and stepped straight into the shimmering air, vanishing. He counted off fifteen seconds, checking the machine and keeping the power levels steady. At last, she returned.

"It's our world," she said, breathless. "But it's very different. People were dressed like you, more or less." She nodded to Felicia and Luke.

"That's all we need to know," said Felicia. "Anywhere is better than here." She took Luke's hand and stepped through. Seamus took the equipment he could while leaving the pieces that kept the rip open and followed Hazel through.

The place was a madhouse. Under their feet stretched a long wooden roadway running on raised pylons along a beach. The sun was bright and the place was overwhelming with a thousand colored electric lights, more than Seamus could imagine being in one place. Giant mechanical structures, one a great wheel with people in dangling gondolas, one a spinning contraption with seats on chains, all spun to a terrible cacophony of pulsing music.

"Thank God, we're home," said Felicia.

She was the only one pleased. Hazel studied the area with a look of mixed fascination and horror. Luke took a step back.

Thunder exploded overhead and people nearby ducked, as if it were a bomb. The air was humid and heavy, but cooled rapidly as a cold wind blew in from the sea.

"I don't like this place," said Luke.

Seamus had to agree.

CHAPTER 40

ELLIOT HAD ALWAYS PAID CLOSE attention to the weather. As a surfer, he knew the tides, and as a ship's captain, he had learned about the sea's currents, the seasons, the wind and the thousand things that could affect a ship's course. So when he observed the wind, its quick change in temperature and direction and the way the sea became rougher, even this close to Santa Maria Island, he became uneasy.

He studied the clouds, dark and heavy with moisture. Everything felt like it was moving, not only physically, but in some other way, some deeper way. Things were moving closer.

Astrid appeared on deck, followed by Yelbeghen, wearing gaudy and ill-fitting clothing from the Luna Park gift shop. Astrid had told Elliot that the drake, a vain creature, always dressed well. Then he remembered the more important fact, that Astrid and the drake were alive and they had recently been in the realm of death. How could he have forgotten, even for so short a time? His mind felt like a wad of yarn, all wound into a big ball, impenetrable and thick.

Astrid said something, and he couldn't remember what he answered, but he answered. Astrid glanced at Sister, and he knew immediately that his response had been off. He tried to remember what her question had been.

The air pressure felt higher, and he sensed the air pressing in on his skin. It went further than that. The whole world was pressurized, compressed, crushed together with something else.

He felt it first, in his mind, and then he saw it happen, half in the sky and half under the sea, the things all coming together. They were small at first, rocks, clouds, then they grew into mountains and great undersea formations. He dropped to his knees.

Worlds and worlds. So many skies! And the seas, all comingling, like the atoms of water were rainbow colored gumballs, all jostling together, vibrating, pressing in, moving through each other. Merging.

He was tired. So tired. He lowered his body to the deck, lying on his back as the sky spun. The sea was below him, then above, the deck of the ship against one shoulder, then against the back of his head.

No one touched him. No one spoke. But there was still sound, the crack of the thunder, and then finally, at last it came. After so long. So very long. The rain. The drops were huge and warm, hitting his body, his eyelids, his lips and teeth, wetting his tongue. They tasted like dust. Like the thousand tiny particles that made everything, the atoms, the sand, the gumballs, the stars, there was no differentiation between them. They all were the same thing, but names and the idea of separation had made them seem distinct.

The things he knew felt far away, and the ball of yarn in his mind loosened. First, it was slow, an expansion, like a great lung filling up, and there was space inside the long, tightly wound thread. Then a piece pulled off, and another, and another. They were like strands of noodles cooking in a pot, tangled and inseparable. Like eels writhing together, or blind white worms deep beneath the earth.

The sky ripped open, and the souls came. The land quaked, the sea tossed, and the wind tore at Skidbladnir's sail. No monkeys hung in the rigging, for even that existed seven times. Seven times seven a thousand times. And again.

For a moment, he wondered if his eye implant was malfunctioning. But this sight was different than viewing a recorded image. He felt everything, smelled and tasted it. He was about to order the implant to record, but a wave of sensation overtook him.

This was unique. And it was also a repetition of something that had happened before. Everything was happening again. His first life. His second one. All one billion people on earth. All seven billion. They pulsed around him like stars, like the lights of an overhead airplane at night, blinking, moving, blinking again. Firefly souls. All of them were alive now, except the dead. Yes, except the dead.

He knew his cousins. He saw Astrid as a baby, black haired and fair skinned, then as a reptilian thing, or was it feline? Then she was a woman with the yellow eyes of an owl. She was nothing and something at the same time.

Sister was here and not here. She was a baby. So ill. So small on her hospital ventilator, the tubes snaking from her tiny body. Then she was bigger, a child, beaten and hurt, her hair and tongue cut off, and she was also young and happy, at the beach, talking with friends. Talking.

Ah, and the others. The golem man, dead and alive again, stone and man. He was not human, no. But Elliot knew now what he was. He was a distillation of humanity, its failings and its curiosity, its passion, its ever-pulsing need to create, to make, to bring into being new things. He existed as a desire for this without its fulfillment and he was also the desire for violence, for freedom, for control, for justice, for strength, for love.

There was a woman from the Library, the place of his imprisonment. How he remembered it now. The kitchens, his small room, the scholars, the endless labyrinth of rooms. And at the center, a woman. Like most of the star lights that were souls, she did not have two lives, but then, she did. Because one of them included him.

How beautiful it was, this destruction, and he was the sole witness from its first moments to its terrible, crushing end.

He saw each universe, so beautiful, like the most intricate of marbles, filled with planets and stars and nebulae and the vast emptiness between them. There were more marbles now, pressed together, like soap bubbles, pushing inward. Then two of them merged. Pop. Now there were six. And pop. Five. The central bubble, his bubble, the one at the center, the hub of the wheel, grew each time, absorbing the others.

Pop.

It hurt, he knew. But births always did. This was a new world being born, and the popping should have deafened the world.

The ship's deck was still beneath him and the water poured from the sky in such quantities that he wondered if the ship was sinking. He tasted it. Dust, not salt. Then a cold wave slapped him. He stuck out his tongue. Salt and the undefinable murky taste of seawater.

He felt the whole sea on his tongue, and the sea was twice, sevenfold, as was the earth, the sky, the myriad things that crawled and flew and swam and leapt. It was the final moment, and the first.

The final soap bubble popped, leaving only one.

The twirled noodle pot of his mind was floating now, the noodles, the yarn threads, splitting into infinity, swirling and breaking apart, like a new cosmos being born. As the world was, so was he.

He understood everything now, the infinity of all things.

CHAPTER 41

I T HAPPENED WHILE NEIL WAS in the pool.

One moment, he was swimming laps in the hotel pool, the next, he was so drowsy he could barely drag himself up the ladder. He fell to the sun-warmed concrete, overcome by a slipping, crushing sensation. His cheek hit the concrete, and it was the last thing he felt before being pulled into darkness.

He woke an instant later, at least it felt like only an instant. He pushed himself up, his mind full and reeling. The memories, so many. There were his ordinary ones, the ones he had received from March, and the ones he had lived himself. And there were others. Memories of people, of friends both human and inhuman. And a woman, his wife. Hazel. Her name was like a little bell, clearing the fog in his mind.

Rain poured from the San Diego sky, the clouds low, heavy, and the air warm. He remembered fleeing March after he chose to withhold the drug that would keep the drake imprisoned. She was free now. He remembered his revolt years ago against March, and he remembered Hazel shooting and killing March. Then March came back in a new body and turned Neil to earth, but Hazel revived him. Death and life for them both, freedom and slavery.

He hadn't seen March since he freed the drake, and he didn't know if his master was alive or dead. And if March was alive, was he free or not?

And then there was the safety of his friends and wife.

He hurried to his room, dried off, changed into clean clothes and grabbed his phone. March's number was still in his contact list, but now there were others, numbers for each member of the Time Corps.

He knew better than to question the reality of what he saw. He had been in the Time Corps long enough to know a time anomaly when he experienced one. But this was different. Never before had his mind been reset. The entire world had been reset. He thought it through. His life had forked into two paths at one critical point, the moment he had met his partner Elliot on a train in the mid-1800s. In one set of memories, he had joined the Time Corps. In the other, he had talked with March and rejoined him.

Two timelines. Two sets of memories.

He called Hazel first, but the call went to voice mail. Then he called Elliot.

"My mud man!" cried Elliot. "The bouillon cube of humanity! You are concentrated mankind, did you know that?"

Elliot said something about the screaming souls of the dead before Neil heard the sound of the phone being taken from him and carried. That must be Sister. Then Astrid came on the line.

"You should come quick," she said. "How fast can you get to LA?"

"I'm in San Diego now. What's wrong with Elliot?"

"Hold on, let me see if I can find you."

A few moments later, she stood in his room.

"Come on," she said. "I've been collecting everyone."

"I thought you couldn't use your Doors for the living."

"Those rules don't matter anymore. Now hurry."

He put on his gun belt and black duster and followed her through the Door and into the Time Corps safe house. Everyone was there, Pangur Ban and her kittens Frieda and Diego, Yukiko, Sister, Julius and his sisters September, June and Red Fawn. Even their brother Augustus had come.

Seamus and Felicia spoke with the members of the Twelve while a young boy who looked like both of them knelt beside Pangur Ban, discussing something. Felicia and Seamus looked like they were in their thirties, which was the age when he had last seen them, before they had become parents. But time travel was odd like that. Next, their son could be older than they were.

"Where's Hazel?" Neil asked Astrid.

"She took Elliot outside. He was upset because you weren't here yet and he started shouting."

Astrid left through a Door, explaining that she had to assist the other psychopomps. Neil went to the backyard and found Elliot and Hazel sheltering from the rain by leaning up against the side of the house. Hazel leaped forward and kissed him, and he knew from her look that she had things to tell him. She too must have experienced a second life. Elliot kicked at the grass, muttering, then gave him a sly look.

"You said you'd take me to Norway," he said to Neil. "To find a woman."

An earthquake hit, but no one seemed surprised. They waited it out, watching to see if it grew stronger. Once it stopped, Huginn, the raven, flew into the backyard, landed, hopped up to Elliot and began speaking with him. Hazel took Neil aside.

"Did you have the dreams?" Hazel asked.

"What dreams?"

"About me and Elliot and everyone."

"No, nothing."

"Are you sure?"

"I didn't know anything was wrong until an hour ago."

She looked away, and he remembered how frantic she had been on the sidewalk with Elliot when the worlds were split. He remembered her terror and how she had begged him to find her. It was not through any fault of his own, but that didn't really matter. He had failed her.

"It's just odd, that's all," she said in the tone that let him know that she was trying to be strong and reasonable. He knew that her second life had not been a pleasant one. "All the other time travelers had dreams. Only regular people remember only one life."

"I would have come for you if I had known. Maybe I had no dreams because I'm not human."

"Pangur Ban and Huginn had them. So did Yukiko."

"They have souls, presumably. What about the Twelve?"

"They remember both time lines through both versions of the world. See, the worlds were split because of us. Because we kept tearing holes. It was mainly the Professor causing it, but there were other things. Astrid using his machine to amplify her Door-making ability to get Elliot out of the Library destabilized things badly. But it wasn't until Luke was conceived that things went very wrong."

"The boy?"

"Yes. Parents from two worlds. He weakened the boundaries very badly and drew the void wyrms. They chased Felicia while she was pregnant, and now the void wyrms are everywhere. The destruction isn't even related to the child anymore."

"Why merge the worlds back? And who did it?"

"The Twelve keep talking about the Five and the Three and whoever. March worked with them to split the worlds, but merging them back together was their own idea. They were forced to it by us. But they didn't do a very good job."

The air shimmered and a void wyrm appeared in the middle of the backyard. Neil leapt forward to force it back when a man appeared and closed the rip. He turned to Neil.

"Ah, one of the golems who tried to kill me," he said. Neil recognized the drake, the one who was friends with Astrid.

"We were told you were damaging the worlds," said Neil. "That you wanted to destroy things."

"And you can now see that is a lie, correct?" Yelbeghen looked at him too directly and too steadily to be within the boundaries of good manners. He wasn't even attempting to act like a human any more, though he looked like one. Yelbeghen excused himself and stepped through another Doorway.

Hazel continued. "Yelbeghen has been closing Doors as fast as he can. Astrid and the psychopomps are working hard at getting the dead souls back where they belong and are closing the Doors through which they come. But there are a lot of souls. The Professor is working on modifying a machine to seal up rips as well. The holes are tearing everywhere. November and Janeiro are the two of the Twelve who can close Doors, and they're out working too."

"March can close Doors."

"Well, I'm not going to be the one to ask him to help. His brothers and sisters can manage him."

"Perhaps if we understood how this happened, maybe we could put it back how it was with multiple stable worlds with stable paths between."

"The paths were never stable. That's the thing. We've been using our own pathways that the Professor calculated, but we've also unknowingly been using those made by void wyrms. The wyrm holes were the most reliable ways to travel between worlds and through time, so we've used them often without knowing it. The wyrms never needed synchronicities like we did with the first version of the time machines. The wyrm holes also place us correctly within time so we don't end up in empty space. With the earth constantly in motion through space, any time travel should have required us to move not only through time, but through space to catch up with the earth. By using the wyrm holes, we've traveled safely. But we've damaged them and torn new holes too. It was all too much."

"Is Santiago doing anything? Does he know anyone who can close the rips?"

"Santiago left town a few days ago, according to Julius. He's not in any of his usual haunts in Vegas or LA or anywhere. He's just gone."

That was just like the Coyote to clear out when there was trouble. Neil's phone dinged and he checked it. One of his brother golems had texted him.

"March is dead, killed by a drake. She fled when we found her."

He told Hazel and explained how he had freed the drake.

"Good riddance to March, I say," she said. "I'll buy the drake a drink for killing him. We'll form a club for people who killed him."

"But seriously, the drake could do anything. She can make rips just as Yelbeghen does, and it's my fault she's free."

"It's all our fault. All of us."

She coaxed Elliot up off the ground and led him back into the house where she checked on the Professor's progress. They were almost ready.

Hazel explained to Neil how she and the Professor had opened a rip from their home world to Purgatory, and from there to Luna Park in the hub world. Astrid had torn a similar Door into and out of death from the hub world. Felicia had forced Janeiro to take her to Purgatory to get her son, and by doing so prevented Janeiro from immediately closing the rip at Luna Park that Astrid had made when she came with Yelbeghen from Purgatory.

"We all did it," she said. "Either out of love or curiosity, we all caused this. We ruined the separation between the worlds."

Neil's phone rang. It was the brother who had texted him.

"There's another drake," he said. Neil wondered if he meant Yelbeghen when his brother said, "Before he died, March ordered us to kill her."

"Where is she?"

"All over. She seems to be constantly making new rips and traveling. She looks human, and one of us shot a tracker and it attached to her shoe."

"Is she endangering anyone?"

"March told us to eliminate all of the drakes."

He noted that his brother had not answered his question. Even after March's death, the other golems would obey their master whether it made sense or not.

"What do you want me to do?"

"Something happened today. March explained it to us earlier. He said you would remember things we don't. That can work to our advantage. The drake is the girl who was on the Mediterranean island with the male drake. I'm sending you her tracker coordinates so you can see where she is. Help us kill her."

Neil didn't need to see the coordinates. He called Astrid on the phone, and she made a Door to the living room.

"They're coming," he said. "Golems are coming to kill you. They think you're some kind of drake. There's a tracker attached to your shoe."

"How many?" She kicked off her shoes and Neil took them.

"Six in total. You can run. Without the tracker, you're harder to find."

"How long have they been tracking me?"

"I don't know, but they said you're moving around a lot."

"I've been here at the safe house over and over. What's to say they won't come here?"

"Time to go!" cried the Professor, shoving his equipment into a bag. Hazel leapt up the stairs to retrieve one of the time machines. Neil heard something outside and pulled back the curtains.

"They're here!" he shouted. "Go!"

Four golems appeared on the front lawn, standing in the pouring rain. They had traveled through Doors, that much was clear, but if March was still alive, he was nowhere to be seen. Then Neil spotted the things on their wrists. Slim and black, he would have thought they were simple wristwatches. But none of them had worn them before. Each of them checked their watches and pressed something on the face and the Doors behind them closed. Now that was interesting.

He thought he understood. If March knew he would be killed by the drake, then he might have equipped his golems with these devices, allowing them to travel without him. But he hadn't given one to Neil. Did the other golems know this or understand why?

Neil counted heads as everyone went through Astrid's Door. Sister pulled Elliot by the hand, Pangur Ban and Huginn went through together. Pangur Ban's kittens were adults now and might be upstairs or somewhere else in the neighborhood, but they would keep themselves safe. Yukiko stepped through alone, followed by Red Fawn, Julius, Augustus, June and September. Last came Seamus, Felicia and Luke.

Hazel stood on the bottom step and met Neil's eyes, and he motioned her to go. He knew she would stand beside him, firing at the golems, relentless and ferocious. But they both knew she was no match for even one golem, let alone six.

She stepped through the Door and it closed as the final two golems appeared on the lawn. They headed toward the front door and Neil shoved Astrid's shoes under the coffee table before opening the door for them.

"They just escaped," he said.

"To where?"

"I don't know. They went through a Door. They don't seem to trust me anymore."

His brother looked him in the eye. "Kill him," he said.

It took an instant for Neil to realize that his brother was speaking to one of the other golems, but it took them a moment longer to understand. He used his time.

Neil dropped to the ground, kicking the legs out from one of his brothers, then leapt backwards, rising to meet a third who barreled toward him. He slipped sideways, but two others grabbed him. They didn't have a good grip, and he pulled them with him to the ground. He wasn't stronger than they were, and they were just as fast.

He rushed for the door, but another golem slammed into him from the side, both of them crashing down on top of the coffee table. One of the legs broke and he rolled with his brother, both of them struggling to pin the other, grappling for purchase, their speed and strength and skill perfectly matched. This went on for a few seconds, long enough for Neil to wonder where his other brothers were. Only one was fighting him. Why was no one tearing them apart and shooting him through the head?

"Push him off," said a woman's voice, and in the flurry of movement, he caught sight of two stockinged feet.

Astrid.

He managed to separate from his brother just long enough for her to do what she had done to the others, to create a Door beneath the golem's feet.

"They'll be back soon," she said and took his arm. They fell through her Door in an instant, and it took him a moment to get his bearings once his feet his solid ground.

Luna Park. The boardwalk.

Rain poured from the sky and something howled overhead. Neil watched as a string of black, diaphanous forms flew past, then broke into groups.

"Those are the souls," said Elliot, coming up beside him. "It's not all though. More will come. I saw them. So many."

Sister took Elliot's hand. She flinched when a great bronze serpent, winged and terrifying, flew low over the roller coaster, dipping down as if searching for something.

"Coaxoch!" Neil shouted, and the drake turned.

She saw him, he knew it, but instead of drawing closer, she turned and flew out over the beach. An instant later, a rip appeared, black and empty. The void.

"I promised you nothing, golem," she shouted, and was gone.

CHAPTER 42

ASTRID FELT THE FAMILIAR PULLS of psychopomp jobs, but instead of the usual one at a time, there were many at once. The sensation was akin to having ten, fifty, a thousand people all calling her name.

Overhead, another rip to the afterlife formed. She changed into an owl, leaving her clothing behind an abandoned snack booth and flew up through the rain, forcing the souls back both with her force of will and by physically shoving them. Though smaller in owl form, she retained her psychopomp ability to force the movement of souls, and she used it without hesitation, digging her claws in, shoving and shouting.

When the Professor had told her that he could not close the Door at the cloister, she had explained that a Door couldn't be closed while it was in use. The same was true now, and she was forced to close this new Door to the afterlife gradually, squeezing it tight until only one soul came through at a time and then clawing and pushing them back until the Door was no longer in use and she could close it.

She sealed this rip, but another opened, and another. They were multiplying on their own now, like cancer cells. She flew through the wind and the rain from one rip to another, closing them, but no sooner had she closed one than two more opened. Some of the rips were closer to the ground, and she noticed Graciela and Robin, both in their black dog aspects, or Gopan popping in to close them. She was relieved to see Graciela and Robin. The group wasn't complete without them, and they were needed.

She caught sight of Sevilen from the corner of her eye. He was working to close the rip to the void that the other drake had opened. She left him to it. She could have helped, but while she could work on all Doors, he could not affect ones to the afterlife. Only she could do that.

"Your phone was ringing a minute ago," Sevilen called to her. She got two more rips closed before diving down, changing into her human form and crouching behind the snack stand to check her messages. Gopan had called, asking her to come to New Orleans if she could. Like her, he was moving all over the world to close rips. She changed into her owl aspect and made a Door.

It was raining in New Orleans, and Jackson Square was filled with souls. She flew up to close three that were too high for the others to reach. Now and then Graciela or Robin appeared below. They shoved souls back and then vanished to attend to others somewhere else.

Astrid moved from Jackson Square to Mexico City to Tangier where she found sidhe, the fair folk, tearing open the hole that Sevilen had closed. She found the drake at Luna Park and told him as much, then traveled to a small town in Ireland and back to Luna Park. Some locations were more susceptible to tears, and they were not only at the places that the Time Corps had torn time rips. There were others, and in each one, dark clouds poured down rain.

She also noticed that she hadn't seen Jeff. She stopped, became human, and called Gopan on the phone.

"He's making complex traps," he said, "like a web. A series of Doors that the souls move through, only to be trapped back in the afterlife. He's at the center, monitoring and adding pieces as necessary."

It sounded a bit complicated for Astrid, who worked better visualizing and moving swiftly and silently.

She returned to Ireland to work with Graciela, splitting the work between sky and land, then returned to Luna Park. She changed into her human form to check another message on her phone. Powerful arms wrapped her like a great iron vice.

Instinctively, she created a Door to the void beneath the assailant's feet, but though the two of them fell, the man did not release her. This was a golem, she knew, one of Neil's brothers. She made another Door between their bodies, pushing it over him until his arms loosened slightly. She squirmed hard, considering changing into an owl and wondering if it would give her an advantage, when she had an idea.

As they hung in the black, silent, empty space between worlds, she worked fast, her fingers nimble. The golem must be suffocating by now, his arms locked around her. She didn't know how long he could survive here, but it could not be indefinitely. She worked the slim black device off of his wrist and clutched it while she made another very thin door in front of her, between his arms and her body. Now, she was sandwiched between her Doors with only his arms on either side. By stretching the Doors around herself, like a cocoon, she managed to escape. She moved a few yards away and turned to see her captor. This was the golem who looked like he was from the Indian subcontinent. No matter, for they were all the same to her, mindless animated matter. All but Neil.

She became an owl, clutched the device in her talons and made another Door to Luna Park, focusing on Neil and finding him. She dropped the black device into his hand. He had only opened his mouth to thank her when another golem, this one of African ancestry, leapt at her. She pulled a Door around herself, like a membrane, so quickly that the golem had no time to react.

The void again, then Luna Park, this time near a small rip from the afterlife. She closed it. Yukiko was now working with Seamus, Felicia, Luke and Hazel, making illusions to distract void wyrms or to confuse the Seelie and Unseelie who had managed to make another Door through.

Sevilen came through one of his Doors and they paused together, her perched on a boardwalk railing.

"I got the Seelie Door in Tangier closed, but they've opened one here as well," said Sevilen. "Also, that Aztec drake wants to let the void wyrms through."

"Doesn't she know it'll kill everyone?"

"It won't harm the wyrms. They'll thrive. And the world will once again belong to the great reptiles."

She was about to ask him what he would do about it, if anything, when the female drake appeared, ripping a large void hole overhead. Astrid immediately closed it from where she sat while Sevilen launched himself at the other drake. The two dragons locked together, jaws clamping and tearing, their tails lashing, their bodies writhing and straining together in their frenzied struggle.

"Astrid!" yelled Neil, and she turned to find one of his brothers almost upon her. She vanished through a Door.

She flew out over the top of the arcade building, wanting to help Sevilen, but not knowing how to do so. Even if she made a Door around the Aztec drake, she would simply return. The void was no problem for her. And if she made a Door to death for her, then Sevilen would be sent there too.

She closed another rip, this one smaller, and spotted one golem, then another. She ducked down low on the roof of the arcade as they gathered on the beach, watching the drakes as they rose and fell, locked together.

The drakes dropped, nearly hitting the water before shooting toward the shore, where they crashed and slid together, wet sand spraying around them, their teeth snapping, their wings opening and closing as they vied for purchase on the earth and sought each other's throats.

The golems watched them and at a word from one, they tore across the sand toward the two of them. Sevilen reared back, breaking free, and in that moment, Astrid made a Door around him, forcing him into the safety of the void.

The golems did not indicate any surprise at this, and they fell upon the Aztec drake. Already weakened, she thrashed as they held her, pulling long knives from hidden sheaths to slice at her. She snapped at them, but two golems held her head while the others set to slitting her throat. Silvery blue blood wetted the sand and the front of her body. After a long while, her tail stopped moving, her wings fell limp and her lifeless head fell forward.

The golems drew back, and though Astrid couldn't hear them speaking among themselves, she knew that they noticed the one missing among their number. She hoped by now that their brother would be suffocated in the void or eaten by a void wyrm.

The golems did not ponder this long, because overhead a new rip opened. Astrid knew it was a Door to the afterlife, she could feel it, but this place was different. She sensed the place before her eyes registered the smoke, the dark, the flickers of orange light.

Then the souls came. Unlike the souls from Purgatory, these ones screamed and howled, some tore at their own flesh and some were already missing limbs, jaws, eyes, hunks of skin or parts of their skulls.

She soared up to the rip, dodging the spirits, arriving at the rip and pushing the closest spirit back. The stench was terrible, and the creatures barely registered to her as human. They were changed beings, things that once were men and women, but now were mad, corrupted representations of human people.

She pulled the Door partly closed, as tight as she could manage while the spirits poured out, and behind them came other creatures, things that felt like the Twelve, but were vastly different in their intent and internal makeup. Within a moment, she knew this was a place of death, true death, and she thought she understood.

She got the Door mostly closed, and only one soul at a time could come through, but she could do no more. Down below, on the boardwalk, another rip opened from this evil place, this one larger. Souls six or seven abreast poured through, and she watched as Hazel yelled for Seamus and Felicia to bring their machine to close it.

Astrid knew that Hazel had no idea that their machine would never work.

Astrid darted down, just in time to see Jeff appear through a Door, barefoot and wearing a ratty green bathrobe that was soaked with rain. Like her, he must have been operating in his aspect form and needed to change clothes quickly.

One of the terrible creatures, the ones that were like the Twelve, approached the Door. The thing was like a burning cinder, but alive and full of such pure malice that Astrid was mesmerized for an instant, her soul paralyzed by the creature's mind as he looked into her face. It only lasted an instant, and she pulled again at the Door, closing it partway, using all her might to keep that monstrous thing trapped inside.

Jeff ran straight up to the Door and she felt his effort as he worked to close it, struggling against the tormented souls that squeezed out, trying to shove the spirits back, sometimes succeeding, but often failing.

Graciela and Robin appeared, both in black dog form, and assisted them, but the monster had already reached the rip. Gopan was the last to appear, and he screamed as the creature forced its way through and took Jeff by the throat, raising him high and looking straight into his face.

The thing spoke words, terrible words in a foul language that filled Astrid with a sickening sensation. She only understood them for an instant, before they faded in her mind, leaving her feeling empty and full of despair.

Jeff disappeared, and for a moment Astrid thought he

had made a Door. But no, she would be able to sense that. Something else had happened.

The creature paused then opened its hand and launched itself into the air, moving so quickly that none of them could have caught it, even if they had desired to. It dropped down to the ground outside Luna Park. Though the park was empty, the surrounding city was not.

Gopan knelt in the rain, searching for something on the ground, frantic, his face contorted in agony.

Astrid heard the screams as the creature moved among the people outside the park. She soared into the air, catching glimpses as it ripped people apart, tearing heads from necks and limbs from torsos.

The violence was bad enough, but the way the thing moved, with pure pleasure, with glee, with delight, was the worst part. It wasn't a terrified being, reacting to an unfamiliar place. No, it understood everything and loved what it was doing.

She tried to make a Door beneath it, to send it to the afterlife, but the thing sidestepped it, then launched itself into the air again, vanishing into the distance so quickly that she couldn't make another Door to try to capture it.

She returned to the ground where Graciela and Robin had finally managed to shove the tormented human spirits back and pull the Door smaller and smaller until they closed it.

"What was that thing?" asked Graciela.

"An evil spirit. A demon," said Robin.

Gopan remained kneeling, cupping something in his little boy hands. The dogs moved in to get a better look, but Astrid, with her owl eyes, could already see. A spider lay in his palm, its legs twisted and its round black body crushed.

CHAPTER 43

SEAMUS HEARD ELLIOT YELLING SOMETHING, but he had no time to comfort his friend. He howled of worlds and more worlds, of how he could see them all, simultaneously separate and unified and of the dark things that tormented him in the recesses of his mind.

Seamus wanted to help his old friend, the man he had worked with for years, the one who had saved his life more than once, who had saved all their lives. But that man was now lost beneath the layers of madness. And unless they found a way to close the rips, it wouldn't matter much anyway.

Seamus had seen the thing that tore across the sky, and now he saw the kneeling Indian boy, the two dogs and the owl.

"Hell is emptied, and all the devils are here!" cried Elliot.

Sister took Elliot's hand and Huginn landed on Elliot's shoulder, speaking into his ear. What an amnesiac raven could tell a madman, Seamus couldn't guess, but Elliot moaned and fell to his knees.

"Seamus!" called Felicia, and he rushed to her, pulling the time machine with him. Luke stood nearby, as Felicia would not let him leave her side, and she glanced at her handheld sensor and pointed out a place where the protective layer between the worlds was thinnest. The human worlds were merged, but other worlds, those of the sidhe and the void and the dead, still opened. The Doors to death he had to leave to the psychopomps, but the rips between worlds he could close.

He set up the machine and started it, noting as Hazel darted past with another sensor, checking on places where the layers were thinning.

"The ship!" cried Luke, pointing out to sea.

Skidbladnir was just offshore, aflame, dark smoke billowing from her sail and blackening mast. Three golems were on board, and Seamus watched as they leapt off of the deck and onto the sand. The monkey crew was a hundred yards off, scampering up the beach, apparently ignored by the golems.

Seamus turned back to the spot Felicia was monitoring only to see Hazel tearing across the beach toward her ship. He didn't call out to her, but raced after her, following her down the concrete stairs from the boardwalk to the rain-soaked sand.

She was fast, motivated both by love and the pure rage he knew she had toward anyone who would harm her dragon-headed ship. But he was not an old man yet, and he pounded over the sand, yards behind her, then only a few feet. He grabbed her around the waist and got a hard elbow in the stomach for his troubles.

She spun around, all hellcat fury, clawing and fighting until she realized it was him, then her anger transformed.

"Let me go!"

"They'll kill you," he said.

"She's my ship." She struggled against him, working against his arms, but he knew she wasn't really trying to hurt him. If she had been, he'd have a broken nose by now. "They're killing her!"

"You can't do anything. She's already moving out to sea."

The ship was sailing out, slowly, the way she did when she had no crew and piloted herself, out into the dark water.

"I'll kill them all," she said. "She didn't do anything to them."

"The golems aren't random. They must have had some reason to want to destroy her."

"They certainly did. She's a dragon, remember? The golems want to kill them all. And she's a dragon with one of your time machines attached to her. She rips holes."

The golems turned toward them and headed up the beach.

"We need to go," he said, loosening his grip on Hazel to see if she would run off toward the golems or act with a bit of sense and flee with him. Thankfully, she seemed willing to do the latter.

Hazel had just reached the concrete stairs when Seamus was knocked to the ground. The sand blew in gritty gusts around him, clogging his eyes and nose and flaying his skin. He caught a glimpse of Hazel hanging onto the railing that ran along the stairs, her clothing and wet brown braid blowing out toward the sea.

He knew what things pulled all matter toward them, the thing that had to be behind him now. He crept toward the staircase, blinded, his mouth and nose choked with sand. The sand slid away under his knees and palms, leaving him unable to get a purchase, and he slid backwards a few feet. He tried again, digging his fingers in deep, keeping his body low and his head down, but amid the tearing wind and slipping sand, he couldn't tell if he was moving forward or backward.

Hazel screamed, and a moment later pain tore through his left leg. His entire being was consumed in an electric sensation, pain, then surging terror and the need to escape. He tried to crawl forward, but couldn't.

The void wyrm must have bitten him, and when he tried to move forward, his left leg refused to move properly. His insides were an acid bath of adrenaline and now he felt dizzy as well.

He tried again to crawl, but his left foot couldn't dig into the sand. Through the sand and pain he looked down, knowing what he would see, but hoping it wasn't so. His left leg ended just below his knee. The terrible head of the void wyrm was just behind him, stretching forward, reaching.

Then something surrounded him, squeezing, a dark thing, metallic but alive. He was lifted, and the wind and sand died down and there was only the pain and the feel of rain splattering over him and the dizzying sensation of flying.

He hung in the claws of Yelbeghen, who landed and carried him, the world swaying around him with each enormous step, blood pouring from his leg. The dragon set him down on the boardwalk. There was shouting and running around him, and he watched as the dragon turned and took off into the sky.

He tried to keep his eyes open. He did. He knew he was losing blood fast and he tried to stay awake. The sun was setting and the darkness came until there was only sound. His wife shouted something, then Luke's voice and Hazel's. His three most beloved, they were. And if voices were to follow him into this dark place, he was glad the voices were theirs.

CHAPTER 44

I T DIDN'T TAKE LONG FOR Neil to figure out how to operate his brother's time ripping watch. After all, the thing was specifically designed for his kind. His mind grasped its structure and function immediately.

He wasn't fool enough to use it, however. Firstly, it would mean leaving Elliot and Sister, who he was trying to keep alive. Secondly, he was only one while the golems were five. Five in constant motion.

He heard the yelling before he saw anything, and then Yelbeghen rose from the boardwalk, soaring into the sky.

"Something is wrong," Sister signed.

"It's all dying," said Elliot.

Sister and Elliot crouched behind one of the concession booths on the boardwalk, and if Neil could think of a safer place, he would have put them there. But according to Astrid, the entire world was affected, and short of putting them in an underground vault, the only way to keep them safe was to keep them close. He tried to keep tabs on Hazel, but the woman was always moving.

Astrid flew past, then vanished through a Door, only to reappear a minute later. She landed near Neil for a moment to rest but didn't speak, then flew off once more the moment his brothers appeared. Neil didn't have to ask what was happening. They were chasing her, wearing her down, as persistent as the most focused predators.

"She'll destroy everything, you know."

Neil found March by his side. He was young and in a

new body, the younger, stronger one. The older version must have been killed, just as Neil's brother had said, and had come back. It could have taken him months or years, but time meant little to March since he could appear whenever and wherever he wished.

March glanced at Sister and Elliot, then turned away, uninterested. He looked out over the boardwalk and along the beach and up at the sky, at the human souls, the Seelie and Unseelie who were coming through the rip from their worlds, and at the other creatures Neil had never seen before. March's movements were precise, insectile, from the top of his head to the movement of his fingers as he buttoned his dinner jacket. Neil had never seen him so inhuman.

"Astrid isn't a drake," said Neil. "She repairs the tears. You have to call off my brothers."

"You have no idea what that woman is capable of. Also, she killed one of my sons. Perhaps two. I'm only able to find four of your brothers now."

"The more you delay her, the worse the tears will get."

"It's already too late. My two brothers who can make Doors can only do so much. And Astrid is failing. So are the psychopomps and Yelbeghen," said March. "It's only a countdown now. We can only watch. Your abilities are useless against this."

Neil hated that he was right. Unless there was a void wyrm or something he could overcome with strength and force, he could do little.

"Why are you here?" asked Neil.

"To say good-bye. I don't imagine you'll survive this."

He was afraid to ask the question, but it rose in his mouth anyway. With March dying, he had to wonder. "Will I die free?"

March regarded him. "Yes."

And then he was gone.

Elliot sobbed quietly and Sister rose and tugged at Neil's sleeve.

"Huginn gave me an idea," she signed. "We're not as helpless as that man says. I can put on Astrid's clothing and tie up my hair so it looks as short as hers. Elliot could tell Astrid to put on my clothes. The golems will not be able to tell us apart."

"They'll kill you."

"Not if you keep me alive. We can buy her time. Maybe you can even kill a few."

He glanced at Elliot.

"You can go," Elliot said without turning towards him. "I won't leave. I can see you anyway. I can see all of you at once."

Yukiko knew she was no fighter. And though she might be a thing of the shadows, of secrecy and illusions, she could still be useful in her own way. The golems and void wyrms, the Seelie and Unseelie, were not immune to her illusions, and she did what she could to keep the Time Corps safe.

The struggle might be futile, she thought. It probably was. The rips were growing more numerous, and while Hazel was using the Professor's machine, and Astrid, Yelbeghen and the psychopomps did what they could, it did not take a far-seer to know what was coming.

The many worlds may be ending, but she would fight to the last moment. Her god, Inarri, might have been proud. Tailless and disgraced as she was, she was still a Kitsune. And she would die as one.

The black drake was skilled at closing void wyrm holes, but while they were open, Yukiko placed illusions of people nearby for the void wyrms to attack. At first, she was shocked that the mindless things could be fooled. Only sentient beings were susceptible to her trickery. But once she understood that they were immature drakes, it made more sense. Even children could be fooled by illusions.

Felicia and her son crouched over Seamus, applying a tourniquet and trying to keep him from bleeding to death. The boy was surprisingly calm, following his mother's orders, squinting through the rain. Seamus was already unconscious, and Yukiko had seen enough of death to know that it was near for the man.

The golems chased Astrid, who alternated between owl and human, sometimes naked, sometimes clothed. Sister made a decent decoy, especially while Yukiko could remove some of her facial scarring. Neil kept the girl close by, using the little black device on his wrist to escape his brothers. By Yukiko's count, only three golems remained, but she might be mistaken.

She checked on Elliot who lay alone behind a concession stand, moaning and mumbling to himself. It hurt to see him so tormented. Although he was a good man and her friend, his mind had always been a little loosely wired, and his time in the Library had not helped matters. Such a pity.

Huginn landed on the counter. "You can go. I'll stay with him."

"I wasn't planning on staying anyway," said Yukiko. "Where's Pangur Ban?"

"With September," said Huginn.

"Are the Twelve doing anything? Or are they watching us like a child observes a kicked-in anthill?"

"Can't say."

Huginn hopped down in front of Elliot just as Neil and Sister appeared from wherever he had taken the two of them. Sister looked exhausted, and Yukiko made seven copies of her, all wearing Astrid's clothing, all running beside copies of Neil.

Three golems appeared and gave chase. Yukiko bent the last remaining sunlight, shining it into their eyes, doing her level best to confuse them, simultaneously concealing herself.

The three golems were well down the boardwalk, chasing the pairs of false Sisters and Neils, when Yukiko hit the ground, something huge and strong on top of her. It breathed into her ear and she knew what it was. The fourth golem.

She twisted beneath him, changing into her smaller tailless white fox form, slipping away and leaving his hands grasping at her empty clothing. She ran, but knew he had a gun. They all did. And they all were perfect shots.

She ran at full speed, leaping and zigzagging, bending sunlight and creating a chaotic mass of white foxes around her, trying to be a difficult target, when she heard the shot. It took a moment for her to register that it had not struck her. She darted behind an empty midway booth and peeked out.

She saw Santiago in his Coyote form attached to the golem's right wrist, snarling. The golem grabbed the handgun with his left hand and smashed the butt into Santiago's skull. But the old Coyote was tougher than he looked, and he glared at the golem through slitted yellow eyes.

Huginn was on the golem an instant later, pecking and clawing his face, and then Elliot gave a cry and leaped onto him as well. His weight was enough to force the golem to stagger forward, and Yukiko saw her chance. She changed into a woman and snatched the gun from his hand, leaping nimbly out of his reach.

She raised the gun, leveling it with the back of the golem's head and fired. He fell. She turned aside and set the handgun on the concession stand counter.

"He's still going round and round," said Elliot. "They all are."

"Well, aren't we all?" said Santiago.

Yukiko changed back into a fox. Elliot and Huginn retreated back behind the concession stand while Yukiko and Santiago ran down the boardwalk to a spot where a void wyrm rip had appeared.

"I thought you cleared out," she said to Santiago as they ran.

"I did. But then I realized I'd miss all the fun. Besides, I think it's about time for me to die anyway."

She glanced at him, surprised. It was the most honest thing she'd ever heard him say. His canine face was unreadable, and his pink tongue hung out the side of his mouth.

"I think you may be right," she said.

"Of course I'm right. But since I have to die today, I'd rather do it at the side of a friend."

"We're not friends."

"Still haven't forgiven me, have you?"

Santiago created an illusion of a row of children, and the void wyrm leapt for them, clamping its jaws on air. Yelbeghen must have sensed the door, for high above, he circled back toward them.

Astrid appeared in her owl form, and Yukiko created the illusion of multiple owls in anticipation of the golems she knew would be following her.

Three more rips opened and void wyrms stretched their terrible heads from all three. Santiago grabbed her by the scruff of her neck and pulled her just out of reach of one.

Thunder crashed, just once, and the ocean waves calmed to nothing and the constant sea wind grew still. Even the rain stopped. The void wyrms ceased their attack, the souls in the sky slowed in their flight and quit their howling. Even Yelbeghen landed and was still.

Yukiko felt her own heart beating and the air moving in and out of her lungs. She could feel the stillness of all creation. The sky tore open from east to west, and beyond it stretched endless black and purple and blue and pale orange, yellow and more blue. Too many skies, too many worlds.

Everyone, even the golems, looked up in horror. The only sound was Elliot in the distance, screaming.

CHAPTER 45

ASTRID FELT THE VOID BEYOND the tear, the void and everything else. Everything. And she understood.

It wasn't simply the worlds being merged, it was everything: planets and space and universes, the places of the living and the dead, the human and inhuman, all becoming one.

But not people. No, for each person was always unique. In every world, there were never any duplicates. Even key historical people were never exact duplicates, but similar people with similar names. And now, everyone was going to die. Every last one.

Elliot's scream broke through her thoughts.

Elliot, her cousin, the epitome of optimism through their years of poverty and struggle through their childhoods. Elliot, the unfailing light who had never turned away or given up on her, no matter how mad things became. She had seen him go from a boy to a young man and then grow up. From a surfer in a trailer to one of the most reliable members of the Time Corps, skilled, resourceful and brave.

She saw him as the Time Corps could not, because she knew what he was. Like her, he was a wounded thing, a damaged being. But while her own damage lay in her heart, Elliot's resided in his head.

She flew to him, the only one to break free of the magnetic hold that the tear had on everyone. The tear held so many things, but with the multitude of everything, it also held the void which was the absence of everything. It might be a paradox, but it was a true one. Only Yelbeghen turned his head to glance at her, and she thought she saw Gopan stir. Yes, the void things were not mesmerized so easily.

Elliot squatted on the concession stand counter, like an ape, staring at the sky.

"It's you," he said to her.

She landed beside him. "Yeah."

"Can you see it too?"

"I can."

"And do you see it the way I do?" His voice shook.

She wanted to change into a human and take his hand, but she would be nude, so she stayed as an owl. Instead, she reached gently into his mind, knowing it was breaking the rule that she must never use her abilities on the living, but hoping that in these last moments that they might face their end together.

Elliot's mind, once only erratic, now was a squirming mass of chaos. But within that was more.

The other members of the Time Corps thought Elliot's words were only the product of insanity, but she now understood that they were beyond that. He saw the worlds, all of them. Together and separate.

Both.

Together and separate.

The golem that Yukiko killed lay on the ground in a puddle of his own blood which ran down between the boards of the boardwalk.

She thought of the golem she had killed using her Doors. Her Doors were her only defense. Her Doors and the void.

So much death. Everything around her was death.

Elliot whimpered, and she reached further into his mind, telling him she was there, that she would not leave him.

And then she saw it, the threads that went from one place to another in his mind, connecting things. The things were all in motion, like spinning planets or electrons orbiting around an atom's nucleus, and Elliot's mind connected them together.

He had an idea, and her mind leapt to another thought with him. The seven earths were one. Their merging had already occurred. But the void, the Seelie and Unseelie worlds, Purgatory and Hell, the other rips to nameless places were only rips. Those places were not yet merged with her world. Together and separate.

Like the golem's arms around her, they pressed in, but they had not yet crushed her world.

That meant something. Inside his mind, she felt Elliot draw closer to her.

You're here, he said.

I didn't want to leave you all alone.

Can you see it now?

I think so. But there's something missing.

She felt him sink farther away, pulled down by his own interior gravity. Or maybe he was pushing her upward. Yes, that was it. He lifted her. She soared.

There were the Twelve. She saw them now, the ones who wanted order and the ones who wanted chaos and the ones between, the ones who had never chosen a side. Angels and demons. Heaven's war.

The kinder ones of the Twelve would not help her.

Would you like me to show you?

She told him that she would.

Inside his mind, Elliot felt more sane. His interior landscape was still a swirling mass, but his voice, his presence, felt as stable as ever.

There are important people in this story. The General, the Messenger, the Healer.

He must mean Neil, the strategic fighter, Yukiko, the one who could speak all languages, and Felicia, the doctor.

There are also a Liar and his helpers.

That must be March and the golems.

And the tortured innocent, the catalyst, father and son.

Sister, innocent, tortured and tongueless, Seamus who had started the rips, and his son, Luke, who had set off the final events.

But if that was what Elliot wanted to show her, why didn't he just show her their friends? Why give them these titles?

See, heaven's war is fought on earth.

But what about us? she asked.

He was silent for a bit.

I don't know.

But she thought she might. The Twelve wouldn't help them. Neither would the Seven or the Five or the Three or the One.

There was only her. Her and Elliot. Him, his mind like a moving map. And her, its navigator.

She moved through his landscape, and things became clearer.

We thought we lived in the hub world, she told Elliot. *But the true hub was the afterlife. There was only one afterlife for all worlds, both the seven human worlds and the other inhuman worlds. Once holes were ripped to the afterlife, everything came rushing together.*

What good does knowing that do us? he asked.

I don't know. The Doors, the rips, they destroyed everything. I don't know what to do.

She felt him move close to her.

But you're a Door.

He receded, and she was left with one thought. It was mad and impossible and she understood.

She felt through his mind, feeling the world, all the people crammed together. So many. There were seven billion of them, when before there had only been one billion. Those were only the ones alive now. There were one hundred billion, including the dead, and that was only the humans. She felt all of them.

Within his mind, she expanded. He stood beside her as the entire place expanded, her mind and his, like the sky, spinning and enlarging, until she saw all of it.

I won't leave you, he said, and she was glad because she was afraid. This was the edge of madness, or maybe the heart of it.

She thought of the golem bleeding on the ground. She had made a Door between herself and the golem. That was the key.

It was time.

She did the same now, using Elliot's mind as the map, finding the spot at Luna Park where the Seelie world touched hers. She slid a Door between the worlds, wrapping a Door around the Seelie world, sealing it. Then she found one of the holes to the Unseelie world and did the same. The small holes to the void that the void wyrms made were easy to find and she sealed them. The huge rip in the sky took a long time, but she worked at it, separating out the components and placing them where they belonged. It took so long, but years and moments were the same within this place. Then, she moved through the world, finding the places where the remaining holes were. There were so many rips, so many, but she slipped Doors here and there, taking her time.

Time.

Space and time are not strictly separate. Not really, Elliot whispered to her.

Yes, and her Doors were holes in space. She could not travel through time.

Seamus's time rips were like her own Doors, but his were through time.

Time. Space. Two parts of the same whole.

Matter, time, energy, all were one. She felt Elliot beside her, laughing, while she marveled in understanding.

The information flew through her mind leaving only an impression as it passed, but she understood enough.

And with this understanding of time, she saw new possibilities. The rips in Fintona, Ireland, in New Orleans, in Los Angeles, they shone like lights in the darkness. Most of the Time Corps were born close to these places, born and raised on these rips. And there were times that were more susceptible too. The early to mid-1800s, the mid- to late-1900s, and others earlier on. Their birth times.

They had been born for their own purposes, but she saw the unifying threads of their lives. She would save her friends. She would save them and all the people.

She moved through the space in Elliot's mind. It was more sieve than map now, a thing of infinite holes, infinite doorways to infinite places. But she did not have any fear now.

She saw the tortured spirits, the suffering dead, and made new Doors around them, around the demonic creatures, the ones who wandered and the one who had killed Jeff. Some of them were recent arrivals, coming through many Doors all over the world. And some had been on earth a long, long time. She found each one and sealed them into their place.

She felt time passing, but she was part of it, touching so many places. And she was outside of it too, for a Door was a thing that was neither one place nor the other, neither beginning nor end. She was the void, the place from which new things were created with only a word. And in that void, she would protect the world, this fragile little blue egg, filled with life.

She felt the precious, tender, fragile world and wrapped herself around it, a Door that had never existed before, encompassing everything, keeping it safe, keeping it sealed from the other inhuman worlds.

The drake and the fair folk, the sea-woman who swam offshore, the old gods and their servants, most of those beings would only be stories to the seven billion humans living in this world. Only myths, tales told long ago, things that could never exist in the modern world. Only stories.

She saved some of them, Pangur Ban and Huginn, Yukiko and Santiago, Skidbladnir, the monkey crew and their people. There were others who could live here peacefully, like Sevilen. Those ones she left in this world, the one they preferred.

She thought of Seamus and his machine, using an invention to tear holes between the worlds while she, like the drakes, did it by natural means. Seamus had led Hazel, Luke and Felicia out of the realm of the dead and into life, while she only sent souls from life to death. Technology and nature, life and death, two poles of a magnet.

And if Seamus had fathered this broken, self-destroying world with his machine, then she would be its mother. He had started the destruction, but she would end it. She reached farther, finding each hidden rip, the ones buried lower, and lovingly closing them, wrapping her Doors around each and every lost being and placing them where they belonged.

I can see now why the Twelve and the Five and all of them won't help, said Elliot. *It's because you are here.*

No, both of us are here, she said.

She felt him smile.

CHAPTER 46

ELLIOT FELT ASTRID BRUSHING THROUGH parts of his mind, her movement as soft as the tip of a feather. He watched as she repaired things, moved things, flitting here and there, doing her work.

It was so quiet in his mind now.

This had to be what the void was like. Astrid had described it to him as a place of silence and peace.

And in this void the two of them now existed. He was both moving and still, and so was Astrid. She repaired things while he observed, his mind the map, the way she located all things.

He felt her move farther away, stretching thin, expanding until she was all around. She was everywhere.

For a moment, he feared he was going deeper into insanity, that his mind was completely unraveling and he was traveling to a place where he would never be able to speak to the people outside his mind again. He thought he was being absorbed into Astrid, but the moment passed. She pulled far away then, almost vanishing, until she felt like a tiny pinprick of light in the dark, a single note in the silence.

What are you doing now? he asked her.

He felt her come closer. *I think I have to do something. I have to save them.*

What can you do?

I have to make a Door. The biggest Door. An inside-out Door that keeps all the other places away from the human world.

He saw the image in his mind, of a Door around the world, the permeable part facing outward so whatever worlds tried to burrow into earth would be sent elsewhere. It was like a mirror, only Astrid would absorb the things and redirect them back out. Then he saw it expand, covering everything, all planets and galaxies and the dark, strange regions of space yet to be discovered. The Door surrounded the entire human universe.

The rest of the multiple universes, for there were far more than the few that he and the Time Corps had discovered, would remain in all their wild and terrible glory, but the earth and its home universe, the one ruled by science and reason, would be safe.

I didn't know you could make a Door that big, he said.

A small part of her was still close. *I can't make one. But I can become a Door that big.*

It took him a moment to understand.

No. Oh, no. You can't.

I can. I can exist outside of space, in the void. I'll be just outside the universe, wrapped around it.

You'll be lost in the void forever, he said.

He felt her smile. *I can't be lost there.*

She was beside him now, and he felt the enormous Door around the universe quiver like a soap bubble.

Then he felt her in his own mind, not out in the wide universe. She set the things inside his head in order, placing thoughts and ideas side by side, removing the cobwebs and confusion, making proper barriers where they ought to be, and openings between the barriers that would let thoughts through at the proper time. She set his thoughts back on logical tracks, organized the sounds and movement that had tormented him, locked away some things, and brought others forward. Though he felt smaller now, the sensation was familiar. He had spent most of his life in this state.

He was, once again, Elliot.

I have to go, she said.

For how long?

She moved out of his mind and was beside him now.

I can never come back.

But you won't live forever, he said. *This solution is only temporary.*

I won't age in the void. And the children are there. The drake children. I will not be alone.

I don't want you to go, he said.

He felt her wrap around him, embracing him. Then she pressed a kiss onto his forehead where it burned warm, then melted into his skin, into his skull and brain, and pulsed through his blood.

The skittish, abused kid from the trashy section of town, the strange, watchful girl who had taken the unwanted mantle of psychopomp, his younger cousin who had cried when he pulled the head off her Barbie, this was now the woman who had saved the world, and no one would know.

It won't be the same without you, he said.

No, I don't think it will be.

CHAPTER 47

FELICIA STOOD BESIDE SEAMUS'S HOSPITAL bed, unable to stop looking at the sheet and the way it lay flat on the bed where his lower leg should have been.

He would live. That was the important thing. She had to focus on that. He had invented a rudimentary prosthetic mechanical leg for Civil War veterans years ago, and he would make one for himself. She knew that too.

Luke was safe. He stood by the window, looking out over the parking lot, watching the cars. She noticed that he kept glancing at the sky, but she had already explained that the world was safe now. He was safe, but she was still uneasy.

Her nephew was in this world. He would receive medical treatment and he would live. Her family was here, the Time Corps, everyone but Astrid.

The moment Janeiro appeared in the hospital room, Luke leapt forward to embrace him. Janeiro scooped him up. Felicia took Luke's arm and gave Janeiro a warning look. He put the boy down.

"Don't touch him again," she said. "Do you understand?"

Luke looked from her to Janeiro but did not move from his spot between them.

Red Fawn followed Janeiro through his Door and immediately went to Seamus. He looked at her and gave a weak smile.

"Hey there, pretty lady."

She looked old enough to be his mother, but Red Fawn

had a feminine magnetism about her.

"You shouldn't have come," Felicia said to Janeiro.

"My sister wanted to see Seamus. She was worried about him."

"A fat lot of good that did when he was almost eaten by a void wyrm. You, all of you, you sat there and did nothing. Astrid is gone and Seamus is maimed and Jeff the psychopomp is dead and you did nothing."

Janeiro sighed and sank into the chair beside the bed. Felicia wanted to pull him out of it and throw him across the room. She felt Luke slip his hand into hers.

"Everything worked itself out in the end," said Janeiro.

"Yeah, why don't you explain that? Astrid is gone. She's in the void. How is that working itself out?"

"She performed her function. We all did. Even you."

"Right, our functions. And yours was to kidnap my son and then stand idly by while the worlds collapsed."

Janeiro rubbed his temples. If she didn't know better, she'd say he looked older.

"The four of us, Red Fawn, September, Julius and myself, we can't do things that the others can. We are restricted in what we're allowed to do. We're watchers. It's our primary function."

"But you intervened when you stole Luke."

"Out of necessity to preserve the stability of the worlds. The worlds your husband and your friend Astrid helped to destroy."

"I think March may have been right after all. Neil explained March's philosophy to me. While you all sat there, while Luke was a piece on a chessboard that had to be removed and while we all performed our functions, while you allowed families and friends to be separated, and worlds to be split, at least March had a vision for the world and acted on it."

"A vision that included destruction. His final vision of the world is no paradise, though he would claim it was.

Also, he wanted to kill the void wyrms and drakes, all of them."

"So did the Seelie. Now, why was that?"

"The drakes were never popular. Humankind didn't get along with them at all, but that was in a version of the world that no longer exists. But it did happen, you understand. The drakes have always been problematic. The Seelie have far-seers, and March knows all sorts of possible futures. The Seelie wanted the human world to stay open to them, so they didn't want Yelbeghen sealing them off. That's why they wanted him dead, to keep their Doors open. They didn't want any drakes interfering with their Doors. They always wanted free access to the human world, and Yelbeghen interfered with that.

"March, on the other hand, wanted Yelbeghen and all the drakes and void wyrms dead because they could open doors to the void. The Doors made by drakes could be used by others, and the wyrm holes were used by you and your friends to travel through time. March wanted to be the only one with such power. He couldn't stop Janeiro and November, but he could act against any others. As odd as it sounds, he wanted the worlds separate and stable. When he had multiple worlds to play in and corrupt, he was happy. Now, he can only act in this one world. It must gall him horribly to be so restricted."

"At least he tried to help humanity by saving us from the void wyrms. He acted from his convictions."

Janeiro looked up at her for so long that she felt uncomfortable.

"Do you really believe that? Do you believe his lies about freedom and self-determination?"

"I believe that none of you know what you're doing."

He laughed then, long and loud, and for a moment, only a moment, she nearly forgave him for what he had done. Then, her maternal anger returned, solid and strong.

"November wasn't idle," said Janeiro. "He took two of

the psychopomps, the black dogs, Graciela and Robin, and had them assisting in other worlds where there were fewer of their kind. He tried to repair the rips before they got too bad. The rest of the Twelve were watching and acting in their own small ways to help. I was keeping you safe, Augustus was trying to keep the Seelie from coming through to Luna Park, June Yee was monitoring San Francisco, September was watching New Orleans in the 1800s. We weren't idle, though you're right that we were flying blind, just like you."

"Do you know more now?"

"A little."

"Then tell me this. From what I understand, purgatory and hell opened."

"One level of hell. Not one of the worst ones."

"Still, it was hell. So why not heaven?"

Red Fawn looked up from her quiet chat with Seamus. "Why would it? Nobody there wants to leave."

Seamus muttered something, but his eyes were drooping closed and Red Fawn stepped away from him to let him rest.

"I see that you didn't bring September," said Felicia. "Seamus told me that he thinks she informed the New Orleans police about McCullen and him being felons. Now, why was it?"

"To prevent them from making the machine. Even with the worlds split apart, March was still active. He might have given the pair of them the blue fluid and the whole mess would have begun again. She didn't know that they'd escape, that McCullen would die or that Hazel would bring Seamus's equipment to Ireland. She also didn't know that he'd be able to make a rip, even without the blue fluid. As the spot was a naturally occurring tear, he simply had to poke it a bit. None of us knew that would happen."

"There seems to be a lot you don't know."

"And that's the honest truth," said Red Fawn. "Now, I

want to ask you something. How did all of you know that time had been reset? All of you searched for each other. It was unexpected."

"We had dreams," said Felicia. "All of us but Neil had dreams about our previous life."

"Ha!" Red Fawn pointed a finger straight at Janeiro. "I told you they were involved. That's got the Messenger's fingerprints all over it. Dreams of pasts that didn't really happen, those dreams didn't originate in their own minds."

"I don't know," said Janeiro. "The dreams were really memories."

"Of a time that never happened. It was the Messenger. I'm sure of it." Red Fawn turned to Felicia. "See, the Seven are subtle. The Three even more so. The Seven aren't like me and Janeiro here. Half the time when one of them shows up, you're going to piss yourself in terror. And if you're asleep when they come, you're as like as not to forget the dream upon waking."

"So this Messenger gave us dreams?"

"Looks like it. Which raises the question: Why would he do it? Why would he want you all to remember each other?"

Janeiro and Red Fawn exchanged a glance, but Felicia understood.

"Because he wanted us to try to find each other," she said.

"Or because the General ordered him to," said Janeiro.

"The General?"

"The Prince of Hosts, the one who, long ago, helped cast out the Liar. He's one of the higher-ups. He's a brother to the Messenger and the Healer. Well, if you really get down to it, we're all siblings."

"So you've mentioned."

"But we're as different as you and the other humans are," said Janeiro. "Some are good and some bad."

"And the bad side won. Astrid is gone."

"She sacrificed herself, but the worlds were saved. And she's not alone out there."

"I'd hardly call void wyrms good company."

"There are drakes too, including her friend."

"She was forced to dine with him as part of a deal. He never released her from the bargain."

"There are always sacrifices," he said, but with such sadness that she wasn't tempted to point out the years of Luke's life that she had missed or her husband's missing limb, Neil's torment over being a golem, Yukiko's taillessness, Elliot's loose grip on sanity, Sister's internal and external scarring from her years of servitude, Hazel's painful past, Huginn's amnesia or Pangur Ban's kitten who died. All of them, even her, had paid and paid again.

Luke studied the readout screen on the computer attached to Seamus's many monitors. Felicia had taught him what a steady heartbeat looked like, what proper oxygen levels were and how the IV bag worked.

He touched his chin, looking far older and more thoughtful than his years should have allowed, and in that moment, she recognized him.

She had met him before, in her past and his future. He had been a doctor.

Of course he had.

The set of his jaw and the shape of his eyes had been familiar to her then, but she didn't know why. Then, in the spirit hospital in Purgatory, she had almost known him.

He had been called Dr. Fairfax back when she had fallen through a time rip and ended up in 1961 in Seamus's universe after St. Louis Cathedral and New Orleans were destroyed by Oren McCullen's hexapod machine. Luke was the doctor who had been there when she awoke in the hospital and who had been remarkably calm about telling her the date, including the year, even when she had not asked. He had known she was a time traveler from the start. He had been one himself.

Luke must have felt her watching him because he looked up at her and then back at his father.

CHAPTER 48

SKIDBLADNIR HAD CHANGED. HAZEL WALKED her deck, but it was unfamiliar and strange. It was made of fiberglass or some other modern material instead of long wooden planks. The dragon head was gone, replaced with a computer inside, and the red and white striped sail, once so glorious when filled with the sea wind, had been replaced by an engine that roared and vibrated through the ship. The Professor's time machine remained. Skidbladnir had been reborn.

This is was what happened when an immortal ship was destroyed.

Hazel wondered about it, as drakes could be killed. But Skidbladnir's punishment, for she now understood that her ship had once been a living drake, was eternal. Hazel would one day die, and the ship would live on.

A few members of the crew sat on deck, playing dice. Hazel opened her mouth to order Mr. Escobar to set a course for his home island, but she stopped herself. He could not operate the navigational computer, and though it was still unfamiliar to her, she was learning. She went to the computer.

"Dragon?" she said.

"Present."

"I have a question. Would you like to be free?"

"I do not understand."

"Astrid told Elliot that Yelbeghen, the drake, said you could live offshore on his island. You were once a drake, like him, and he said you might like to be free."

"I do not understand."

"Then tell me this, what do you want?"

"I want to sail on the sea."

"What else?"

"I want to see the world, to feel the wind, to go over the water, and into the sky, if I can."

"Do you want to stay with me as your captain?"

"You are a skraeling, but none of my other captains have sailed me as far as you have. I desire you to stay with me."

She waited to see if the dragon would say any more, but she did not. Hazel set the coordinates. "How long will it be before we reach the coordinates I just set?"

"Six days."

"Let's go then."

Neil and Elliot chatted about something at the stern while Hazel and Mr. Escobar walked out to the prow.

"The crew members don't know what to do with themselves," said Mr. Escobar.

A ship like this didn't require a crew. Even one person could sail it effectively. Hazel did not fail to notice the way Mr. Escobar looked out over the waves. She knew that he was thinking the same thing she was.

"How long have you been a sailor?" she asked.

"Nearly twenty years."

"Will you find another ship?"

"I don't know. I've been with Skidbladnir so long that I don't think I'd like another ship. Besides, the seas are dangerous in the mid-1800s, and I wouldn't want to be in any other time."

She understood. They both came from the same era, albeit different worlds, and without a time machine, he would have to pick a time within this single merged world, and stay there.

"Did you have a mate? A sweetheart?" She wasn't sure what term to use.

"I did."

He said nothing more, and she did not press him. Her first mate kept his own counsel.

Days later, when they reached the crew's home island, Hazel paid the crew in gold, as was their custom, and each crew member lined up to shake her hand. It was a human gesture, and she appreciated the thought. They scampered off into the trees until only Mr. Escobar was left. While the rest of the crew changed out with new crew after their contracts expired, Mr. Escobar had been with her from the start.

"Time to go home," she said and set the time machine for 1867, Mr. Escobar's home year. She flipped the switch, and they moved through time.

He went below decks and returned with a little bundle of belongings tied up in a blue handkerchief.

"You know how to contact me, don't you?" she said. "I'll check that hidden spot in that rock formation. If you need anything, if you get bored or want to sail again, you leave a note. You wouldn't be crew this time, you'd be my guest. My friend."

"I am already your friend."

He took her hand and bowed over it, like a gentleman from her own time, and turned, walking up the beach and into the trees. She saw him pull off his vest, the one he had always worn because it had pockets, and toss it onto a bush. Then he leapt into a tree and was gone.

CHAPTER 49

I T WAS CHRISTMAS AND NEIL went to his quarters to retrieve the gifts he had purchased for Elliot and Hazel. He opened the storage compartment over his bunk and pulled out the canister of high-quality surfboard wax to go with the new surfboard he and Hazel had gotten Elliot. Now that almost two months had passed since Astrid had gone, it was time for Elliot to get back to his old pleasurable pursuits. Once they returned to Julius's house in Los Angeles, Elliot would find the new board waiting in the garage. It had been Hazel's idea to give him something to look forward to instead of ruminating on his cousin.

It would be Elliot's first Christmas without Astrid, and though his friend did not say anything, Neil noticed his occasional distant looks. Elliot kept Astrid's sketch books in his quarters, and once, Neil had found Elliot paging through one of them. There was nothing wrong with that in itself, but Elliot's internal light had dimmed a bit, and Neil wanted to see it come back. He also knew that these things took time.

For Hazel, Neil had purchased a few books of sheet music and a garnet pendant. Looking at them now, they seemed uninspired, but he knew that nothing he could purchase would really suffice.

He wrapped the gifts using some old newspaper, as none of them had remembered to bring along real wrapping paper, and took them to the cabin.

"You know Neil wants you to," said Elliot to Hazel.

"Wants her to do what?" asked Neil.

"You want her to play something on her violin."

"I always want her to play something."

"I will after we finish with the tree," said Hazel.

The tree was a small artificial tree that Hazel had picked up in a drugstore before they left. It came with a set of red and green plastic decorations. It was tacky and ugly and, to Neil's eyes, perfect.

The ship rocked gently as the sun went down, and as soon as it vanished over the horizon, it was officially Christmas Eve according to the old-fashioned way Hazel reckoned time.

Elliot joked about the tree and made Hazel laugh. She sang an old Yule song and Elliot joined in for the chorus. Neil sat in a chair to one side, his feet stretched out in front of him, the scent of sea air in his nose and an unfamiliar feeling inside. Then he named it. Contentedness.

The world was not ending. No unstable time loops threatened lives. His friends were adjusting to their new lives. The two people he loved most, his best friend and his wife, were with him, and he was a free man.

Sure, he was aware of the emptying hourglass of his life. While the others would die and go to the afterlife, he might blink out. Bang, like a candle, as the character Tweedledum had once said.

But though Hazel had breathed life into him, and Elliot had whispered to his earthen form that he wanted Neil to have a soul, there was no way for him to know for sure if he had one or not.

He was a thing of earth, made of river earth and blood, sacrifice and fire. He was of the earth, like the other golems, which was why he supposed the void wyrms could not pull him into their rips. He was rooted to the earth, while humanity was part spirit.

He alone among the Time Corps had not received the dreams. Maybe it meant he had no soul, so this Messenger person did not bother with him. If he had remembered Hazel begging him to find her, he would have torn apart heaven and earth to do it. He might have forced March to take him to her. He might have tried to make the captive drake do it, if she could. He would have done anything.

He understood the struggle of the Twelve, of the sides in the great war, of the conflicting philosophies of restraint and kindness or of freedom that included cruelty.

He thought of March, out in the world, in a young body, and for a moment he missed him and their philosophical talks. But even though March would make rulelessness sound appealing, Neil no longer agreed with him. He wondered about the idea, but Hazel and Elliot were finishing up the tree, and it was not time to discuss it.

Hazel left and came back with her violin, and Elliot dropped into the chair beside Neil. Hazel played, and as always, she was transformed into something greater than her slight, freckled, physical form. He watched her fingers dance over the strings, the push and pull of the bow, the press of her chin against the instrument.

He might have no soul, but he still hungered for life. He wanted to hear every piece of music, to view and ponder every piece of art, to feel every sensation and breathe the cold, clear air under a starry night sky. He wanted it all.

And if he had no soul, then he would never be the wiser. It would not stop him from living. But another thought occurred to him. Astrid had said that there were various parts to the afterlife, some populated by humans, some by other creatures like the drakes and the sidhe. He might have a soul like theirs, or one inhuman and unique.

Elliot listened to Hazel play, his head slightly to one side, his gaze far away. Neil didn't think Elliot looked sad. No, he had a look of longing. This wasn't the way he looked when he thought of Astrid. Neil knew the woman who occupied his friend's thoughts at this moment. Elliot hadn't seen her in some time, not since his captivity in the Library.

Neil let his eyes close. Elliot and Hazel were two poles, between which he could exist. They would anchor him to the regular world. Or maybe they were the axis upon which his world spun. For whatever he might be, he knew he could love and be loved in return. Perhaps any knowledge other than that was unnecessary.

And if he had an inhuman soul, then when he died, he would take a long walk through the afterlife, and find those he loved best. And they could sit together again, just like this.

CHAPTER 50

"TELL ME HOW SHE IS," Elliot said to Yelbeghen.

"Don't you want to come inside first?"

"Fine, but we don't intend to stay long."

Elliot, Hazel and Neil were on Yelbeghen's island, and Elliot knew he ought to be on his best behavior. The drake was now his only link to Astrid. But like Hazel and Neil, he was not fond of the man. The creature rang an interior alarm bell of mammalian self-preservation, and Elliot wanted to get as far from him as he could.

"She is well," said Yelbeghen, turning toward the house and heading up the path. Elliot fell into step beside him. "She's a mother of sorts to our young."

"Neil said that the other golems were instructed to kill her because she was some kind of drake. Is that what they meant?"

"Well, she's not one of us, but she is kin, in a fashion. If March could see possible futures, he might have seen this. She's not floating in space, not precisely. Like the void wyrms, she exists there, but there are places in the void that are physical locations. You yourself were held captive in the Library which hangs in the void. There are other places there, some very much like this one. These places are like islands. Astrid can have visitors, as the other drakes can take human form. Even if they could not, she does not fear us in our natural shape. She has a place to live, and she can create original art. She is content."

"But she can never leave."

"Her vigilance keeps your world safe. She exists as an immense Door and as herself simultaneously. But no, she cannot leave."

"The things I saw in my visions, when I wasn't right in the head, they came true. All but one. I saw Astrid when she was all dead and rotted, like a corpse. Does that mean she'll die some day?"

"Perhaps. You saw many things, from what Astrid tells me. She said she was in your mind, and it held much more than visions of her death."

He tried to remember, but all he knew was that the universe had felt so large and that he had understood things. But it was only a memory now. He retained little.

"Could you take me to her?" Elliot asked. "Astrid managed to bring people to the Library. Maybe you can do the same."

"You would die quickly. Her island is a void place."

"Could it be changed to one I could inhabit? Or could she come to the Library to see me?"

"You would return to that place?"

"Only if I had a way back and I was sure the Librarian wouldn't try to kill me."

"I can ask one of my sisters about it. She might know. She is far older and wiser than I."

They had reached Yelbeghen's house, and he opened the front door. Elliot glanced back to see Hazel and Neil walking through the garden in the central courtyard.

"You miss her, don't you?" said Yelbeghen.

"Of course."

"I have something for you. It's for you and Sister both."

Sister was back at the Time Corps safe house in Los Angeles, but she and Elliot e-mailed and texted regularly. Yelbeghen took Elliot into a sitting room appointed with a black marble sculpture of a woman and an angular white sofa. To one side, right under the window, sat an antique writing desk. Yelbeghen pulled open a drawer and handed Elliot an envelope. He recognized Astrid's handwriting immediately.

"I'll deliver your return letter to her," said Yelbeghen. "Writing supplies are in the top drawer."

Elliot slipped the letter from Astrid between the pages of her sketch book and slid it back onto his bookshelf. He didn't understand everything in it, as parts of his mind that she had accessed were now closed off. She said she understood about the General, the Messenger, the Healer, the Liar, the tortured innocent, the catalyst, the son and his father. At first, she thought he meant the members of the Time Corps, but roles existed twice. Many things happened twice. She said she understood it better now.

She also explained about the bubble world he had slipped into when the Seelie had drugged him, so long ago at Luna Park, and how Felicia's home world was similar, a bubble world off of one of the seven main worlds. That was why Seamus could never find a way to get her home. The point was moot now, but he would tell Seamus and Felicia when he saw them again.

"We got final confirmation from Huginn and Pangur Ban," said Neil from the doorway. "We have an exact date and coordinates."

Elliot's stomach jumped. "Are they sure?"

"The chieftain died young and the widow disappeared a week later. We have a clear window for travel."

Bennu was waiting, the woman from the Library. She had been promised as a wife to a Northern chieftain and forced to move far from her African desert home. Unable to leave the Library or take her with him, they had been separated. He had never ceased to think of her. She was clever and fierce, protective of her people and willing to sacrifice herself for them. She had married the chieftain, he knew that much. But if the chieftain was dead now, then her duty to her people was complete.

"Are you ready?" Neil asked.

"Let me shave and change my shirt."

Neil gave him a knowing look, almost a smile, and left him. When Elliot was finished, he went up on deck, and Hazel set coordinates for a time in the past where a warm-skinned desert woman waited in the cold and snowy North.

CHAPTER 51

HISTORY WAS STRANGE, SEAMUS THOUGHT, as was the future. Some of the Time Corps' past mapping of time still held, but with the new merged world, much of it did not.

The president during the American Civil War had been one Abraham Lincoln, not Breckinridge, as in his world. The first man on the moon was Neil Armstrong and in this world, the atomic bombs had been dropped on Hiroshima and Nagasaki and the widespread use of steam engines in the nineteenth century had never taken hold. Some famous people he remembered had risen to historical significance while others ended up leading unremarkable lives.

His feet, or remaining foot, rather, was just as it always had been, more apelike than those of the others. Hazel's feet were the same, as were Luke's. But they were the exception to the rule. No one else had feet like them. And few people had the lighter-colored eyes that people in Felicia's world had. The physical differences between people in the different worlds had been averaged out, and in some cases, erased entirely.

His parents and siblings still lived, though they were still in their proper time in the 1800s. His parents had been shocked to meet Luke and Felicia, but had embraced them as their own, naturally. Though skeptical at his tales of traveling in time, they had been convinced by the technology involved in his prosthetic leg and his digital watch.

With a few months of work and some input from Janeiro, Seamus had modified his time machines so they were less damaging to the world. He managed to automate the machines to close their own rips. It was imperfect, but workable.

There were only a few trips through time left to make before he could rest. First he went to 1961 to deliver his favorite time machine, the one to which he added brass embellishments and decorative touches, to an older Hazel in New Orleans. Inside a little door in the body of the machine waited a book of coordinates in his own handwriting. That machine and that book would be the start of so many things.

The book and the machine had been part of a time loop. He had received the two from an older version of himself, and thus neither had been properly created. He copied his own device, then gave it back to a younger version of himself. It had no stable origin. Many of their friendships were the same, people meeting each other because one of them knew the other from previously meeting them. But Astrid had fixed things when she healed the rips. The world was more stable than it had ever been, according to Janeiro.

In New Orleans, Seamus gave an older Hazel the time machine, which she took to the attic. They had lunch together, and then it was time for him to go.

He traveled to the hospital where, after research on 1960s' medical practices, a much older Luke spent months working, waiting for the day when his young mother, nearly drowned, would be brought in.

But there was another person Seamus was keen to see.

"Is Oren here?" he asked Luke. Oren had also been nearly drowned in the Mississippi.

"He is."

Luke took him to Oren's room where his old friend lay unconscious. Seamus knew he would wake before Felicia.

Some of their personal time threads remained unchanged. But the man lying there was not the same one who had given his life to save Seamus's. This was the man who wanted to destroy parts of New Orleans, who had stolen Seamus's engine designs, who wanted to jump start the Civil War. The man who was his friend was truly gone, for he had never existed.

"Now take me to your mother."

Luke led him down the hall. Felicia was as still as death, her lips white. She would wake, and she would come to him using the very machine he had delivered to Hazel's house. Even now, Hazel was visiting the hospital, claiming to be Felicia's aunt. And when Felicia woke, Hazel would be there.

"She looks so young," said Seamus.

"So do you."

Seamus rested his hand on his son's shoulder. "And you and Hazel are older now. And when I get home, you'll be young again."

That was how it always was, with lives lived asynchronously. Even now, an older Felicia was in the future, working in an advanced medical laboratory with a younger Luke.

"It was good seeing you, but I think it's time for me to head home," said Seamus.

CHAPTER 52

"WHEN WE GET THERE, I want you to tell me what you see when you look at them," Santiago said to Yukiko.

"Who, the prostitutes?"

"All the people. But them too."

It was a winter night in Las Vegas, too cold for comfort. Santiago had spent part of the evening gambling and had won a fair sum.

"Give me the money," said Yukiko.

"I already gave you some."

"The deal was all of it except living expenses."

"I can spend quite a bit on living expenses."

She put out her hand, and he pulled sixteen one-hundred-dollar bills from his billfold, a ten and some ones. The faces on the bills were different from the ones in her old world, but many things looked a little strange to her now. Like all of the Time Corps, she retained her original memories. She would adapt. She always had. It was how she had survived so long.

"Now," Yukiko said, folding the bills in half and handing them back to him. "You're going to give it away."

"To the hookers?"

"Them or the homeless. Take your pick. But I have a soft spot for the prostitutes."

"I can't imagine why," he said.

"You've done worse things, I'm sure."

He gave a little shrug and after walking down the street

a bit, Yukiko saw a pair of women. She knew what they were immediately. Sure, their clothing gave them away, but more than that she knew the way they held themselves.

"C'mon. It's more than sixteen hundred bucks," said Santiago. "We could get one of the fancy hotel rooms and drink champagne all night together."

"I'm not interested in you or the champagne. Now give it to them."

She stood back while he approached them, and they smiled and turned to him. His back was to her, but she watched him give them the money and walk back to her.

"What a waste of money," he said. "Both of them could have come with us. They'd have a good time. I have centuries of experience."

"They're not for sale."

"Sure they are. Everyone is if you name the right price."

"You really can't see them, can you?" she asked.

He put his hands in his coat pockets and shrugged. "I told you I wanted to know what you saw."

"People. They're just people. That's what I hoped you'd see. Doesn't helping them do anything to you?"

They walked in silence for a long while.

"I can barely see them," he said. "When I'm with them, with a woman I mean, I can see her. I can feel her then. But she's like sand through my fingers. A tide rolling out. A clock ticking down to the grave. The older I get, the less real they are to me."

"Maybe that wouldn't be a problem if you stopped being a womanizing son of a bitch."

"You'd think that, wouldn't you? But actually my mother was—"

"That's not my point."

It was long past midnight and they walked back to the parking structure where Santiago's sports car waited.

"It'll be sunrise in a few hours," he said. "We could drive out into the desert and have a nice nighttime run.

Maybe see if we can catch a few jackrabbits."

She was tired, but the idea did have its appeal. It had been ages since she had gone hunting.

"Come on," he said. "An old guy like me needs the young."

Few other beings would have called her young, but she understood what he meant without him saying more.

"All right," she said. "I think we have enough time."

CHAPTER 53

FELICIA GLANCED UP AT LUKE. He was in his early thirties, but she found that no matter how old he was, she always felt he was much younger than she was.

"We're done, right?" he asked.

"That's it. Now we just bring it to your father."

Together, they packed up twelve vials of synthetic drake blood. It had taken them months to get it right, but now that they could make it, they could run the time machines indefinitely.

"I've been studying limb grafts in my spare time," said Luke. "The technology will be viable in a few years, and in sixty more, we can grow Dad a new leg and Sister a new tongue."

"No clones," said Felicia. "I'm not harvesting things from clones."

"No, I know you wouldn't go for that. I mean single limb generation, grown over a synthetic bone. The skin color might be a little off from the natural leg, and it won't have birthmarks or scars. It will look like baby skin until it's attached and the hormones make it grow hair, but it'll function."

"We'll talk to Seamus when we get home."

"And Sister?"

"Her too. Though she seems pretty content as she is."

Seamus was too, if she thought about it. He was always reengineering his leg, working on perfecting the joints and foot shape. The man wasn't happy unless he was tinkering, and his leg provided a never-ending focus for that energy.

Felicia set up the time machine, and the two of them returned to the early twenty-first century. They found the car they had left parked the day before according to the car's time line, but months before according to theirs, and Luke drove them home.

On the way, her phone rang.

"I've found a number of clear paths to some times we haven't explored yet," said Seamus. "Some really promising ones. How did your trip go?"

"I have enough blue fluid for you to make many machines. And we can synthesize more."

"How is our boy?

"I couldn't have done it without him."

"Tell him I miss him."

"You can tell him yourself. We're on our way home."

AUTHOR'S NOTE

I love hearing from my readers. To drop me a note or to learn about my other books, please visit www.heatherblackwood.com.

If you enjoyed this book, please post a review on the retail site where you purchased it.